GARY
CHARLES
EVANS
IS
KLOCKS

Adirondack Heist

Jeffrey G. Kelly

Creative
Bloc
Press

FIRST EDITION, MAY 2002

Copyright © 2002 by Jeffrey G. Kelly

Published in the United States by Creative Bloc Press
Saratoga Springs, New York

Distributed by North Country Books, Inc.
Utica, New York

Printed by Sheridan Books, Inc.
Chelsea, Michigan

Cover design by Susana Dancy

Library of Congress Control Number: 2002090946

ISBN: 0-9663423-2-1

9680

for Linda
with love

With thanks to...

A special thanks to author and cartoonist Chris Millis and editor Marilyn McCabe for a thorough reading of my first draft and for advice on what to leave in and what to leave out. Graphic artist Susana Dancy designed the cover. Sculptor Noah Savett briefed me on the finer points of how to dismantle a bas-relief set in stone. During the research phase, I spoke to many North Country souls – at the Hammond Library, at the Crown Point Historic Site; to a student writing a paper on the lighthouse, to a former tollkeeper and others. I thank them all.

One

Klocks propped open the screen door with his chunk of iron ore and unlocked the oak door. It wasn't even ten o'clock, and he was already sweating from being outside. The walk from the river to his store did that.

Once inside, he moved around behind the glass case, careful not to knock over any of his junk. He raised his free hand to the long horizontal painting and tapped the sensuous curve of the naked lady. That was his morning ritual. Tap her butt, then pull the string for the ceiling fan.

Wearing his beloved muscle shirt, he sat on a worn stool behind the counter and got comfortable. His antique store, as he liked to call it, felt almost cool from the night air of the Gulf. He spread out the weekly Apalachicola Times and sipped his ice tea. This was his favorite time of the day. These precious morning hours were a brief reprieve from the unrelenting heat that would peak around two. Then the streets of Apalachicola would be empty, except for the rare tourist or itinerant couple who were convinced they had found the new off-the-beaten-path best place. And they had.

Apalachicola wasn't like the rest of Florida and the locals liked it that way. So did the doctors from Tallahassee and the boys who rented Klocks his boat. Nobody asked too many questions, and if you didn't become too obvious a drunk, it was the best place to live on the Panhandle. Though it was damned hot in the summer and downright damp in the winter. The Forgotten Coast, the locals called it.

Klocks frowned at the sound of an engine, and a car door opening and closing. That meant someone was about to walk in. And he hadn't even had a chance to turn on his computer and check eBay.

Drumming his fingers on the display case, he waited. Sure enough the stooped figure of an old man carrying a cardboard box appeared in front of his dilapidated store. Klocks closed the newspaper and snapped the lid back on his tea.

The chimes jingled and his first customer shuffled in. "Good morning. You're open, I see."

"Correct," Klocks enunciated.

"May I put this here?" The old man slid the box onto the counter, under Klocks's nose. "I'm cleaning out," the man said. "Help yourself. Tell me what's good and we'll dicker."

Klocks looked down. You never know. That's why he played the lottery. Just like the young actors from the Dixie Theatre on Avenue E said, "You never know who might see a show and launch a career." The older ones didn't say that. They knew the odds. They were here for the open space and the slow pace. They accepted that their glory years were behind them.

Sadly, Klocks was feeling that way too; that the good times were behind him. He found himself thinking about the past, which wasn't like him. Maybe he had been down here too long, sleeping too much.

Klocks leaned back and took a gander at the old man, whose body trembled. He seemed pleasant enough, handsome in his day. His thinning white hair was combed back. He was wearing a seersucker jacket, glasses dangling around his neck on top of a bolo tie inlaid with a gold nugget.

"Nice tie."

"Yes, thank you. People say that."

Klocks expected him to elaborate, and was annoyed with himself for giving an obvious compliment to a man who had heard it many times before. Did Klocks ever tell a woman with beautiful eyes that she had beautiful eyes? No, he didn't.

See, he thought, I'm slipping. I'm losing my edge.

The old man nodded. "Go ahead. I'll let you pick through the box, if you don't mind. My hands aren't that good."

Klocks gulped his ice tea, savoring the honey and lemon taste. He inhaled the stale air, puffed his cheeks and blew out. "Alrighty," Klocks said, satisfied that this stranger meant him no harm and was not inquiring into his past. And, who knows, maybe there was money to be made.

First he pulled out three framed pictures - two paintings, and a photograph. In one darkened painting four men sat in a saloon playing cards. Klocks liked the scene. The other painting was a pastoral setting that didn't appeal to him. The old man said they were painted by an Austrian friend of the family who died in 1972.

Klocks examined the signature.

"His name is Gerstenbrand. He was born in 1898," the old man said.

Klocks leafed through his book of artists while the man spelled out the name.

"Alfred," the old man said.

"I liked the poker one," Klocks said, "but he's not in my book and it's damaged. Right here. It's torn." He put the two paintings back inside the box, on edge, the way he had found them.

"Yes, I'm aware of that. Okay."

The black and white photograph appeared old. It was of a bridge crowded with cars and people in hats, maybe a parade of sorts, with a biplane flying underneath. Most of the cars looked like model As. The bridge had a symmetry to it, as bridges do, and the village in the background caught his eye - tweaked his memory. Klocks placed the photo to the side.

He went on to the items wrapped in newspaper. Chinaware. Several small boxes of various shapes and sizes - one made of seashells, one the shape of an elephant.

"That one's from Burma," the old man said. "They're all from my box collection."

Klocks didn't know much about imported jewelry boxes. He had only been in the antique business a year. It was something to do, a front of sorts, while he kept a low profile. But he did know other dealers in town. Each had their specialty. If something caught his eye, he'd check with one of them.

Another box was a blue Noxzema jar covered with a colorful combination of sparkling stones, tiny chains, and beads.

"That's from Zocalo, the big square in Mexico City."

"You've traveled a lot, have you?" Klocks remarked.

"Yes, quite a bit."

That was a good sign. That meant there was some money there, even wealth. Klocks was waking up now. He was feeling better. Maybe it was the caffeine kicking in.

Klocks picked up the last box, ornately carved and hand painted.

"India?" he guessed.

"You're right, very good."

Something inside clinked. Carefully, Klocks lifted the lid. He removed an elaborate piece of jewelry. It immediately spoke to Klocks. Years ago he had seen one on a gentleman at the Thoroughbred track in Saratoga, and, in hopes of lifting it, had struck up a conversation. Those were innocent days when he was a simple pickpocket.

"What, is there something in there?" the old man asked. "They're all supposed to be empty."

Klocks tilted the box towards the old man.

"Oh, hmmm, I remember that. I used to wear that attached to my watch. Even then I was a bit old-fashioned, a bit pretentious, I'd say. Nowadays, I don't think suits even have those little pockets."

The item was an 1880s watch fob. It was about four inches long with a horse's head and horseshoe made from mother of pearl. A tiny gold farrier's nail cleaved the horseshoe, a few gold links away from a golden bridle and a few more gold links to a clasp. It was the kind of showy jewelry that Sean Connery might have worn in The Great Train Robbery.

Klocks had no idea of its value, but he loved it. Trying to conceal his interest, he closed the box and without saying a word placed it next to the photograph of the bridge.

"So, Mister . . ." the old man began.

"Deed, Jonathan Deed," Klocks informed him.

"I'm Harry Southard, Mr. Deed. What interests you?"

"What interests me?" Klocks repeated, pulling at his scraggly red beard, stalling for time. Immediately turning to the item of lesser value, he held up the photograph. "Tell me something about this photo."

"All right, I will. I'm actually in that picture, closest to the New York side. Right there," he said, touching the photo. "I think that dot on the bridge is me," he chuckled, "as a boy."

"What was the occasion?"

"It was an historic occasion. August 26, 1929, two months before the crash." As he spoke he puffed up with pride. "It was the grand opening of the Champlain Bridge between Chimney Point, Vermont and Crown Point, New York."

Klocks had heard of Crown Point. "Is that a village there, in the background?"

"Sure, that's Port Henry on Lake Champlain and those are the Adirondack Mountains."

Klocks was dumfounded. Port Henry, of all places. The timing was too much. He eyeballed the old man, suspicious that he was some sort of sorcerer.

The old man grew more animated as he spoke, pacing around the creaky floor, gesticulating with his arms, raising his voice. "I was right there at the center of the bridge when Governor Franklin Roosevelt stepped out of his car on the New York side and Governor Dewey on the Vermont side. Honor guards ramrod straight. The governors strode towards each other and shook hands. Bands played. Boats and floats all around, planes overhead, and forty thousand people, a few passing out in the sun, and then when that stunt pilot flew underneath . . . " Wistfully, he stopped as if seeing himself there as an eight year old boy. "Why it's the greatest day Essex County has ever had; two governors. One a future president."

"Why would you want to sell this? I can see it means a lot to you."

"Well, I really don't want to sell it. I want to know how much it's worth."

"Oh, you want it appraised? But you don't want to sell."

"Yes."

Klocks's shoulder muscles tightened. This old man was wasting his time and trying his patience.

"And that little watch chain, do you want to sell that?" he snapped.

The old man scuffed his feet together as if he were in the marching band on the bridge, reliving his dramatic childhood moment. He narrowed his eyes, fixing them on Wallace Klocks. "Possibly," he said.

Klocks rolled his head, listening to the crunching sounds in his wrestler's neck. The gentleman had placated him. If Klocks came out of this with a deal, fine. If he didn't, he was going to be in a nasty mood.

Klocks was trying to practice restraint. He was trying to change his ways and take advantage of this second chance that he had sewn for himself through his own guile and will power; the one thing he possessed over every other human creature - a will that wouldn't quit.

"Calm down," Klocks whispered.

"What was that, Mister Deed?"

"I was talking to myself." He took a deep breath. "Back to business, shall we? I liked your story. But though they're in the picture, these governors . . . " He paused. "Is it signed by either one?"

"No, I'm afraid it isn't."

"You can't really make out their faces. Though the condition of the photo appears to be good. No mildew and it's been kept out of the sunlight. The whites are still white." Klocks scrunched up his face. "Twenty bucks, not much more."

"Twenty bucks, eh?"

"Just keep it. Hang on to it."

"And how much for the watch fob?" the gentleman asked.

"Is there any history to it?"

"Probably my father's."

"And who was he?" Klocks asked.

"He was a state senator from Albany, up in New York. We didn't get along that well."

"That happens," Klocks said, shrugging his shoulders. "I didn't get along with mine either. Didn't even know him."

Klocks was thinking that it's good the gentleman didn't get along with his dad because as of yesterday gold was three hundred dollars an ounce. He hefted it in his hand. He guessed it weighed at least two ounces.

It was the end of August, and in Klocks's mind, a plan was taking hold. The day's heat was seeping into his rickety oasis. A drop of sweat ran down the side of his forehead. He glared at the ceiling fan and pulled the string again, switching it to high. He refused to pay for air conditioning.

Unseen behind the counter, he moved his left cowboy boot to the top of a brass button protruding from the floor, and with his toe pressed down. He and another antique dealer, around the corner at the only stoplight in all of Franklin County, had worked out a system for contacting each other.

In two minutes the phone rang just as Klocks was ambling around the counter, examining the watch fob under the dim light of a heavy, standing lamp. Klocks pretended as if he were surprised by the interruption.

"Hey, Mack, how you be? That's right, that's right. No, I don't. Say, I've got a gentleman in here with a watch fob, yellow and white. Is it worth anything?" After a few seconds of silence on his end, Klocks answered questions of authenticity and condition, pausing in-between. "No. No. Yes. It appears to be. I will, definitely." Then he hung up.

The old man eyed Klocks. "Well, now you have a second opinion, don't you?"

"Yes, I do. I'll give you fifty bucks for it."

"Excuse me, Mister Deed. Fifty bucks for that fob is ridiculously low."

"Old man, what did you bring this crap in here for?" Klocks took a deep breath. He was taking this game of haggling too seriously. He retreated in tone and price. "All right, all right. Seventy bucks for the fob."

"I'll take $100. That's my price."

"Your price," Klocks scoffed. "Seventy-five," Klocks countered, opening his National cash register as he spoke. He took out four twenties and a ten.

"A hundred dollars, I said." The old man's Parkinson's was shaking his bent body.

"Ninety, final offer." Klocks held the bills out to him.

8

The old man balked, then with surprising quickness, swiped the bills out of Klocks's hand as he said, "Deal."

For a moment Klocks felt like he was the one who had been taken, the old man had such a sly grin on his face. But Klocks knew where he could sell it for five times as much. Up north in New York State at Lawson's on Broadway near the Saratoga flat track. As long as he got it to his old stomping grounds by Labor Day weekend.

The worldly gentleman knew it was worth more than ninety bucks. But years ago when he had worn it, it had given him bad luck. About some things, he was superstitious. That's why he stuck it away in the blue India box, never to be worn again. The money was secondary.

The old man gathered everything together in the cardboard box, except for the framed photograph. He was holding it before him, caught in the past. "You know, right here, near this bridge, there's an old lighthouse they turned into a monument to Champlain, the explorer. This girl and I, Helen, we climbed the lighthouse stairs. I still remember the steps, damp and slippery. So I held her hand. Believe it or not when you're fifteen that's exciting. We carved our initials in one of the stone balls on the top. As far as I know they're still there. It ruined my Buck knife, but it was worth it. She was my first love." He looked up, staring at the fan. "Once in a while I still dream about her."

Klocks could relate to that, no problem. Besides, his mother was named Helen.

The old man wedged the photograph into the box, straightened himself up, turned around and faced Klocks.

"You know, you might be interested in this. Surrounding the lighthouse is this incredible monument, and at the base of it . . . " He eyeballed Klocks. "At the base of it, there's a Rodin sculpture."

"No kidding," Klocks said as if going along with a tall tale. "The Rodin. Auguste Rodin from France?"

"Hard to believe, isn't it? Right there in Crown Point where I grew up. Been there since 1912 when the French crossed the Atlantic with it, to honor Champlain's discovery of the lake three hundred years before, in 1609. They didn't get the monument done until three years later, so 1909 became 1912. They had a fancy word for the celebration - tercentenary. No one expected the French to bring a Rodin, but they did. You know, hardly anyone knows about it, and the people up there in the North Country don't give a damn."

"How big is the sculpture?" Klocks asked, unable to temper his rising curiosity. He knew Rodin was probably the most famous sculptor in the world. Before Klocks had immersed himself in the business of antiquities, even he, with his ninth grade education had heard of The Thinker by Rodin. He remembered the picture in his social studies book of a bronze statue of a naked man leaning over, his head tilted down, supported by his fist and forearm, his elbow on his knee - thinking. Thinking was something that Wallace Klocks's teachers had told him he wasn't good at. "Think, Wallace, think," they would say. He hated school. But he always remembered that statue and the name of the sculptor who made it.

"How big is it?" the old man repeated, trying to recall. "It's more like a big plaque. I'd guess you'd call it a bust. It's embedded in granite. It's a bust of some woman. It's half the size of that painting of yours behind the counter, the one of that naked lady and the tiger."

"No kidding? A Rodin sculpture."

"No kidding."

"You're dead serious."

"I'm dead serious."

Klocks began to whistle. He swung open the oak door with a flick of his toe, and another blast of moist heat, sealed his decision. August in Apalachicola made August in the Adirondacks awfully appealing.

He put his arm around Harry Southard, slipping two fingers into the old man's breast pocket, lifting the bills. Just to see if he could do it. He escorted this sorcerer, who had rekindled the thief in him, to his car. Klocks held the cardboard box while the old man fumbled for his keys.

Klocks admired the car, a 1977 two-door Cadillac Coupe de Ville, and noted the Florida license plates.

"Where do you live?" Klocks asked with all the innocence he could muster.

"Near the bay off Avenue B." The old man was distracted. "My money. Where's the money? I put it here with the keys."

"Oh," Klocks said, as he thrust the cardboard box back into the gentleman's arms, "you must have dropped it when you gave me the box." Klocks reached down and appeared to pluck the folded bills off the cracked sidewalk.

The old man, angling his head, regarded him a bit oddly, and said, "Thank you, sir." Klocks couldn't recall when he had last been called "sir." His hand in his pockets, Klocks fondled the lucky fob, as he would come to call it, calming his racing mind.

Back inside his store, Klocks beheld the lamps and paintings and then gazed into one of the standing mirrors. "Being a thief is an honorable profession," he announced. "I've got work to do."

Two

The horse scene in Saratoga Springs and the bust of a woman in Crown Point beckoned him, while the August heat of the Florida Panhandle propelled him. Klocks was ready to be Klocks again. If his Oldsmobile wouldn't make it, maybe he'd FedEx himself from Apalachicola to the Adirondacks, with a brief stop at the Saratoga track to pick up some money, not by playing the ponies, but by selling the fob.

For one year Wallace Klocks had remained anonymous. That was his plan and so far he had succeeded. But you know what? He missed where he had escaped from. He missed upstate New York. He missed having a reputation. At age forty-two Klocks was learning that everyone wanted to be somebody.

It was hard to believe, that he had been gone a whole year. The only item in the shop of value to Klocks, that he needed to find a home for, was the Beauvais painting of the tiger and the nude. Which wasn't a problem. The Gibson Inn, two roadhouses, and the Oyster Cove on St. George Island had badgered him about hanging it behind their bars.

Klocks needed the cash. This time rather than press the floor button, he phoned his buddy near the stoplight, who agreed to give him a thousand bucks up front in return for brokering the painting and the rest of the contents of his antique store. Klocks was not planning on returning.

With that transaction complete, Klocks emptied the cash register of all the bills and quarters. He grabbed a satchel and threw in a few items, including an antique chisel. Wallace Klocks pulled the string on the fan for the last time, and walked out backwards into the sweltering heat. On impulse as he exited, he reached back in and snatched a faded leather jacket hanging from the antler coat rack.

With the heel of his boot, he kicked away the doorstop. He had brought that chunk of iron ore all the way from the 21 Mine in the hills above Port Henry. He was always impressed with the weight of that hunk of magnetite. He picked up the iron ore, reopened the door, and stuck it in an urn.

Klocks walked around behind the shop, his shirt clinging to his back, to check on the pulse on his 88 Oldsmobile, for which he had no insurance and no registration. Klocks wasn't one to insure anything. Paying money for "what if," now there's a racket.

The 1954 Rocket 88 started on the first try. He sat there letting it idle, knowing that come nightfall he planned to drive away in it. The engine sounded all right, so he turned it off, and plopped his head back, thinking about the past. The one thing he loved about his old car, other than it started, was the chrome ornament of North and South America on the hood and the trunk, above the license plate.

The New York plate was part of the reason he never drove the car. The week after he arrived from the Adirondacks, he was forced off the road, twice. The first time a red pickup driving towards him swerved into his lane. The second time, some jerk in a Camaro zoomed up from behind, hanging two inches off his bumper, until Klocks veered off the road onto the crabgrass. As the car roared by, a confederate flag on its bumper, the guy riding shotgun leaned out and spit. Ordinarily Klocks would have retaliated, but he was on the run.

A year ago, not a soul knew him down there in the Panhandle, and he was puzzled by the incidents. By the end of that week, he had it figured out. This was the deep South, not like the rest of Florida. The Panhandle was really an extension of southern Georgia and southern Alabama. Outsiders called it the Redneck Riviera. The locals didn't like Yankees they didn't know, especially New Yorkers.

The source of the harassment was his New York plates. First thing he did, two weeks after his arrival, was take off the front one, which wasn't required in Florida. Then he faced a dilemma. He didn't have a Florida license or registration, and wasn't sure about his forged New York driver's license identifying him as Jonathan Deed. The last thing he needed was to have a clerk on a computer run it through a national database and turn up a discrepancy.

His landlord agreed to let Klocks leave the Rocket 88 out back against the slanted shed. Instead of a car, Klocks delighted in renting a sixteen-foot skiff with a thirty horse Evinrude. For a place to stay, he found a dingy houseboat upriver on Bonatee Bayou. The walk from the dock at Benign Boat Works on Water Street to his store on 6th Street was only three, deserted blocks. He had loved his car, but not the hassles.

The better way to travel in the Panhandle was by water and Klocks grew accustomed to it. He learned that once you were on the river, you were accepted. His penchant for fishing was a big part of that. Soon he fit right in. He even developed a bit of a drawl.

Klocks took a long breath, sighed, and got up out of his Olds. He made his way through the tall weeds, glancing back, taking his last walk from the store to the boat. He knew he would miss the fishing, especially at the Cut. In the 1950s the Army Corps of Engineers cut a deep channel from the Gulf of Mexico through the barrier islands and the shallows of Apalachicola Bay into the harbor. The Cut was the best fishing spot on St. George Island.

Klocks fished there with the night bartender at Gibson's, who lived at the Plantation near the Cut. The tiny no-see-ems were the only drawback, pestering them on the walk out to the breakwater. For bait, they used pinfish, cigar minnows, live shrimp and sand fleas. Every kind of fish was out there; tarpon and shark feeding on redfish and pompano. Those good times would be missed.

As he stepped onto the marina dock, Klocks snapped out of his daydreaming. "Hey, Butch," he waved. "I'm heading out. I'm leaving tonight, and I might not be back for awhile. I'll settle up with you in a few hours."

"You leaving us? Here we were getting right comfortable with you," Butch said, trying not to expend too much energy in the heat. "We gave you an anchor too, right?"

"Right, that'll be in the boat." Klocks stepped gingerly down into his skiff.

"What did you do, find some babe, some Tallahassee coed?" Butch cooed. Butch was one of the gay boys who worked at the marina.

"Nope. I did find a job I couldn't pass up."

"Well, send something my way, will you, sweetie?"

Klocks smirked and tossed him a look. He yanked the cord of his Evinrude and the outboard sputtered to life. He waited for the shrimp boat, the Pelican II, to pass. It was coming in from the Gulf, through the Cut, across the bay, up the river, heading for Scipio Creek Marina, trailing a cloud of squawking seagulls, a sign of a good catch. He undid the figure eight from around the stanchion and eased out into the current, bow upstream. He ferried across, knowing enough to avoid the sand bar in the middle, before opening the throttle and heading up the Apalachicola River for the last time.

Forty minutes later, just past the railroad-bridge, he throttled down. He had caught so many catfish in and around those piers he had lost count. Upstream from the railroad, he seldom saw another boat, just alligators and miles of dense green shoreline. The sloughs of the floodplain forest were thick with overhanging vegetation. He remembered which meandering creek was his by a patch of beach on the opposite shore, where the gators sunbathed. Even EcoVentures couldn't find his place. They ran estuary tours up the river, through the marsh and deep into the swamps. But their chartered boat, the forty-foot Osprey, was too big for his bayou.

Klocks tended to get whacked in the face by tupelo tree branches camouflaging his opening to Bonatee Bayou. This time he carefully parted the bushes and vines, and watched the neighborhood white egret flap away. There, on the far side of the backwater, sat his tilting houseboat.

His fishnet hammock hung on the rotting sliver of a deck, where he had spent a few glorious Saturday afternoons, drinking beer, tossing the empties at fire-back crayfish, listening to the radio as Coach Bobby Bowden and the Florida State Seminoles clobbered some rival.

The cost for the houseboat was one hundred dollars a month and there were no such things as human visitors. He didn't know who owned the land, designated a natural resource to help keep the oysters pollution-free. Maybe the State of Florida or the Nature Conservancy owned it as part of the estuary.

Above Klocks's houseboat, which from the air looked like a decaying stump, mosquitoes dropped down in clouds. Klocks had concocted a makeshift system of netting to defend against those suckers.

But those days are gone, thought Klocks, as he rummaged around in his mind for what to pack, feeling more energized than he had in months. He cherished having a clear-cut goal. He always traveled light, one bag. He never knew when he might have to get up and move quickly, or flat out run.

Going back to where he had pulled the perfect prison escape was reckless. But a man, at his core, never really changes.

He makes adjustments borne out of necessity, then during times of total freedom or total desperation reverts back to his basic nature.

Klocks cut the outboard by pulling out the choke and drifted in alongside his moldy houseboat. A fearless gray kingfisher fluttered out of the rotten, wooden mailbox, which was a decorative, backcountry joke. No mail was delivered in the bayou. Klocks stepped out of his boat.

He examined himself in a broken shard of mirror fastened to a mangrove tree. Scraggly beard, with a gut. Losing his edge. Dying of the heat down here in the Panhandle. Craving the cool air of the Adirondacks. He was thinking, nobody's seen me with a beard up there in New York at Moriah Shock Incarceration.

In the prison library he had studied old maps of the mining tunnels in and around Mineville. He chose the most harrowing of all mines, the 21 Mine, to run down into. Somehow, without drowning, he found his way out of the maze of tunnels and shafts.

Inside the living quarters of his houseboat, he took two steps towards a cupboard door which at one time swung open during the night. At three in the morning, after too many beers, he would get up off his mattress to piss, nick the top of his head, and wake up the next morning with a bump. Finally he had just taped the damn thing shut.

He ripped the duct tape off the cupboard door, tossing aside empty bottles, while looking for a certain can of stewed tomatoes. From the can, Klocks pulled out a roll of twenties and shoved it into a front pocket of his jeans. Into his satchel, made of thick, Arabian carpet, he stuffed a couple of black T-shirts, his box of cobia jigs and casting lures, and a fishing knife.

He wanted to leave before nightfall. He patted his shirt pocket for his cell phone. He had his fake ID. One last thing. He peeked in his mailbox, which was full of sticks, doubling as the

Kingfisher's nest. He was curious to see if the babies had hatched. Among the grass-lined twigs, he caught sight of three pinkish eggs blotched with brown.

Upriver, off St. Marks Creek, in another abandoned houseboat lived another swamp rat like Klocks. Klocks would have liked to say good-bye, but he wasn't about to try to locate the hideaway after dark, when primeval creatures, real and imagined, slithered around the river bayous.

If all went well, an hour from now, at dusk, he'd be back at BayKing Charters standing under a galvanized roof, saying good-bye to his fishing buddies, before heading north on Route 98.

Three

Twenty-five hours later, on Thursday evening, Klocks turned off Northway exit 14 onto Union Avenue in Saratoga Springs to score some cash, catch some shut eye and rest his Oldsmobile, which was leaking oil. He drove straight to Bobby Benson's Antiques on Broadway. Benson had recently hit the big time by going on-line. He once was the typical upstate antique dealer until the Internet came along, and then all the junk, collectibles, and genuine antiques that had been collecting dust suddenly sold on eBay.

Klocks parked in the loading zone and checked his pocket watch for the time. He gazed at the watch fob that he had grown attached to on the ride up from Florida. But business was business and he had one thousand one hundred and sixty bucks left to his name. He was looking for another four hundred.

Assuming that the watch chain was early 1900s and twenty-four karat gold, Klocks guessed that a swell, one of those dashing, fashionable horse worshipers, might pay five hundred bucks. That would be an optimum price.

It was nearing 6:00 and a lady was inside Benson's fiddling with the glittering window display. Klocks hurried to the door. Summer hours were tied to the track, and the last race was over at 5:30. By 7:00 most of the shoppers had met up with their mates at the track and were dining, many around the corner at Sperry's and One Caroline St. Bistro.

Klocks pushed on the door but it was locked. He caught the lady's eye and taking out his prized fob, swung it back and forth with a big smile on his face as though trying to hypnotize her with the watch. A man in the back of the store motioned to the lady to unlock the door.

"Hello, I phoned ahead. I have an item that Bobby said he'd like to take a look at."

Benson had already turned on his examining light. "Where did you get it?" he asked.

"A Florida estate. It belonged to a man's father - a state senator. The man was old, old. "

"Hum," Benson said, turning it over in his hand, under the bright light, examining it again through an eyepiece. Unbeknownst to Klocks, he was looking for the minuscule initials of its designer. "How much do you want for it?"

"Five hundred bucks," Klocks said. He was a little road weary, not his usual sharp self. Generally he segued into a transaction, enjoying the dialogue, before jockeying for an advantage.

"I can't give you five hundred dollars. I have to make a profit, and on jewelry I try to make a minimum of fifty percent." Benson could be frank because most of his money was made on-line. "Five hundred dollars is what I would sell it for." He put down the fob and inspected Klocks. He wasn't the prettiest sight in blue jeans, an old leather jacket and a scruffy growth of beard. But with the track crowd one could never tell. Some were seedy, some were rich, and some were seedy and rich.

Benson elaborated. "This watch fob is attractive because of the horse motif. I would definitely display it, here, under this glass, next to these diamond studs. I'd say it comes from the 1920s, an era that people, particularly the horse crowd, are enamored with."

"Another dealer down south, a friend of mine, said flat-out it's worth five bills." Klocks said.

"I know that, but I have to make a profit." Benson took out a calculator. "I'll cut my profit in half to $125."

Klocks eyes widened in disbelief until he realized that wasn't the price he was being offered.

"How does $375 sound? Pretty generous, I think. Too generous, really. But now that I've said it, I'll stick to it - for about one minute."

Klocks was nonplused. He was usually the one in control. He sensed the guy wasn't kidding. In fact Benson was looking down at his watch.

"All right. I'll take it. I'll take the deal." He reached for Benson's hand to shake.

"Mary," Benson called through the slot to the back room, "could you get me $375." He turned back to Klocks. "You've done well. I haven't paid that much for something off the street in a week."

In a week, thought Klocks, is that an insult or what? Klocks walked out counting the bills.

Benson wore an equally glum look. He never gloated. "Mary, display this for the weekend. Put $575 on it. If I can turn it over quickly, I will. But it is signed Schlumberger and the Sotheby's fall jewelry auction is coming up. I hope we haven't missed the deadline for the catalogue." Schlumberger was an esteemed designer of Tiffany jewelry.

Meanwhile Klocks was beat from the long drive, feeling he had grown soft down in Florida, too many Hurricanes (the drink not the storm). He folded the bills in half and slid them in his silver money clip, which he inserted in his hideaway behind the ashtray. The track was out and Broadway was packed. The temperature was right - high sixties, and he had just made almost three times what the fob cost. You never lose money by taking a profit, he reminded himself, trying to assuage his pride.

A convertible Mercedes with Florida plates slowed to allow Klocks's Oldsmobile 88 to pull out and then immediately glided into his parking spot. Klocks stopped at the red light on

Broadway and Lake. He turned right on Lake, then right on Maple. He had made a big U-turn of sorts and came to the intersection of Caroline and Maple where it looked like a block party was going on, reminding him of New Orleans.

His face was drooping, his eyes downcast, his chin hanging. He crawled through the crowded four-way intersection passing the Ice House bar, where one wall was open to the outside, much like a garage with the door up. Ten yards farther loomed the sanctuary of a large library parking lot. He turned in.

Some college kid wearing white shorts, black loafers and no socks in a crowd of preppies yelled at him about no turn signal. Klocks rolled down his window, and realized he barely had the energy to speak. His turn signal didn't work. Should he run after the little shit? No, the kid didn't know whom he was dealing with. "I'm an escaped convict, you fool."

A baby-blue convertible Cadillac backed out of a space. Klocks braked and pointed to the spot. The driver touched his hat and didn't move forward out of the lot until Klocks had maneuvered his Olds into the spot. Klocks was fading. With effort he cranked up his window almost to the top and reaching, pressed down the four door locks. He tossed his cell phone in the glove compartment, climbed up over the top of the front seat flopping onto the back seat, pulling the satchel up off the floor to use as pillow. The last thing he remembered before he was awakened by a cop in the early morning was the juke box from the Ice House bar playing the Stones' I can't get no satisfaction.

"Can't spend the night here," the cop stated. The bundle in the back didn't move. "Hey, wake-up. You! Move it. Get out of here." The cop circled the car, as Klocks sat up in the back seat.

He was trying to shake off the cobwebs and make out what was going on. For a moment he wasn't sure of where he was. He wasn't in Florida anymore, where he never saw a cop, especially after he swapped his car for a boat, and the road for a river. He didn't want any trouble. This was New York, one hell of a regulated state. Klocks was convinced that big brother kept tabs on its citizens through cars - registration, picture IDs, and traffic tickets; all a means of surveillance.

To make his point the cop whipped out his pad, as if he were about to write a ticket.

Klocks piped up, "Yes, sir. I'm leaving, sir."

Klocks noticed the people were gone and the music had stopped. Only a few other cars remained parked in the lot. He checked his pocket watch and winced, realizing he no longer owned the golden fob. It was 6:30 in the morning. As Klocks pulled out of the lot and headed north, the cop put his pad away.

Wallace Klocks couldn't believe how unprepared and foggy he had been. He winced again, reminding himself that he was driving an unregistered, uninspected vehicle, with "borrowed" Florida plates from gentleman Harry Southard. He stopped to think about where he was, and who he was. For a year he had been Jonathan Deed, starting a new life with a new attitude in the Florida Panhandle. But the closer he got to upstate New York, to Troy, to Saratoga Springs and ultimately to Port Henry, the more he reverted back to the Wallace Klocks of old, the one whom all of upstate thought dead and drowned in the treacherous 21 Mine.

"My finest achievement. Pure will," Klocks purred.

Four

K locks did his best thinking while driving, but right now he was stymied. He was trying to outrun the cloud of uncertainty that was overtaking him. On the one hand, why was he hesitating? On the other hand, what the hell was he doing, once again, risking all? At first, all he wanted was a chance for a new start. Lately, he felt guilty about the second chances he hadn't given his partners in crime, the thieves he pulled jobs with. He didn't dwell on that. He was human. He made mistakes.

Was this another mistake? The alternative was to be a nobody. Klocks missed his notorious reputation. Living alone in Florida hadn't been all it was cranked up to be. Klocks liked to picture himself as a man of action. He walked the walk. A man built a life on what he did, not what he said. So here he was, venturing back upstate.

With his right hand, he checked behind the ashtray for his stash. Still there. "And what about a woman? I've got no woman," he murmured.

After an hour and a half of the hilly, winding roads of the southern Adirondacks, he saw the sign, "Bridge to Vermont, to Rt. 17," and made a right past several parked cars. He accelerated up over a railroad overpass. He was on a four-mile spur off routes 22 and 9N, on a wide peninsula made up of farm land, marshes, and lakeside cabins, which at the end jutted out into the lake to within a quarter mile of the Vermont shore, forming a narrow channel.

The historic French Fort St. Frederic built in 1734, and His Majesty's Fort built in 1759 marked the tip of this strategic peninsula. When it was built, the British fort was the largest in the New World. The forts lay in ruins due to fire and the gradual disintegration of the soft limestone rock of which they were made. The only intact structure was a nearby light station built in 1858. The lighthouse became the Champlain Monument and in 1912, the home of a Rodin sculpture. The Champlain Bridge, built in 1929, was the one featured in Southard's old photograph. The State bestowed the name the Crown Point Historic Site on the tip of the peninsula.

Klocks braked for a porcupine waddling across the highway, sending a plastic quart of Mobil oil sliding out from under his front seat. Back in the Florida bayou, he had plucked the quills from a dead porcupine, to make a tiny tepee. The quart reminded him that the seal of his engine block was probably shot, which signaled the beginning of the end for his Oldsmobile 88. Klocks took the waddling porcupine as a bad omen.

Even in August the Crown Point peninsula looked desolate and deserted. Klocks guessed the town was somewhere else, and he was right. The town of Crown Point was an outgrowth of the French control of the peninsula and in the 1730s was the first community to be settled in Essex County. He had passed through it coming north from Saratoga.

The town of Crown Point got its name from a battle early in the 1600's where the victorious Algonquin Indians took scalps. This battle, where the Indian custom of scalping began, occurred near the channel, at the tip of the peninsula, on the "point." The French called the place "Scalp Point." When the British translated the phrase, it came out "Crown Point."

The sign for the Champlain Bridge said four miles and he had already driven two, passing by the Bridge Deli & Market, tempting him to stop for some beef jerky.

From the village of Port Henry which was on a bluff overlooking the lake, the bridge was a peaceful sight, especially on a warm summer night when its twinkling white lights outlined its center arch like a starry constellation on the horizon. Officially the name was the Champlain Bridge, but in the neighboring towns in the Adirondacks it was known as the Crown Point Bridge, and then as you got closer as simply, "the Bridge."

As he approached, Klocks's mood was darkening. He had no woman, no friends. His only encounter on the drive up had been with a pushy patrolman. What happened to the good old days when people used to meet and make friends on the road? Instead he met with days of solitude, nights of sweat and worry. Or was he confusing his rosy prison dreams about life outside with the reality of life outside?

That's usually how he operated. Back himself into a corner, until he had no car, no money, and no friends. Until he had to act. "I wonder how high it is?" Klocks mused. "I used to jump off bridges."

He drove onward on a smooth, well-maintained road sweeping around a curve past some yellow and brown state signs he didn't read. Then came the bridge. He hadn't planned to go over, but the bridge was pulling him forward, reeling him in like a carrier pigeon with a message.

He saw some tents and trailers and on the left the foundation of the French fort. It was a narrow bridge, no toll, no room for walkers or bikers on either side, no traffic. He was driving ten miles per hour, purposely not looking at the lighthouse, though he caught sight of it two hundred yards to his right. He checked his rear view mirror as he climbed, still nobody behind him. He reached the crest of the bridge, and came to a rolling stop.

The old-timer who had been in his antique shop in Florida drifted into his thoughts. He imagined a biplane zooming under the bridge. All at once he was peculiarly exhilarated. He spied a plaque across the other lane at the top of the bridge. He shifted the car to park, left the engine running, and hopped out.

It was windy. Looking both ways, he crossed to read the plaque, mouthing each word with open lips. It was an accomplishment getting a bridge built at the cost of a million dollars the year before the Great Depression. He was impressed that it stood unchanged since the stock market crash. Maybe somebody jumped off back then on Black Tuesday. At what height does jumping into water become fatal?

Distracted, as if watching himself, Klocks took a step up onto the narrow, raised walkway. A noise jolted him. A cement-mixing truck was coming from the New York viaduct. The driver could not see over and beyond the rounded crest of the roadway into the oncoming lane. The behemoth chugged by, avoiding the open door of Klocks's Oldsmobile. The ruddy-faced driver fixed Klocks with a perplexed, alarmed stare. After the driver passed the height of the span, gaining momentum down the Vermont side of the bridge, he craned his neck and yelled back, "Don't jump."

Dazed, Klocks braced himself against the wind by holding on to a grime-covered guy wire attached to a tall lamppost. He squinted out, over and down, at blue waves in the black water below, rippling with strings of white foam. An innocent sight, like a child's dream. He released his hand and squeezed his palms. His chest tightened. The water did draw him.

The bay was blurry and beautiful. He spied a sailboat. Was it a nice day? He thought it was. He turned around, looking at the open door in wonderment. He wasn't the careless type. Is that why he left the car door open?

I'm losing myself. Is it the pull of gravity? Is it a death wish? Only a slim edge to stand on, then miles of space. What's the word? Not dizziness, but I'm afraid I'll fall.

The sun lighting up the green above the first red leaves of autumn. Swatches of hardwood, paths of maple. The mountains winding down.

Below me, the blackness of the water, the whiteness atop the waves - a chalk drawing calling me closer. Are they large waves or small waves? I need to see someone in a canoe, then I'll know.

I step off, but don't seem to fall. I float. Am I rising? Is the magnetic, beauty of the Green Mountains pulling me upward? I feel the cold wind opening my mouth, pushing the skin around my face. I'm flying, flying to heaven. Three seconds can be a long time.

A noise, not the wind, not himself hitting the water, interrupted his trance. It was the noise of another car, this one from Vermont, stopped with the door open, just like his. Two people ran towards him, a big boy and a big girl. They were hugging him. No they were pulling him back from the edge of the bridge, tackling him. The boy was yelling in his ear, "You're okay. You're okay."

Klocks was rocking back and forth.

"You all right? I'm not letting go." The boy turned to the girl, "Kim, drive to the campsite. I've got him. I'll take his car and meet you there."

Then he said to Klocks, "Okay buddy, easy does it. I'm driving your car, first to Chimney Point right there, where I'll turn around and drive back over the bridge."

"That's fine," Klocks mumbled, his expression saying, what's all the fuss? "I was just reading a plaque. I'm not that fast a reader. And then I looked over the edge. And then I don't remember."

"Mister, you were leaning out with your arms spread. If you weren't about to jump then you were about to fly."

It was sunny and sixty, but Klocks was shivering. He noticed he was inside his own car but this college-age kid was driving while holding his wrist. The boy eyed him like a doctor as Klocks meekly slid his hand away. Klocks stared at the lake aware something had happened.

The boy pulled into the Crown Point campsite next to a Subaru with two kayaks on top and a worried girl standing straight with her arms crossed. She opened the passenger door and offered Klocks her hand. "We're here to help you. We're from Middlebury, from the college."

"He's shaking, Kim. Give him one of our blankets."

Klocks leaned forward. He was struggling to come back from wherever he had been. "Give me a minute." He tried to snap out of it, to relax, to breathe deep and slow. He saw the lighthouse in the distance. He knew it meant something to him, but he wasn't sure what.

The couple let him sit there, but the boy, Matt Jenkins, who liked to think he was pretty savvy in these situations, kept the keys to Klocks's car. He and his girlfriend Kim walked around to the other side of their car, out of earshot of Klocks.

"I told you that concrete truck blinked its lights for a reason."

"Was he trying to jump, really?"

"I'd say so," Matt said. "Christ, it was pretty scary."

"It was," Kim said, as she glanced back over at Klocks, who had his head back and the blanket in his lap. "Is there anything else we should do. Should we call an ambulance or something?"

Matt turned and surveyed the bridge. "I wonder how high it is. I don't think you'd necessarily die. How high is Barn Rock? Seventy-two feet right? How much higher is the bridge?"

"Higher, way higher," Kim said. "Anyway, you learned you have to land just right." Kim thought for a minute. "The museum director told me there was a guy in a pickup truck, with his wife and kids in it, who stopped at the top and jumped off. Like five years ago. He died. Then the Vermont troopers found out this guy had jumped off other bridges for thrills. So I don't know, if it was, like, ruled a suicide or not."

"I think I could do it. Be just like jumping a humongous waterfall in my kayak."

"Sure, Matt. But your plastic kayak hits first, not your body."

"I'd still like to find out the exact height."

"Don't worry. When my internship is done, I'll know all about this place - the forts, the bridge, the lighthouse. I almost wished they still charged tolls."

"Let's talk to our patient," Matt said.

Klocks was up now, walking slowly towards them. "Do you have a cigarette?"

Matt raised his eyebrows and said, "Nope."

"Wait a minute," Kim said, "I might have, in my purse."

She got her purse from under the front seat. "Yeah, I think I do."

"What! What are you doing, smoking?" Matt asked.

"Relax, Matt, I just brought them with me in case, I don't know, in case the job is boring and there are no tourists asking questions."

As Kim passed Klocks a Marlboro and matches, Matt shook his head in disapproval.

Klocks took a drag. It seemed to soothe him. "Listen, thanks. I don't know what happened up there. I'm exhausted. I just drove all the way from Florida, alone. I don't know what the hell I was doing up there. I'm okay now. I'm Jonathan, Jonathan Deed."

"Do you want us to call an ambulance, Jonathan?"

"Noooo," Klocks crowed. "I just flipped out, spaced out. I don't know." Klocks closed his eyes and rubbed his forehead. He wanted to change the subject. "What do you know about this place, can you camp here?"

"Sure. Yeah, we're going to, for one night anyway. Starting tomorrow, I'm working for two weeks as an intern at the museum across the road.

"She's an archeology major," Matt added.

"Over there?" Klocks saw a roof line a couple of hundred yards off.

"Yeah, that's it. Across from the entrance to the park."

"Is it expensive to stay here in the park?" asked Klocks, still woozy.

"I think it's three dollars a night, and twelve dollars a week. Maximum stay of two weeks, unless you're disabled. Then you get some pass and you can stay as long as you want. But," she wagged her finger, "remember the park is closing in a few weeks. October 15th, something like that. The weather usually sucks in November here in the North Country."

Kim looked at Matt and said, "I can't believe I've lasted four years up here." And to Klocks, "I'm from Rhode Island, right on the ocean. Maybe that's why I'm drawn to Lake Champlain."

Klocks flipped the cigarette butt onto the parking lot pavement. He was returning to his old self. He checked out Kim and Matt.

Physically, Kim was broad shouldered and athletic like a swimmer. She was open and trusting, gullible and educated. Young men found her disarmingly attractive. Matt at six feet was only a couple of inches taller, shaggy brown hair, and sharp, observant blue eyes.

"Thanks again, kid," Klocks said sticking out his upturned palm. Matt stuck his hand out to shake hands, but Klocks pulled his away. "My keys," he said.

"Oh, right," Matt said, quickly fumbling in his front right blue jeans pocket.

"So listen, I'm good. Maybe I'll see you here at the park this evening. The beers are on me." Klocks smiled as best as he could, disappointed in himself. Something inside had crumbled, or at least short-circuited. He had always thought of himself as an independent, solo artist. Maybe that was because physically, on the outside, he kept himself in good shape with push-ups and sit-ups.

But there's an inside. Will power has its limits. He wasn't one to wallow in regret. Maybe that was his problem. He wasn't one to let something fester inside him. Klocks believed that holding onto bitterness could do a lot of physical damage, even make you sick. He needed to distance himself in time, before he examined the meaning of his trance, his blackout at the bridge. He needed to admit a few regrets. Not just the bad things he had done to other people.

He corrected himself, no, they weren't "people," they were criminals, just like him. And they were taking a risk, just like him. Klocks saw honor in being a thief. Among the underworld, it was an honorable profession. Ordinarily no one got hurt. That's why bank robbers were romanticized, especially if they didn't shoot people. No one got hurt. Banks were insured. No individuals lost their money. And citizens could relate to robbing banks because that's where the money was. The motive seemed so simple and pure.

In a way Klocks yearned for the days when he was just a thief. Being a thief was okay. In the hierarchy of the crime world, being a thief had a certain 'elan to it. He was a like a cat, sneaking inside strange places at night. Klocks had routinely burglarized antiques from the Heritage Village on Route 7, outside Bennington, Vermont. At night, he'd pull up in his pickup truck and load the antiques from the stores into his truck. Afterwards, if the cops were looking for a green pickup, he'd paint his blue. He was always painting his pickup different colors. Those were the days.

Klocks was reeling from the incident on the bridge. Sitting in his Oldsmobile, he twirled the scraggly hairs of his reddish beard between his thumb and forefinger. He recalled the saying "the habit makes the monk." Was it the beard? He had grown the beard as part of his Florida quest for anonymity. He kept the beard so no Moriah Shock correction officer stopping at Stewart's or crossing the Crown Point Bridge, would recognize him as the notorious Wallace Klocks. With a beard he looked more like a woodsman or a carpenter, or a North Country community college professor. As a disguise, the beard was working, but otherwise it was sewing the seeds of self-doubt - the type of second thoughts that buried a man of action.

Klocks had his pick of campsites. He backed up his Rocket 88 Oldsmobile next to a picnic table and stone fireplace that overlooked the lake, on a high earthen bank called Grenadier's Redoubt. He liked the view and he liked that it was right next to the lighthouse that had been made into a monument to the French explorer, Samuel de Champlain.

Klocks looked down at the driver's seat beside him and noticed the blanket the Middlebury girl had tossed over him. He should return it. She was cute too, in an athletic sort of way. He was tempted to crawl over his front seat again, curl up in the back with the blanket and close his eyes.

Instead the monument was calling him. Out on the bridge from the center of the channel the lighthouse had looked so small. Now up close it had a presence.

The monument was the physical manifestation that had propelled and pulled him back up here. The mythic Rodin sculpture was the right catalyst at the right time. It was his reason to retire from being anonymous. What happens when you're anonymous? You grow grumpy and lonely. Being anonymous is romanticized, just like being famous. Neither extreme is desirable, but if he had to choose one, he'd pick fame. Otherwise why would he be back up here when he had pulled off the perfect escape?

The one development that would piss him off was if the old gentleman in Apalachicola had deceived him. He had no tolerance for deception. To deceive Klocks was to invite retaliation. If there was no Rodin sculpture, and he had been made a fool, then he had one choice. Drive back to Florida to retaliate.

Five

K locks didn't know where he had been or what mental state he had been in the last hour. He gazed over the water at the bridge. No one else was around. His eyes followed an oil truck crossing the bridge past a Victorian house on the Chimney Point side. He looked up at a V of geese honking overhead, gliding in for a landing somewhere south of Crown Point where the lake spread out again. Below him a pair of mallards paddled out from the weeds. He squinted at a cluster of rotten logs poking up out of the edge of the water. At first he thought they were a large assortment of ducks. Then he decided they looked like the remnants of pilings from a pier.

Klocks was stalling to allow his head to clear and his mental state to mend. The lighthouse monument was less than a stone's throw away. The glamorous side of the monument where his prize awaited was on the opposite side from where he stood. Though he wasn't trespassing, Klocks looked around to make sure no one was watching.

Klocks purposely started on the side facing away from the lake, saving the best for last. He walked closer until he could see the individual panels of the hinged iron door leading to the spiral limestone steps up to the watch room.

In 1915 the illuminating apparatus for the lighthouse was a fifth order Fresnal lens made up of various reflecting and refracting prisms which gave off a fixed white light. A single-wick mineral oil furnished the light that had an intensity of 360 English C. P. (candle power). Before the lighthouse ceased operation in 1926, the focal point of the Fresnal lens, ninety-two feet above the water, could be seen from a distance of fifteen miles. Now, the only illuminating apparatus was a seventy-five watt lightbulb, which only came on if a tourist was up there and pulled the cord.

Klocks was walking around the monument's circular granite apron. By 1912 the old limestone lighthouse tower was encased and encircled by the granite monument to Champlain. Klocks stopped halfway around. Twenty feet above him on a pedestal in front of four heavy Doric columns was the side view of a French voyageur, a "coureur-de-bois," gripping his hatchet, crouched, leaning forward, squinting at the southern horizon. Klocks stepped back.

Next to the soldier in a coat and helmet stood the imposing twelve-foot figure of Samuel de Champlain. His left arm was thrust forward, hand on his arquebus, his right arm cocked at his waist, his long hair falling from under his plumed hat, over his robe, his view directly ahead, dominating the lake, his lake. Champlain sported an upturned mustache and tufted chin. On the other side of him, next to his forward foot, an Indian crouched - a Huron warrior, an ally of the French, his hair bristled up on his head, peering north. Laden with furs, the bow of a birch bark canoe protruded beneath them, splitting the waves. The three commanding figures looked as if they're were scanning the lake for the enemy of the Huron, the Iroquois. It was a striking assemblage of three warriors.

Klocks moved directly in front of the monument, looking up at Champlain. He wasn't aware of historic details, and this statue wasn't what he had come here to see, but he was struck momentarily by the force of the three men. They spent a good part of their lives struggling to conquer a raw and untamed land. There was will at work, thought Klocks.

Below the trio of men, but above the canoe, the heads of two dogs, or wolves, guarded the triumvirate, their tooth-filled jaws open, ears and nostrils alert for whatever they might pounce on. The eyes of the animals bored into Klocks's pupils. Klocks rubbed his forehead. The sight of the creatures, the dogs, spooked him. He felt they guarded the statues, their masters, like slaves guarding a pharaoh's tomb.

The mass of the monument towering above him impressed Klocks. He brought his eyes down to the stone steps behind him, fearful he could stumble backwards recoiling from the imposing aura of the statue. The sky had changed from blue to a blurry, grayish white, reminding him of the sky when he was incarcerated in Moriah Shock. Klocks gave his head a shake, as if to clear a cobweb that was fouling his thinking.

He leaned on the rough granite, stained green in streaks from ninety years of harsh Adirondack weather washing over the darkened bronze feet of Champlain and the knees of his companions, dripping onto the Fox Island granite below. A plaque four feet by two was facing him. It stated "1609 - To The Memory of Samuel Champlain - 1909: Intrepid Navigator - Scholarly Explorer - Christian Pioneer. In Commemoration Of His Discovery Of The Lake Which Bears His Name."

The first battle involving Samuel de Champlain occurred at Crown Point in July of 1609. He aided the Huron and Algonquin Indians in defeating the Iroquois by firing his arquebus and killing two Iroquois chiefs and mortally wounding a third. Most likely this was the Iroquois' first encounter with a European with a rifle and gunpowder, and it left a lasting impression. The Iroquois spent the next ninety years trying to drive Champlain and the French from the shores of the Lake.

The magnificent triumvirate of Champlain bounded by soldier and Indian, atop the jutting prow of the canoe, the furs, the canines - all this was the work of an American sculptor, Carl Heber. (Heber's heroic trio was cast in Brooklyn, where he also cast a statue of Champlain for the city of Plattsburgh, farther north on the Lake.) Though Heber's creation was much larger and more dramatic than what was set in the stone beneath, it paled besides the fame of the sculptor who created that small bust below.

Below the larger than life statues, though higher than Klocks could touch, centered over a stone pedestal, was the bust, or bas-relief, of a young French woman. It was surrounded by a French tribute to Champlain etched in the bronze, ending with the name of the sculpture, "La France."

Klocks swallowed, his nerves tingling. Frantically he surveyed the small bas-relief, desperate for the legendary signature. Quite clear in the lower left corner, angling up from left to right was the signature, A. Rodin. The letters were printed, except the "i" and the "n" were joined by a cursive line. Klocks leaned against the granite stones, closed his eyes and sighed, whispering, "Auguste Rodin."

When Klocks opened his eyes he stared upward at the woman's face. He was observing Rodin's lover and fellow sculptress, Camille Claudel, the woman who had modeled for "La France." Her head was in profile and she possessed a beautiful, serene yet vacant look on her face. Her turban-like headdress and the suggestion of an arch above accentuated her face.

He walked around the lighthouse in nervous energy coming back again to what was vital to him: the signature, which was so clear. It was unbelievable that here on a northern woods peninsula jutting out into Lake Champlain existed a genuine Rodin sculpture.

Now, how to remove the bust? Removing it without damaging the plaque, that would be the tricky part. Klocks paced back and forth, looking up between footsteps, scrutinizing Rodin's Camille, drawing on his knowledge from previous jobs.

His first problem was that Rodin's bust was about eight feet off the ground.

He peered higher up at the heroic statues of Champlain, the Huron and the Voyageur and at the elaborate bow of the canoe, and found himself again in a staring contest with one of two wolf-like dogs, half its stone head stained dark green by decades of drippings off Champlain's bronze boot. The magnificent Champlain controlling and discoloring his dogs, even in statuesque homage. On either side of the prow of the canoe, the two dogs glared down.

Klocks glared back. I'll use them to my advantage, he thought; the keys to gaining entrance to the tomb. He could rig something off the dogs and the bow of that canoe. He would need a good thick rope to throw over the bow and hoist himself up to the plaque. He would construct a webbed chair out of rope, a type of boatswain's chair, and then pulley himself up so he could work face to face with Auguste's mistress and disengage her from her stone mortuary.

Six

K locks thought, it's small, easier to steal than the statues above. He opened the rear door to his Oldsmobile and climbed back in. He reached over the leather top of the front seat and grabbed the blanket, wadding it up to use as a pillow.

Twenty minutes later a light tapping on the window awoke him. Two young faces peered at him like he was an endangered panda bear.

"Hi, it's us," Kim said. "How ya doin'?"

At first he was looking around, disoriented, until he saw the lighthouse monument in the background.

"What are you doing this afternoon?" she asked.

"Me, I'm here. Man, I'm camping here for two weeks, for as long as I can."

"Matt has this crazy idea. He's rented a speedboat from Velez Marina in Port Henry. Over there," she pointed.

"I know where Port Henry is," he said. "Listen, thanks for coming along when you did today, but don't feel like you have to stick around to take care of me."

"No, that's not it. I start work at the museum tomorrow morning and this is our last day to play. So Matt's rented a boat for the afternoon. Why don't you come along? It will be fun."

Klocks loved the water and boats. For him they meant freedom. No double lines to cross, no rules once you left the marina, and no cops. He'd never been stopped on the water.

"Isn't three a crowd?"

"Oh don't worry about that," she said, giggling. "During the summer he works on the lake at Camp Dudley. He's all about the guys right now." Kim hesitated. "Well, Matt thinks you have a fear of heights - vertigo. He doesn't think you were trying to, you know, commit suicide or whatever and neither do I. So come with us. He's going to jump off Barn Rock and so am I . . . maybe."

Kim realized it was kind of weird them inviting a guy who sleeps in his car to come out and play. Nice kids didn't hang out with unshaven strangers. But Matt and especially Kim were tired of being predictable. Weren't the college years when you were supposed to experiment?

And, this was the end of summer. You're meant to take chances in the summer, hang out with people you ordinarily wouldn't hang out with, make love to people you ordinarily wouldn't make love to. At least that's what happened in some of the trashy books she read. And finally Kim felt sorry for him, whatever his problem was, all alone.

Klocks sat up straight and stared out the through the front windshield, shielding his eyes because the sun had broken through the haze, blinding him. He sagged back down until he was sprawled across the back seat, propped up on one elbow.

"You know what, I will join you," he said.

Wearing shorts only, he crawled out the back door head first, using his hands like an animal's forepaws. He was horizontal, all the way out of the car, except for his feet, suspended over the gravel and grass. He did twenty push-ups, his usual number, and felt better.

Kim watched the first few, mesmerized by the crisscrossing scars and tattoos on his muscular back, then busied herself elsewhere, turning her head back to the windshield. She read the inspection sticker and noticed it had expired.

He hoisted himself into the back seat, agile like a trapeze artist, his feet never having touched the ground. She turned and said, "You'll need a bathing suit."

Klocks raised his eyes and cocked his head. "Will boxers do?"

"Not really," she said. "Barn Rock is high. If you want to jump - you don't have to, but if you do, you're going to need protection. Wear your blue jeans. That way if you land wrong, aside from what else you might hurt, your legs will be protected. A week ago it was 90 degrees here, and a bunch of us went from Basin Harbor. This one kid, Harold, had too many beers. He landed in the sitting position," which Kim half-demonstrated as she rattled on, "and, I mean you could hear that slap echo off the lake. He was still moaning when he climbed out of the water. He was wearing a bathing suit and the bottom of his thighs were bright red."

Klocks's forehead furrowed. "How high is it?"

"Seventy-two feet. That varies a few feet with the level of the lake. We haven't had a good rain in a while, so it might even be higher."

Klocks's expression changed. Two little grooves between his eyebrows replaced the wrinkles.

"At the most, a couple of more feet. It's always August when we go cliff jumping. Otherwise, the water's too cold. Look, don't jump from the top."

Klocks didn't have a sense of how high seventy-two feet was. "How high is that lighthouse?"

"That's the kind of stuff I've been learning for this internship. Part of my job is to be a tour guide. That's what they're going to do - promote tour guides for the two forts, the big British one, the older French one, and for the lighthouse monument."

"So how high is it?"

"Let's see, the lighthouse itself is sixty-four feet. And it sits twenty-eight feet above the lake."

Klocks had never heard a girl, a woman, talk so fast, and with such confidence about everything from protecting his balls to the height of the lighthouse. From Klocks's viewpoint, anyway, she was gaining in sex appeal and stature.

Klocks regarded her and then the lighthouse. Neither looked too bad. He glanced out through the sumac and the yellowing leaves of the oak trees to the graceful lines of the bridge. "What about the bridge? How high is the bridge?"

"The museum has such a great view of the bridge, tourists always ask about the bridge. It's ninety-two feet." The Museum director had printed up a single sheet of vital statistics, and Kim remembered the height of the roadway at the center of the bridge was the same as the deepest part of the channel, ninety-two feet. "That's odd," she said, realizing that the top of the lighthouse was also the same height above the lake.

"Twenty feet higher than Barn Rock?"

"Correct," said Kim the tour guide.

Seven

"There he is," Kim cried out. "Oh, I've got to get my suit. Help him dock." Kim ran to her Subaru, calling back, "Get your blue jeans."

Klocks changed and walked past the monument and down the granite steps to the long concrete wharf covered in a green slate roof. Prior to 1929, before the bridge was finished, Kim had told him the wharf was used for steamboats ferrying people and supplies across the channel.

Klocks watched the motor boat pass between the first and second bridge piers and then swing out to avoid the remnants of a dock - the rotting pilings that Klocks had mistaken for ducks.

Matt was steering, standing shirtless in the afternoon sun. He cut quite the muscular figure, as did Klocks in his own blue-collar way. Klocks's tank top showed his white, hairy chest, contrasting with Matt's, which was tanned and smooth.

Another dump truck, this time empty, rattled across the bridge on the way back from Vermont. Probably from the same job the concrete truck was delivering to. To Klocks, the morning incident on the bridge seemed far off, like it had happened to someone else long ago.

Leaning into the turn, having some fun, Matt zipped by the wharf, which was shaped like a capital T. On the next pass, he slowed down, and cut his engine a few feet away. He tossed the bow rope to Klocks, who looped it twice around a large iron stanchion bolted to the corner of the dock.

Just as Matt asked, "Where's Kim?" she appeared beneath the lighthouse monument, in her green tank suit, full of energy, looking as if she were auditioning for a lifeguard on Baywatch. She trotted down the steps and to the dock her hands full with towels and a cooler.

She plopped them down. "The sun," she exclaimed opening her arms wide, titling her head back, radiating youth and beauty.

"I've been in the woods too long," commented Klocks, who understood that he was in the "old enough to be her father" category.

"Come on, get in," motioned Matt, his arm outstretched.

Klocks had to accept the situation. He wasn't in charge. He'd have to change. Change is good, right. Sit back and enjoy the ride. He did notice that the boat was a fiberglass, sixteen-foot Bayliner, which couldn't compare to the twenty-four foot, glistening, wooden Hacker-Craft in which he rode out of town a year ago.

When they left, Matt steered the boat directly under the center span, ninety-two feet above the water. Under the bridge orange streaks of rust poured down the sides of the concrete piers, like drippings on a painter's canvas. Up close, the stained and patched piers, in the shadow of the roadway they supported, seemed dark and foreboding. As they motored by, Matt pointed to a narrow, metal ladder running forty feet down the side of the pier, stopping above the waterline.

"Too high for a swimmer," Matt commented.

"But just right for someone in a boat," Klocks replied. He was figuring out the logistics for transporting the Rodin. He was trying to foresee any contingency.

Kim and Matt weren't old enough or experienced enough to be jaded and suspicious of strangers. But perhaps they should have been. Klocks wasn't like Kim and Matt's friends or their fathers' friends. On the one hand, he was an unshaven deadbeat who slept in his car and hadn't bathed in days. On the other hand he was a street-savvy hustler who viewed himself as risen from the impoverished to become a purveyor of antiquities and antiques - basically an art thief.

In the summer near the water, the superficial trappings of class distinctions were less obvious, especially if one were young and trusting. Vacationers wore cut-off jeans and bathing suits, more fun to look at but fewer clothes to judge by. Besides Kim and Matt felt sorry for Klocks, so beset with doubt and loneliness that he had apparently contemplated suicide by jumping off a bridge.

Klocks tolerated the long and bumpy ride to Barn Rock because he had never seen the lake north of Port Henry. He sat alone in the stern near the outboard engine. The noise prevented any conversation. The lovebirds up front sat arm-in-arm the whole way.

Matt took the west channel hugging the New York shoreline, which was undeveloped compared to Vermont's. The only landmark Klocks recognized was the mountainous heap of tailings above Port Henry in the hills of Mineville.

During the heydays of the iron ore mines in Moriah, the Witherbees and Shermans, who owned the mines, bought the point of land where the forts had been built, with an eye towards preservation. In 1910 they presented the point to the State of New York with a deed that said the ruins should be preserved for all time.

Along the eastern shore of the historic lake the railroad tracks of the Delaware & Hudson had been laid down in 1875 as the Northeast corridor between two great cities, Montreal and New York. North of Port Henry, at the edge of the town of Westport, they veered inland. This westerly turn in the tracks was due to the influence of a local state senator who appreciated the value of an unobstructed shoreline in the upscale, lakeside community of Westport.

When a blackened orange engine pulling two yellow D & H freight cars sped north from the freight yard in Port Henry, Matt pushed the throttle of the Bayliner forward, trying to keep up. Kim stood, and in a suggestive manner, swayed her hips side to side, waving her arm back and forth at the engineer, her hand seeming to float in the air. Klocks found himself staring at the motion of her body.

"Good thing the engineer is on tracks, otherwise he might crash," Klocks quipped.

Matt turned around, knowing Klocks had said something. Matt tapped his ear indicating he couldn't hear, and Klocks flicked one hand indicating what he said wasn't worth repeating.

"Poor guy," Klocks mumbled, thinking of the engineer. "That's a different life." One that wasn't exciting enough for Klocks.

Next to the bed of the tracks were slabs of shale and toppled blocks of stone making up the shoreline known as "the iron mines." Long ago workers had quarried the cliffs above, the blocks left to be transported by barge to be used elsewhere.

Matt skimmed across the smoother water near shore. Directly in the path of their boat, a point of land with one camp jutted out into the lake. Matt was forced to turn easterly towards Vermont. They were losing anyway. As they pulled away, their view was of multicolored freight cars riding on rails cut into a tan cliff, the powerful orange locomotive disappearing behind the green peninsula.

On the other side of the little peninsula was Mullen Bay. From there Matt made a beeline for a distant point of land. Klocks spied an island and a beach. Sailboats abounded. Slick cabins, backed by manicured playing fields, overlooked a miniature harbor that included a pool full of swimmers. Matt swerved into Cole Bay around Albany Island skirting three moored yachts from Montreal. He fishtailed back out by some marker buoys, raising a large wake. This was the Camp Dudley that Klocks would soon hear about.

Matt was an alumnus of Camp Dudley, a cub and eventually a leader and coach of the lacrosse program. Dudley was like a big fraternity, and Matt liked that. Every counselor of any renown had a nickname. Matt's was "Check" because he was known for his brutal cross-checking in lacrosse. He had even returned to their annual New Year's Eve party, but now he had a girl, "K," who wasn't as keen on the Dudley scene.

Matt glided by the woodsy brown boathouse and then gave North Point a wide berth. He was looking for the backside of a totem pole carved by his buddy, Daddy Wags who was one of the old-time counselors caught up in the back-to-the-country movement of the 1970's. After thirteen years of summers at the camp, he settled year-round in the Adirondacks to build houses.

Once past Dudley, Matt headed for the open water of Lake Champlain. They bucked through larger waves, the hull slamming down every three waves, jarring Klocks's back and mind. He felt like he didn't belong in this boat with these two preppy-types.

Kim wrapped a towel around her shoulders and tossed one back to Klocks, almost flinging it out of the boat. The spray was soaking Klocks and he crouched down and moved up under the protection from the windshield. Matt was standing and pointing out the four largest Westport estates, that, when the leaves were gone, were all visible from the center of the lake. "The Mansions of the Matriarchs," he called them, but neither Kim nor Klocks were listening. "If we were in closer near the Yacht Club," Matt said, "we could see the homes of the Three Widows along the shore, too."

Matt steered out across Northwest Bay aiming for Partridge Harbor near the end of Westport's North Shore. Ten minutes after reaching and skirting the sheltered, wooded harbor,

Matt yelled "Thar she blows!" He pointed dead ahead to a light gray rock face that didn't look so incredibly high, at least not from a mile away.

The three of them could see across the mile-wide channel to Basin Harbor in Vermont. The ride from the Champlain Bridge to Barn Rock had taken maybe forty minutes. As they motored closer Kim grew fidgety, a little nervous, not sure about jumping from the top. Her watch was waterproof but she took it off anyway.

In the fringes of the afternoon, the imperial Barn Rock commanded its own harbor in the growing shadows cast by the large cedars and white pines arching out from the cliffs on the other side of the cove. Slashing below Barn Rock's angular top, a broad, whitish band of granite stood out. As they cruised closer the darker brown grooves and gashes from top to bottom accentuated the height. It was an impressive hunk of rock, shaped like the Rock of Gibraltar. When you were on the top, looking down, most jumpers moved back and climbed lower. Those who jumped from the top only jumped once, except for a few like Matt.

Kim wished one more boat were around, especially with a rookie jumper with them. She knew that Klocks was different than they were. Which wasn't necessarily a problem, she told herself. She embraced diversity in her studies, though in reality the atmosphere at Middlebury College promoted a certain packaging for the "in crowd." She could see he was from a different class, a concept she seldom verbalized. She didn't want to accept that a class structure existed in American society. America was supposed to be a free, open society; that's what she believed. Klocks's age too separated him from Kim and Matt. They had guessed that he was almost twenty years older.

Kim felt that in his own way, Klocks had let it be known that he was thankful for their help at the bridge, and she felt good about being there for someone else. Privately, she thought that they might have saved his life, that he really had been trying to commit suicide.

That's why she was unsure of Matt's plan of having Klocks confront his own demons by jumping from Barn Rock. Matt was always experimenting, taking risks by jumping off high places and kayaking dangerous rivers. Not everyone was like that.

Unbeknownst to them, Klocks took his own risks on the dark side that Matt and Kim never dreamed of taking. But right now as they dropped anchor below Barn Rock, Klocks was as nervous as he had ever been, still rattled from whatever had possessed him at the bridge. And he wasn't much of a swimmer.

Underwater was less of a problem. As a boy, he learned to swim underwater in the Poestenkill Gorge in Troy. Whenever he climbed the rock walls and got stuck, he'd fling himself down into the Gorge, legs apart like some jungle frog. He'd repeatedly pop up, gulp a mixture of water and air, and then sink below the surface, eyes wide open, frantically frog kicking and breast stroking to get behind the falls. One time a lady watching him called 911, thinking he had drowned.

A choppy surface unnerved him. He had to fight to stay calm. One thing he knew he could do though was hold his breath for a long time. If he started to panic, he dipped underwater where all was serene. The water cradled and hugged him. There hadn't been a mom or a dad to hug him or teach him how to swim, and there hadn't been a swimming pool. His pools were the Poestenkill and Hudson Rivers and now Lake Champlain.

Eight

K im threw the drag anchor off the stern, and it went down, down, until Matt said, "We're too close, it's too deep here."

Hand over hand, Kim pulled up the anchor, leaving it hanging off the bow, until Matt maneuvered the outboard away from the deep cove below Barn Rock. Farther out in the lake, he throttled down on the slanted side of the mountainous rock facing east across to Vermont. That's the side they would climb up.

Kim let the anchor go until she felt the rope slacken. "It's on the bottom."

"Good, now let out twice that length," Matt said.

From where the boat was bobbing in the water, Klocks couldn't swim to shore in one breath. He always tried to swim underwater in one breath. He was resigning himself to letting the college kids know that he didn't grow up taking swimming lessons at a country club. Then the boat drifted, until the hook on the Danforth anchor caught, and the distance to shore was cut in half, leaving them two boats lengths from the slanted rocks.

Matt cut the engine and dove in off the bow. Kim followed him with a racing dive. Klocks stood up. He was wearing regular blue jeans, his "I Win" tattoo prominent on his right shoulder. His hairy chest and back were an unappealing white. Klocks was definitely from the other side of the tracks.

Matt, who was treading water, told Klocks he should wear his running shoes. Then he wouldn't have to worry about cutting his feet on the zebra mussels. And shoes would make it easier to climb up and cushion Klocks's entry - if he jumped.

Klocks declined by shaking his head. He never made last minute changes in his gear, for a stunt - and that's what he considered this. When you changed equipment, there were always unforeseen consequences.

He gingerly climbed over the windshield onto the bow. He didn't dive and didn't want to learn. He jumped out as far as he could.

Kim was onshore on the slippery rocks, crouched half in the water, her right hand jammed in a crack between two slabs, holding her in place. With her left hand, she reached out for Klocks.

Matt watched Klocks's progress underwater.

Klocks came up gasping, his bare feet sliding off the slimy, submerged slabs. He grabbed Kim's hand and she yanked him onto the granite outcroppings. "Put your foot there and your hand here." She showed him the best spot to gain handholds and footholds on the wet rock. She started to climb and called back, "Once you're on the dry rock, it gets easier." She scampered up on all fours, Klocks following her curvaceous butt up the rock.

Part way up, Klocks was breathing hard. The three of them stopped as soon as they were out of the shadows formed by the forested cliffs on the other side of the cove. In places Klocks could stand, in others the angle was too steep. He basked nervously in the late afternoon sun, shaking slightly, his arms covered in goose bumps.

"Lake Champlain's always cold, especially beneath the surface. If you stay on the top two feet, you'll do better," Kim advised.

Klocks viewed a widening horizon. "How high are we now?"

Matt scrambled over to the edge, holding onto an exposed root of a scrawny cedar clinging to a ledge. "Twenty-five feet, I'd say."

"That's it, huh," Klocks said with a downcast look.

"I'm afraid so. You can do it. There's another way up, though. Over there, " Matt said jerking his to the other side of Barn Rock.

"It's not up I'm worried about," Klocks quipped.

"I can't believe I'm going to jump," Kim exclaimed. "Let's go."

Silently they climbed higher, the top of Barn Rock coming into view. None of them looked down again. They glimpsed the emerging tops of the Adirondack Mountains and, across the lake, the Green Mountains.

Higher and higher they climbed until they walked upright onto a patch of couch grass and packed earth backed by a tall, wind-blown white pine.

"Remember," Matt cautioned, "no one has to jump."

Slowly, deliberately placing each foot, Matt walked on a worn path out to the highest triangular ledge. The path wasn't from jumpers, there weren't that many. Inland hikers from the road to Essex trekked to this lookout spot on the New York shoreline to enjoy the view, have lunch and then turn around.

Matt came back from the edge, his breath making a hissing sound between his teeth, the adrenaline beginning to flow. "No other boats are down there so we don't have to worry about that. When you jump, use your arms for balance. You have to stay vertical. Right before you hit, you have two choices - arms plastered to your sides, or up over your head. Not out to the side. Go in straight. Point your toes. Go in like a dagger and you'll be fine."

Matt's chest was heaving. "You can't wait too long," he said, as he touched his toes in perfect pike position. From scouting rapids on rivers, he knew if you waited too long, you psyched yourself out. "I'll go first. I'm diving." He pointed to Klocks. "Jonathan, do not dive."

53

Kim was running in place, her elbows working at her side priming herself. "If you're going to jump where he is, you have to get a running start. It's set back. Come here," she motioned to Klocks, "a rock sticks out, below Matt's spot. He's pretty good. If you don't like the idea of a running start, you can jump from that rock." They moved closed to the edge. She startled him by nudging his elbow. She pointed to the spot. "It's only five feet lower. You're still jumping from the top."

Matt was motionless preparing to dive.

Klocks and Kim crouched to one side, hushed.

In the northern sky above the palisades a peregrine falcon screeched and dove. Above the hills closer to Westport, a turkey vulture soared. A fleeting patch of sunlight warmed the rock. A weekday in August, yet only two boats were visible near the Basin Harbor Club across the lake.

Matt glanced at Kim and winked. Klocks was uneasy watching this close to the edge. Matt crossed his chest. He bent his knees and threw out his arms. He sailed out into space. Kim's hand went to her open mouth. He was in flight. Seventy-two feet was high. His dive was in slow motion. Interminable seconds later, he landed like a thrown spear, piercing the water, his head down. The impact bent his arms and pushed his hands back. The water smacked his head like he was diving through a picket fence.

Moments later he punched up through the ruffled surface, raising an arm in glee. "Yaahhoooww!" he yelled, pumping his fist.

Kim waved to him from on top, happy he was safe. Except now it was her turn.

Talking to Klocks, she pointed to the jutting, triangular rock slightly below her. "Jonathan, jump from there. That's the best thing."

He didn't answer, and she didn't care. Already the afternoon sun was blocked behind the towering pines atop the cliffs. Clouds were blowing in from the north. With her head down she walked up to where Matt launched from and kicked away a few pebbles. She looked down and saw the speck that was Matt treading water, waiting.

"Come on, baby!" he yelled up.

She was biting her lip, bobbing a little bit, reminding herself to point her toes. "Here we go," she said to herself. She snapped her arms down to her side, practicing her landing. She walked back about fifteen feet, spun around, bolted down the path, like a guard on a breakaway lay-up.

"HonchooO, bonchooO," she screamed as she took off from the very top of Barn Rock, inadvertently turning her body sideways to the face of the rock wall, flailing her arms in the air, like a rogue hummingbird, trying to keep her body straight up and down. Hers was a first time jump, and like first time love-making, there wasn't a lot of poetry to it. At the last possible moment she snapped her arms to her sides and went into the water like a pencil.

She shot through darker, colder layers of water. She waited for her buoyancy to take over. Finally she stopped plummeting and worked her arms and feet, propelling herself upward to the daylight dancing on the water.

She burst through the surface and for one marvelous moment an unbroken veil of glassine water clung to her hair and shoulders, as if she were a sea creature, sensual and timeless.

"Weoo, oh wow, oh wow!" She gaped at a wall of rock that was fourteen times her height. The winter and summer water marks on the anorthosite granite gazed back at her, impassively.

"All right!" she screamed, splashing around in the water. "I was sooo scared," she hollered to Matt with her mouth wide open in delight.

"Yeah, baby!" he congratulated her. "You all right?"

Mentally, she checked herself out. "The bottom of my feet sting. But that's it. So much for pointing my toes."

From the top of Barn Rock, a stranger named Wallace Klocks stared down at them, standing on a triangular rock five feet below where she had taken her running jump.

She and Matt both yelled, "Jump!" They were soaking in their own glory of jumping off the fabled Barn Rock, and had forgotten part of their mission.

Treading water, they waited.

Klocks didn't move. He peered over the edge, as if he were looking for something he had dropped.

Matt yelled up, "Use your arms for balance."

Klocks couldn't hear. He was up there, somewhere else in his mind. He recalled the Crown Point Bridge. This wasn't as high, he was sure of it. Klocks's eyes floated upwards in search of birds. The circling turkey vulture was gone, lofted away on a plume of hot air rising off the parched inland fields.

Dark cumulous clouds were moving in from Vermont. Klocks couldn't remember when it had rained. He hadn't used his windshield wipers once on the drive up from Florida.

Klocks liked the shape of a raindrop, though he had never examined one on the way down. If those dark clouds brought rain maybe he would twirl down next to a raindrop his eyes wide open. He thought of a tear. A drop must be the shape of a tear. He liked the sound of the word tear. He repeated the word to himself. Then he spoke:

I don't cry, but I'm a tear. I drop. I'm the first teardrop. I'm the first raindrop. I'll bring water to the lake. I'm a teardrop, and I will fall.

Without rocking back, Klocks stepped off the ledge, silently. It wasn't a deliberate step. It was a hazy, summertime motion as if he were stepping off his backyard porch.

Down below, the muscular and manly Matt and the confident and carefree Kim were caught by the quiet suddenness of his jump.

Klocks fell close to the wall, the white and rust colored blotches of the aged granite cliff flying by his crooked body. Klocks had his arms out wide. He was dropping in the shape of a cross, and when he landed he never completely closed his arms. He plunged into the water at an angle, his large splash splattering the rocks.

Klocks twisted into the hard water, which tore at his limbs. One arm was fine, the other wasn't. Something was wrong. He was hurt.

He hadn't bothered to hold his breath. Teardrops don't have to hold their breath. Raindrops don't have to hold their breath. Instinct took over at the end, but the law of gravity was too fast for his lungs to inhale air. Instead he inhaled water.

Instantly, Kim and Matt were swimming over to his lopsided landing.

Klocks wasn't rising. His left arm dangled by his side as he twirled in suspended animation, sputtering beneath the surface. He was drinking water. "I'm drowning." That single thought triggered a fighting response. He was choking, kicking, struggling to rise. Pulling himself up with his good arm while another arm reached down from the shining heavens above and grabbed his wrist.

It was Matt, swimming underwater, as desperate as Klocks to avert this tragedy. In his risk-loving college naiveté, Matt had pushed Klocks to this. Matt had been trying to combine physical risk with emotional gain, with Klocks as the guinea pig.

Another hand scratched his distorted face, grabbing him under the chin. "I can't breathe." That was Klocks's last conscious thought before he blacked out.

Kim and Matt pushed and pulled Klocks through the water. Getting him up and into the boat over the stern was tricky. Matt and Klocks bumped and banged each other and the Evinrude. Klocks's left arm flopped around like the arm of a rag doll. Matt started mouth to mouth while Klocks's lower half was still in the water.

Klocks retched. Stringy mucous dripped from this mouth. Matt turned Klocks's head to the side, while he and Kim kept dragging him into the boat like an endangered sturgeon that must be kept alive. Gurgling and gasping, Klocks opened his eyes.

Matt laid him across the stern seat and Kim shoved a towel under his head. She looked hard at Matt who had rocked back on his knees, bloody from scraping the side of the motor. Matt's chest was heaving and his face was red, as if he might cry. "Oh, thank God," he said, closing his eyes.

The sun had left them. Klocks looked up. "My shoulder," he moaned.

Still huffing, catching his breath, Matt said to Kim. "Get him on his side."

Kim, the lifeguard, was already hanging his arm down, positioning his elbow. "He's dislocated his shoulder. We've got to pull evenly, until it pops back in."

Klocks lay on his stomach as raindrops started to dance on his back. "It's raining," he mumbled. "I was the first drop."

"What did he say?" Matt asked.

"I don't know," Kim said, her jaw set and her teeth clenched. "Something about the drop."

She surveyed Barn Rock one last time, as she increased the downward pressure on Klocks's elbow and his mumbling turned to groans of pain.

Nine

In tense times when he was cornered, Klocks had been able to find clever ways out. As a high school dropout, he discovered he could think. And then for one summer he had gone to every country auction in Greenwich, Cambridge and Schaghticoke. He learned by watching and listening to the unkempt antique dealers who hung out at the corners of the tents, learned how they waited to bid only on items they could quickly turn over.

Klocks was like every "plain Joe," in that he accumulated knowledge others would never guess he possessed. Every deadbeat has something he admires in his miserable life, some sliver of respectability he aspires to, some kernel of knowledge he holds dear. For Klocks, his tinkering in art and antiques was that sliver, that kernel.

When trying to sell the objet d'art Klocks had bid on, or stolen, he took a certain pleasure in the higgle-haggle with art dealers. He had learned about negotiating, about the importance of an authentic signature. He recognized he would get more money for a piece in fine condition than in fair condition. He had gained some rudimentary knowledge, and a smidgen of appreciation for fine art and antiques. He liked Gustav Stickley furniture, Rockwell Kent paintings and Andrew Wyeth drawings. Of course, Klocks knew he was raising the stakes with a Rodin. His New York contact, the dealer Bobby Blodgett, had told him that.

After Klocks heard about the Rodin, but before he drove up from Florida, Klocks phoned Blodgett. A former museum curator, Blodgett was now a nefarious art dealer in Manhattan who didn't ask questions and shipped art of questionable origin abroad to collectors who paid huge sums for the works of famous artists. He told Klocks anything with a Rodin signature was worth millions, but, if stolen, difficult to sell. Rodin was almost too famous, he said. But he assured Klocks a few brazen, wealthy collectors would pay for an authentic Rodin sculpture regardless of the origin. Klocks was counting on Bobby Blodgett and his connections.

Prior to teaming up with Blodgett, Klocks's modus operandi had been to steal urns and stained-glass windows from tombs and then sell them to local antique dealers. Eventually Klocks only stole Tiffany stained-glass windows from mausoleums and then only sold to Blodgett. The windows were easy pickings for Klocks once he adjusted to working at night around the dead and buried. No buildings to break into, no security systems to disarm, no guards to watch out for, except for the cemetery apparitions who from time to time did appear - from crypts of Civil War soldiers and others who had died violent deaths. On one occasion, after Klocks had pried out a soot-covered, flowered Tiffany (which eventually sold in Holland for $22,000), a warm, yellowish, iridescent cloud enveloped him on the way back to his pickup.

These ghostly moments were unnerving, but he never felt he was being menaced or warned away. Rather he saw the apparitions as tormented souls who had unfinished business on earth, but not with him. For those who died naturally, he believed in an eternal and peaceful afterlife. After the third or fourth heist from cemeteries in Washington and Rensselaer Counties, Klocks grew quite comfortable working at night around the occasional roving spirit.

Blodgett always asked the date of the deceased, which sometimes was hard to verify. Klocks had gathered from Blodgett that the proper era for Favrile glass, commonly known as Tiffany glass, was from the late 1880s to the late 1920s. After a while, if Klocks couldn't read the weathered digits, he just made up dates within that era. Mostly Blodgett wanted to verify the authenticity, that Klocks personally had acquired the Tiffany windows.

Blodgett worked out of a discreet second floor office on Madison Avenue. After the first couple of transactions with Klocks, the man seemed to take an interest in Klocks's downtrodden lifestyle. They'd go for coffee at the corner deli, where they'd sit in a booth, and Klocks would entertain him with his stories of crime. In turn, Blodgett would educate Klocks about the seamier side of the elite art world.

It was Blodgett who told Klocks about Camille, the model for Rodin's bas-relief "La France" at the Champlain Lighthouse. He explained that sometime in the 1890s, at the behest of Rodin's wife, a tumultuous affair between Rodin and Camille ended. The separation proved painful for Rodin, who for a time afterwards assisted her financially whenever she would permit it. For Camille, the separation proved devastating. She became progressively disturbed and was committed to a French asylum in 1913. She spent the last thirty years of her life in the psychiatric ward, dying there in 1943.

That story pained Klocks. But the rest of Blodgett's information fueled his scheme of stealing the Rodin. Much to Klocks's growing delight, he learned that all the great museums, the Metropolitan on Fifth Avenue, the Getty Museum outside of Los Angeles, and even the Rodin and Louvre museums in Paris had at one time owned and displayed fakes and forgeries.

Blodgett confided that on one occasion he had purchased a fifteenth century drawing by a colleague of Raphael's that he suspected beforehand was a fake. The blotching and discoloration on the edges of the paper appeared too obvious, too cleverly haphazard, and he suspected the hand of a notorious British forger. Whether the drawing was a forgery or not,

Blodgett, then a curator, had been uncertain about the provenance. In hindsight, he said he had felt pressured to come up with a "find" for the museum to make its largest donor happy.

With a penetrating wink, Blodgett the dealer informed Klocks that the forger had recently had his skull crushed in Florence, Italy. The murderer was never found, but it was understood that his death was all part of the underworld in the high-priced art scene - where a penciled sketch by a fifteenth century master brought six figures.

The notion that this vignette, about the skull being crushed, was meant as a subtle warning to Klocks - lest he divulge anything, lodged in Klocks's mind. His reaction was, you're not threatening me are you? Because if you are, I'll strangle you. Crossing Klocks was a mistake. He was a revengeful, eye-for-an-eye kind of guy.

When Klocks contacted Bobby Blodgett about any possible interest in a Rodin sculpture, his reply had been a terse, "I'll call you back."

When Blodgett called back, Klocks heard a familiar background din of cabbies' horns and Greek accents. Klocks imagined Blodgett, with his pockmarked face, on his cell phone sitting at the familiar corner table of the deli.

Blodgett's voice had an edge that Klocks hadn't heard before. Was it the masked eagerness that comes from a potentially big acquisition? Or was it the plunge in the values of Christie's and Sotheby's on the New York Stock Exchange? The blue-blooded presidents of both storied auction houses had admitted to collusion on prices, eliminating costly, high-end bidding wars for the most desirable works of art, thereby deceiving their clients.

Actually, Blodgett's edginess was due to the fact that in his long, sullied, yet financially rewarding career with museums, auction houses and antique dealers, he had never brokered an authentic Rodin sculpture. Never actually touched one that was indisputably an original Rodin. He always liked to do what the public couldn't do - handle priceless works of art.

Blodgett correctly assumed that the acquisition of Klocks's Rodin would be under questionable circumstances. Blodgett wanted to know the whereabouts of the sculpture so he could determine ahead of time that it wasn't a fake, that it was a genuine Rodin. Klocks refused to divulge the location of the sculpture. Once he took possession, Klocks assured him, the episode would be in the papers. For better or worse, he'd read about it in the New York Times.

In discussing his options with Klocks, Blodgett at first eliminated museums as a market. Museums would not knowingly buy stolen items. Or would they? For the good of the public? To resurrect a treasured Rodin? To bring it back in circulation before the public? They might. But Blodgett knew he would be stretching even the avaricious nature of museums. Realistically, the fact that it was stolen would eliminate museums and collectors in the US as potential buyers, at least in the immediate future.

But being stolen didn't eliminate the Arab world and the French. The French resented any outside ownership of their treasured painters and sculptors. And Auguste Rodin was a French treasure. Wealthy French patrons with grande maisons would be willing to wait a decade or so before reselling a Rodin, in a circumspect manner, of course.

The Arabs of Kuwait and Saudi Arabia, flush with oil money, were always in search of a deal - a one of a kind, world-renowned deal that only huge amounts of cash could buy. If, unbeknownst to the Arabs, a piece of art was verified as stolen, so what? Maybe the French would buy it back.

Klocks grasped some of these things and intuited the rest. He knew if he could pull it off, if Blodgett could broker a deal, he would be set for life. Blodgett had refused to quote him a figure, but Blodgett admitted the ultimate buyer of the Rodin would pay millions. Conservatively, Klocks figured he would net two hundred thousand dollars for delivering the Rodin to the first of many middlemen. Enough money to maintain his dreary, downbeat, ever-changing life style forever. Or, if he started to live like a normal person, he calculated two hundred thousand would last him six years. Six years was an eternity to Klocks. It was only recently that he began to think beyond the next week.

Ten

After several painful attempts in a rocking boat, Kim and Matt positioned the shoulder back in its socket. Klocks lay pale, shaking and sweating. An hour later they were back at the campgrounds, cold and wet.

It was Friday evening and RVs and trailers had arrived. Like unleashed springs, kids burst from the their vans with pent-up energy. Ten-year-olds bounded around in the rain, running in circles, racing their bikes or razor scooters up and down the parking lot.

Away from the kids, a group of men smoking Marlboros, wearing denim jackets, set up two canvas tents and stretched a blue tarp above a picnic table for late night poker. They heaved a case of beer on the table.

With Matt's help, Klocks hobbled to his car and lay down across the back seat. "One last favor," he said as he opened the ashtray on the back of the front seat, scraping out a crumpled wad of bills. "Here's a one. Ask those guys for a beer, will you?"

Matt dutifully trotted over and came back with the beer and a dollar. "They wouldn't take the money."

Grimacing, Klocks held the beer out the window, saluting them, bobbing his head.

"Well, now you're an expert jumper," Matt said.

"Yeah, I know everything not to do. Craziness comes over me when I'm up high like that."

"Kim starts her job Sunday, but we'll be back before then."

"Well, don't wake me," Klocks said.

Matt's voice faltered. "You know, you almost drowned."

Klocks gulped his beer, looking away. "I knew I wasn't here for a while."

"I shouldn't have brought you there, to Barn Rock. I know that."

"No problem, fella. That was my choice. My choice. Hey," Klocks raised his arm to gesture, but the pain stopped him. "Hey, I'm back and it was one hell of a ride. A real trip."

* * * * *

Twelve hours later, Klocks woke up, crawled over the front seat, turned the key, and headed for the Miss Port Henry Diner. It was 6:30 Saturday morning and he was hungry and sore. He could raise his left arm as high as his shoulder, but that was it. With the mist rising off Lake Champlain and logging trucks barreling by, Klocks crested the hill onto Main Street. He eased into the parking lot next to the diner.

Damian Houser had told him about this place. When Klocks finessed his own disappearance, he had coerced him into helping. Damian was a young, naive inmate who had been sent to Moriah Shock for selling marijuana. After he was released, Damian stuck around Port Henry, deciding he liked the notoriety of being about the only black person in all of Essex County.

The oil light was on in Klocks's Oldsmobile. He turned off the engine and scanned past the parking lot to the gas pumps at a Stewart's convenience store. He'd find out if Damian was still working there. He picked the quart of oil off the floor and tossed it onto the front seat. He'd put it in when the engine cooled.

Klocks got out and slowly rotated his shoulder, then stretched his legs, walking past the diner to gaze out at the expanse of water that had welcomed him back to the Adirondacks.

Lake Champlain was one hundred and ten miles long, four miles across at its widest, and four hundred feet deep at its deepest. The lake was broad there because of Bulwagga Bay. For the most part, though, the lake was long and narrow like a river, like the Apalachicola River, and that comforted Klocks.

Klocks raised his head and marveled at the mountains across the Lake, Camel's Hump and Mount Mansfield of the Green Mountains of Vermont. He turned inland to see if he could spot the gray, manmade, towering pile of tailings in the hills above Port Henry. The Lee House, once a grand hotel, blocked his view of Mineville's signature mountain. Just as well, he thought. For him it was a reminder of doing time at nearby Moriah Shock. For the locals it was a reminder of better times, when the iron ore mines were booming.

Lastly he looked southeast across the bay toward his ultimate prize and what was nearly his demise - a graceful, silvery arch suspended on the cotton-covered water. Out of the morning mist rose the riveted steel arch of the Lake Champlain Bridge, lights still visible, illuminated and alluring like a distant cruise ship. From dusk to dawn, the superstructure and the center span were lit. The bridge with its arch floating in the night sky, was the village's most treasured view.

The Miss Port Henry diner was tucked in off Main Street in the center of the village at the edge of the Grand Union parking lot. (Even though the supermarket had changed hands and now said TOPS in big red lettering, everyone still called it the Grand Union.) The diner wasn't much to look at, cream colored with green trim, but it had a following and a history. It was once a horse-drawn lunch wagon, ten feet by thirty-two feet, built near Buffalo and delivered by rail in 1932 from Glens Falls north to Ticonderoga, where it couldn't fit through the tunnel and was shifted to a truck.

A large clock, which was typical of diners of that era, was added on top above the name Miss Port Henry. The 'Miss' is also historically accurate, attached to encourage a woman to enter what had always been a man's domain. One of the four original wheels was mounted outside on an electric motor, spinning.

Klocks brushed aside his momentary gloom and walked into the diner. "Good morning," said a young lady behind a marble counter.

The place was tiny. It looked like a diner resurrected from the 1930s, which it was. A half dozen small, wooden stools were bolted to the floor. On three of them sat five rather large rear ends, overflowing.

Each guy expected the stool next to him to be left vacant for elbow room. Klocks saw nowhere else for a single person to sit. He definitely felt like an outsider. As casually as he could, Klocks sat between the last big guy and the cash register. Same type of National register that he had used in his antique store.

As he squeezed in, the young waitress was pouring coffee. "Black?" she asked.

"Sure," Klocks said. He eyed the register and guessed 1915.

The bald guy sitting next to Klocks moved his cane aside and slid his menu over to Klocks. Klocks gave a nod of thanks. To his right both booths were occupied, one by a girl younger than the waitress, holding a baby, and one by a big guy reading the Valley News, holding a piece of pecan pie in his hand.

The waitress observed this stranger in the scraggly red beard as he glanced at the man with his paper and pie. Easily could be a local, she thought.

"Here you go. Here's the daily. The Press Republican," she handed it to him from under the counter. "It's today's. The Valley News is three days old, right?"

"Right," the big fellow responded.

"What d'ya have? Sunnyside? Easy over?"

"You have any pancakes?" Klocks asked.

"Sure do. Bacon? Sausage? Home fries?"

Klocks smiled. "All three."

"Cakes with the works," the waitress called out to the galley kitchen.

The balding guy next to him named Conway McMahon preferred to think of himself as having a shaved head. He was in his late fifties and was engrossed in a conversation with one of the guys from the phone company.

"He's made money. Plenty. Christ he was one of the owners of the Lee House when they sold it to the ARK," one lineman said.

Conway was always fishing for information. Never took anything at face value. Nothing was as it seemed. The Kennedy assassination was a Communist conspiracy; that or a CIA hit. Definitely one or the other. James Earl Ray did not kill Martin Luther King. Clinton: A whole series of deaths surrounded Clinton; fifty people who knew too much had come to accidental or self-inflicted deaths. He did concede, however, that the United States had actually landed on the moon, that it wasn't staged for TV.

"I figured he had money," Conway said. Conway was new in town, having been in Port Henry two years. Even then he was always traveling back and forth to Ireland. But he had made his mark quickly, buying up three properties in a town that was always waiting for the next entrepreneur to come along and save it.

Conway wasn't wealthy but he was street smart and handled everything himself, up front and in person. He told the lawyers what to do. Here was a guy with a sixth grade education, born in Dublin, who hadn't learned to read until he was twenty-seven, writing the contracts of sale for the closings on his properties.

"Now," Conway asked, "wasn't what's-his-name in with Cohen for a while? You can't tell me Cohen made all his money selling meat from his grocery store."

"You know that Cohen delivered meat - this is a long time ago now, maybe the 1950's and 60's - to Camp Dudley in Westport," the lineman said.

"I heard that," Conway said as he stole a look at Klocks.

"Well, he grew to love the place. It's a YMCA camp, a Christian Camp. This guy Cohen was a Jew, you know. He dies. In his will he leaves six hundred acres to Camp Dudley, more than half a mile of lake-frontage, right next to Dudley. Largest gift of property they're ever received. Worth millions."

"There was something else going on there," Conway said, "I know it. There's no way he made that kind of money living in the house he lived in, buying the land he bought." Conway pointed to his porcelain cup and Darcy the waitress came by with more hot coffee, as the linemen walked out chewing their toothpicks.

"Thanks babe." Conway swiveled around until he was facing Klocks and continued, "Cohen was local, I'm an import. But once you live through a couple of winters up here, and, I don't know, you run into each other at Haps in Crown Point. Here in Port Henry. Wherever. Ernie's in Westport. Pretty soon, you think you know each other. But do you? I don't know." Conway looked out the window. "How was the food? "

"Terrific," Klocks replied. "So this is the place."

"Yeah, this is the place to come and shoot the shit. I'm in here every morning at 6:30. I stopped drinking years ago. This is where I come to get the gossip. There's also Stewart's over on the other end of the parking lot."

"Say, does a young fellow, he's black, work in there?" Klocks asked.

"Yep, ever since he got out of Moriah Shock."

Conway sipped his coffee and waited for Klocks's response.

Klocks struggled for a moment to come up with the least damaging answer.

"Yeah, I heard that. I used to know him down in Troy. Heard he decided to stay here."

When Klocks lied he always wove in some truth. Klocks did grow up in Troy, but he didn't know Damian from there. Damian grew up in Harlem. Klocks only knew him from prison.

Klocks felt like he had to leave. He pulled out his pocket watch to check the time.

Conway was eyeing his every move. "Quite a watch. Let me take a look."

Reluctantly, Klocks leaned over and handed it to him.

"Gold, huh?"

"Yeah, I bought it at a pawn shop down south."

"Where?" Conway asked. He didn't care if he offended a stranger.

Klocks felt his forgotten past, his nasty self, surface. "Florida," he said.

"Where in Florida?" Conway asked, persisting.

Finally, Klocks drew the line. "I forgot, buddy."

Conway wasn't rattled. Conway was used to confrontation. He had once been a New York City cop, until an ambulance plowed into the back of his leg, giving him a limp and a permanent disability pension.

Klocks paid and departed for the sanctuary of the Champlain Bridge and its park.

Conway was left to ponder the stranger, uneasy about one of his responses. Most out-of-towners, when you mention Moriah Shock, they ask, 'What's that?' The stranger didn't seem baffled by the term. Conway suspected Klocks was well aware Moriah Shock was a prison. And he knew Damian.

Conway was replaying the conversation in his mind, trying to substantiate his suspicions. It could be that the stranger just wanted to hide the fact that he was in prison. That's not uncommon. But it could be more, too.

Conway swiveled around and faced outdoors. Not ten feet away from him, out the window, was the brick wall of one of the properties he owned. He had bought it from a town judge. Then for a couple of thousand, he bought the right of way that one end of the Miss Port Henry Diner was encroaching on. He should see if the carpenters were working on the mantelpiece of the fireplace of the judge's chambers. He swooped up his ivory handled cane, left a two dollar tip, paid his bill at the cash register, and gingerly walked down the steps without using his cane, limping slightly.

Conway had grown attached to the cane the way some Saratogians grow attached to their hats. That was one of the few nice things about growing old, you were allowed affectations that you couldn't carry off when you were younger. But he disdained attention. He preferred that no one knew his business, and had to adjust to the visibility and notoriety that comes from living and working as a landlord in a small town.

Conway ambled towards the entrance to the judge's old building, a grand distance of about thirty yards. He remembered too that one of his upstairs tenants was complaining about the noise from the carpenters below. Then there was the Chinese Restaurant, whose vent was leaking brown tar. And the florist next door whose toilet wouldn't flush and screen door needed fixing. Ah, the life of a landlord.

Conway furrowed his brow, preoccupied. He decided those complaints, those annoyances, could wait. For some reason Conway had an itch of a different sort. In his mind he was playing an intellectual game and something was nagging him. Nothing big and complicated like a chess game. More like a game of checkers, and it was his move.

He stopped and his eyes wandered across Main Street, his mind going two directions at once. He liked this town. He liked the low prices. No real crime. Only deer hunters with rifles and duck hunters with shotguns. Three buildings, that was enough. In the village of Port Henry, besides the ARK, a non-profit agency, he was the largest single property owner.

Conway resumed walking. He placed his cane out to the right, hesitated, and swung his body to his left towards the Grand Union parking lot that separated him from Stewart's. He meandered through the vast parking lot, enjoying the summer temperatures, on his way to ask the young black manager a few questions.

Eleven

D amian was the most popular guy in town among the girls. But Damian didn't play that card, for fear of alienating the rest of the community. He and Chantal were on the rocks. She was the foxy daughter of Heidi Beauvais, the artist who had painted the picture of the nude and the tiger that Klocks stole. Damian decided that she was too old for a young stud like him, too many ex-boyfriends around too many corners.

Conway sauntered in and picked up his copy of the Daily News, the same paper he used to read as a New York City cop. "Damian, got a minute?"

"What's up?" Damian said, as he ripped off five lottery tickets for a logger.

"I want to talk to you about something," Conway said as he motioned with his head to the corner table, away from any customers.

Once the logger clomped out, the store was empty. Damian called to the back room, "Molly, cover for me, will you?

"You want coffee, Damian?" Conway asked.

"No, I'm good. What's up?"

Conway leaned closer and spoke in a whisper. "You know that buddy of yours, that crazy guy who escaped down into the mines?"

"I used to. But he's gone for good, remember?"

Damian knew Conway would think he meant that he was dead. Only one other person in Essex County knew that wasn't the case, and that was Spike Taylor, who had just gotten a promotion from drill instructor to captain at Moriah Shock.

"Yeah, well okay. But didn't he have a tattoo on his shoulder that said Betty."

Damian stared at Conway in disgust. "I have a tattoo that says Betty. He has one that says 'I win' - above a skull."

Damian grew annoyed with anyone who poked around that part of his past. He still felt the whole thing was unjustified - being sent Upstate for selling pot. In the year since he was released and decided to stay in the sticks, as he called Essex County, Damian had grown even more resentful. He discovered that half the hillbillies smoked marijuana, and it was no big deal. His being sent to Moriah Shock for selling the weed reinforced the notion that his incarceration was a racial thing, him being from Harlem and all.

But he tried not to dwell on that. His new mantra was forward, forward. Forget the past and move forward. And now this bald, hippie-entrepreneur, who had waltzed in from Ireland and owned half the buildings in town, was dredging up his past.

"Anything else, Mister Conway?"

"Relax Damian. You know me. I just like to poke around."

"Suit yourself, man. Why don't you go down in the mine and look for his body."

Conway understood where Damian was coming from. He put down his tea. "I don't think I could make it down there anymore," he said tapping his cane.

Conway's geographic background was a triangle of three distinct places. He spent his childhood in Ireland in a cottage at the edge of a mountain meadow. He immigrated to New York City where he became a cop. Disability in hand, he relocated to Jamaica where he honed his skill as a landlord and the captain of a small freighter transporting bananas, vegetables and other sundry goods to and from the Caribbean Islands. On the bridge, in a compartment meant for a fire extinguisher, Conway had carried a loaded 12-gauge shotgun to discourage pirates from taking an interest in his cargo. So he had been around.

Now for six months a year Port Henry was his home. How or why he picked Port Henry no one knew. Once he started buying buildings, in his blue jeans and faded green corduroy jacket, he proved himself a man to be reckoned with.

He could see he wasn't getting anywhere with Damian. Conway tried opening up. "Hey, you know there really are good cops and bad cops. Sometimes I saw it. In the Bronx, I ran with a gang. You had to back then. We survived those teenage years, somehow, without OD'ing, or getting shot, or getting sent here, Upstate. From that gang three of us became cops. We were punks. All of us were punks to start with. And you know someone gives you a gun and sooner or later you use it. I saw cops firing when they didn't have to. And I saw times when a cop could have fired but didn't. Justified. Would have held up in court. In the Bronx I knew if I stayed a cop, I'd either shoot or be shot. And if I were shooting, I'd probably be shooting at someone I knew, someone from the neighborhood, from the old gang. I just reserve judgment, I don't know. But I'll tell you one thing, crime is like drinking, it's hard to stop. I've done both, and I've stopped, but I'm the exception. For most, there's no stopping." Conway had opened, expecting Damian to follow suit. But Damian wasn't biting. "All right, Damian. Look, fifteen minutes ago a guy walks into the diner. A newcomer. A down-and-out guy. Naturally, I talked to him. Before he left, he asked me if a black fellow worked at Stewart's. This guy says he knows you from Troy."

Damian had been nibbling on a saltine while Conway told him about his morning encounter. Damian got up and leaned over to sweep all the crumbs off the table into the palm of his hand.

"I know lots of guys in Troy," Damian hissed, "white guys. Friends of mine used to ride the bus up from the Port

Authority to the Greyhound station in Albany. They'd sell in Arbor Hill and on Fifth Avenue in Troy. Sometimes I'd run with them. So I know guys there."

Two women who had filled up at the gas pumps walked in. "I got it," Damian called out to the back room. Turning to Conway, Damian said, "When you got more than that, come back and we'll talk."

"Most definitely," Conway said.

Damian's tone was confrontational, which was out of character. Conway picked up on that. Damian was behind the counter now, smiling at the North Country women, showing his perfect teeth, running a Visa card through the machine. Damian gave Conway a malevolent look, escorting him out of the store with his eyes. The phone rang.

"Hello, Stewart's," Damian said. "Hold on, sir, I'll be right with you." With one hand, Damian held the phone to his chest and completed the Visa transaction with the other. He didn't resume talking to the caller until Conway was well across the Grand Union parking lot and the women were gone. He was paranoid.

"How do I know it's you and why are you calling me? You supposed to be far away." Then Damian was silent but for two "yeahs."

Finally, after peering around behind him, making sure the door to the back room was closed, Damian uttered the caller's name in a harsh whisper. "Klocks," Damian shook his head side to side, his jaw tightening. "You're a fool to be back here. You were dead and buried."

Gradually, Damian composed himself and his grimace turned to a slight smirk as he realized that this time he held the cards, not Klocks. "A local fellow is already on to you, Klocks. He was just in here asking questions."

Damian didn't expect an answer but he asked his one question, taunting Klocks, "By the way, where are you?"

Twelve

"Let's sit at the counter. There are seats," Matt said. For lunch, he and Kim had decided to whisk up to the diner. They sat on the wobbly stools next to two big, disheveled guys, who had a copy of The Press Republican on the counter between them. On Saturdays Conway did breakfast and lunch at the diner. He perked up when the young couple walked in. Outwardly, he appeared blasé. The other man was Putnam (Putty) Witherspoon. He too was a newcomer in the grand scheme of things. A Hollywood escapee who had found in Port Henry everything opposite. Once a soundman for the movie Star Wars, he bought the vacant Starlight Roadhouse and became a potter, throwing ceramic pots on the wheel and, if dissatisfied with the results, throwing them against a concrete wall.

A letter to the editor complaining about the decline of fishing in Lake Champlain had sparked a rambling conversation. The writer said the cause was the zebra mussels and pollution.

Putty and Conway disagreed about the causes. "It's the lake trout, the salmon, and the cormorants," Putty said, "and over-fishing. It's happening all over the world."

"Yes, it's the lake trout. No, it's not the salmon. There aren't enough of them. And what the hell are cormorants, may I ask?" said Conway, rolling up a section of the paper.

"Cormorants, my friend, are scavenger birds. They look like black ducks and they eat the fingerlings, just like the salmon and the lake trout do," Putty said.

"The salmon have always been here," countered Conway. "They're native. So you can't blame them. Years ago, when the fishing was good, the salmon were here. Now, the lake trout, that's another story. They're imported. They eat the walleye, the perch, the fry. Lake trout are killers."

"Yeah, but we're imports and we're good guys." Putty said, smiling.

Conway poked his finger at him. "Listen. What the DEC did, is they made a commercial decision. They traded walleye for lake trout. The lake trout are big, they're exciting to catch, and they're deep in the lake. The average sports fisherman doesn't have the boat or the gear to troll, doesn't have the downriggers. So, he pays for a guide."

Putty shrugged his shoulders and reached for the sports section.

Conway swallowed coffee, and gazed in the mirror behind the counter. "The sad part is the pan fish are going - the perch, the rock bass. Nothing for the kids to catch from shore. Christ, a dad can't take his kid fishing. Money, money. Does it always come down to that? The damn lake trout, the god damn DEC," he said, slapping the paper down on the counter.

Conway had worked himself up. He was rubbing his forehead, his chin, massaging his temples. He breathed deeply, swiveling on his stool, regaining his composure. "More coffee, Darcy, will you?"

Moving on, satisfied that they dismantled the letter and dismissed the writer as an environmental zealot, Conway turned to the newcomers.

Seeing their wet hair, he commented, "It's raining that hard, eh?"

"Well," Matt said looking out the same row of narrow horizontal windows that were available to Conway, "it is." Then he thought of something to say. "We're camping at the Crown Point campsite, near the lake. Think it will rise much?"

"If it rained straight for three days, maybe a few inches. The lake is low now," Conway declared.

"Yeah, we found out. We jumped from Barn Rock yesterday, and it seemed a wee bit higher," Matt said.

Conway looked at Kim and asked, "I've heard that's a hell of a jump. Did you jump?"

"I jumped, he dove," Kim said. "First time for me."

Putty busied himself reading about the Giants training camp in Albany. He wasn't as open to visitors as Conway.

"Yeah," Matt said, "I used to work at Camp Dudley, so I know all the spots. At Split Rock Falls, in New Russia, I dove from the pine tree overlooking the top pool."

"Really," Conway said.

"That was stupid," Kim said. She knew about one fellow who had gotten hurt trying a similar stunt from the route 73 side, not jumping out far enough, landing in three feet of water at the edge of the bottom pool, breaking every blood vessel in his body.

"Too bad you don't get paid for it like Nacho Man did, hanging upside down from a bungee cord to snatch that chip between his teeth." Conway cocked an eye. "He's a Dudley guy. After that ad on TV, he retired from Hollywood, to guess where? Here in the village, on the sly side, down the hill off Lake Ave."

Putty had heard all this before.

"Yeah," Matt said, "I heard that he was a Dudley guy. I didn't know he moved here for good, to Port Henry?" Matt scowled, slightly incredulous.

Conway had figured him for a Camp Dudley guy, already tagging him with a higher socioeconomic background. Generally the natives of Essex County sat on the other end of the economic spectrum. Governor Mario Cuomo had once referred to them as the "abject poor." Even if they weren't tilting towards the poor side, Essex County natives pretended they were, by disdaining the trappings of money and downplaying the property they owned. They called themselves "land poor."

In that regard Conway fit right in, living in a wood-heated home, driving a six hundred-dollar clunker. His one goal was to leave his sons what he never had - a substantial amount of money in the form of property. Conway viewed Port Henry as his last stop.

While Kim and Matt scanned the menu, the cook in the back was glancing at the forecast on the TV monitor. In a mountainous region like the Adirondacks, abrupt changes were the norm. Like any local diner the weather was a safe and friendly icebreaker, and the waitresses, for the sake of conversation were always well versed.

"Take your time. You don't want to go back outside anyway. It's supposed to rain for days," the waitress said.

"Really, is that the forecast?" Kim asked.

"Reggie the cook told me," motioning with her head to the kitchen.

"I'll take the meat loaf, corn and mashed potatoes," Matt said. That's how he survived when he was away from home - one large diner or truck stop meal and munch on GORP (good old-fashioned raisins and peanuts) the rest of the day. Kim ordered a salad, baked ham, applesauce and green peas.

Kathy, the waitress, called in the order. The cook, who was a short guy, stood at the end of the aisle behind the counter, wiping his hands on his bib before planting his hands on his waist, arms akimbo. "They've issued a storm warning," he said glancing at Kim, checking her out. "Here, I'll turn it up." The cook disappeared back in the kitchen. The four of them, Conway, Matt, Kim and Kathy stayed motionless and listened.

"A low pressure system is stalled off the coast of New England and it's moving slowly westward, while a higher pressure system is moving eastward across the Adirondacks. This is a real nor'easter and the potential exists for several inches of rain, if the two systems collide in the mountains. The National Weather service has issued a flood watch for New Hampshire and Vermont, and the Adirondacks in upstate New York."

The cook poked his head around the corner, to look at Kim, and said, "Well, we needed rain."

"You're right, there," she said pointing at him.

Matt was downright excited. This would bring high water to the rivers, for sure. He even felt a tinge of butterflies in his stomach as he thought about running the Hudson Gorge at high water. He'd have to call one of his paddling buddies in Middlebury or just hope to run into some kayakers once he got to North Creek. Tomorrow was Sunday, so there would be a lot of boaters at the put-in on the Indian River. If not, he could be the sweep boat for one of the rafts.

The rain and the report of more rain triggered random thoughts in Kim and Conway. He was momentarily distracted thinking of his Cohen building. It had a tar roof which slanted inward on both sides, draining through a pipe down the center of the building inside a wainscoted wall of the stairwell. In the past when it rained hard, that pipe had leaked.

For Kim the forecast was depressing. She had been looking forward to pitting her knowledge against questions from curious tourists. Rain meant fewer tourists. Except for the actual museum, the forts of the Crown Point Historical Site were both outside, as was the monument, which before it was a lighthouse, was the site for a windmill for the forts.

Conway waited until Kim and Matt had been served their meal before he resumed his subtly probing questions.

"A lot of people don't know about that campsite at the bridge. It's cheap, the fishing's good, or used to be, and you can stay for weeks - two weeks, I think. Run into any strangers, any characters over there?"

Matt peeked over at Kim before he answered. "To tell you the truth, we rescued a guy off the Crown Point Bridge who was about to jump off. At least that's what we think he was doing. So I thought, oh you want to jump do you? Come with us to Barn Rock."

"Did he jump off Barn Rock?"

"Oh yeah, he jumped off Barn Rock. It wasn't the prettiest sight. It was my fault, though, I shouldn't have brought him there."

"Correct," Kim said.

"Did he get hurt?" Conway said.

"Yeah. Dislocated his shoulder."

"Was he from Port Henry?"

"I don't know. But he was staying at the campsite."

"In an old green and beige car," Kim said.

"What did he look like?" Conway continued quietly.

"Older guy, on the short side, pretty good shape. Kind of wiry," Matt said.

Kim interrupted Matt again. "Dazzling blue eyes and a tattoo on his shoulder."

"I didn't notice his eyes," Matt commented looking at Kim out of the corner of his hazel eyes.

"Guys don't notice other guys' eyes. Girls do. Besides you're too self-absorbed."

"I am, am I?" Matt said, thinking she'll pay for that comment. He was hurt.

Tattoos were fairly common on loggers and out-of-towners, who drifted through, and even on some of the high school seniors at Moriah Central. They had become an acceptable way for the older teenagers to separate themselves from adults, a rebellious symbol, similar to the way long hair functioned in the 1960s and 70s.

Conway was playing with his tapioca pudding, twirling his spoon, while he contemplated one more question. He was scraping the sides of the glass dish, gathering enough sweetness for one last spoonful before he cut out and checked on the leak in the Cohen building.

"I suppose my youngest will want a tattoo soon. But he's going to have to wait until he's eighteen. My oldest is into computers. I don't think computer nerds and tattoos go together. Who knows, maybe they do. What did this guy's tattoo look like?"

"It said 'I win' above a skull and cross bones," Kim said, looking at Conway.

Conway had closed a lot of deals. His face was difficult to read in negotiations, in poker, and in life.

"That's what it said, 'I win?'" he repeated as casually as he could.

"That's what it said," Matt confirmed.

Conway sat up straight, the ends of his mouth turning up slightly as if he were about to smile. "Thanks, Kathy. See you in the morning, rain or shine."

"You betcha. I won't be here, but Darcy will."

That bit of forgetfulness, that Kathy didn't work mornings, was the only miscue of Conway's that might have revealed how flabbergasted he was. He was convinced that Wallace Klocks was still alive, and had returned to the scene of his great escape.

Conway wasn't one to go to the police, but he wasn't a crook either. Conway walked home, pushed open the side door, sat down in front of his empty Ashley wood stove and lit his pipe. Moriah Shock had a new superintendent in the year since Klocks fled, and Conway hadn't heard any more talk about Klocks's disappearance. Though his body was never found, the authorities had pronounced him dead and drowned down in the 21 Mine. And that was that.

Conway had some decisions to make. Damian had resisted answering his questions at Stewart's. In due time Conway would need him for verification. Conway decided that today, Saturday, come evening, he would drive to the campsite at the bridge to confront Klocks, one on one.

Thirteen

After their frosty lunch at the Miss Port Henry, Matt and Kim had been sufficiently annoyed that that they hardly spoke on the drive back to the bridge. Once at the campsite, Matt located his cell phone wedged next to the driver's seat of his Subaru. He keyed in the number 465-2227 and listened intently to the gauge reading on the Hudson. After a long, muffled electronic sound, he counted the beeps. Eleven, twelve, thirteen . . . that's the highest reading he had ever heard. Pure flood stage. Pete Skinner, the river-running lawyer from Albany, had run it at thirteen feet. With this rain, by the time he drove to the put-in, maybe the Hudson would be at a record level. Matt was pumped.

He clenched his right fist. "Thirteen feet," he said to Kim. "Let's forget about our argument." He leaned over and kissed her long and hard.

"Now you're all lovey-dovey. Now that you're leaving." She knew kayaking and cliff jumping were his thrill-seeking addictions. "Promise me two things, take your cell phone and don't run it alone."

"Whatever you say, babe."

Matt stopped to think. He tilted his head up and ran his hand through his surfer hair. Safety concerns were tempering his flippant attitude. This was the first time in a while he had the jitters just thinking about a run, knowing how incredibly high the Hudson was flowing.

She was right; he shouldn't paddle alone. He keyed in the number of a kayaking buddy in Middlebury, who had been hanging around after graduation, putting off the inevitable - work.

"The Hudson's at flood stage. I need a partner. What do you say?"

The gist of the conversation was that his buddy had already planned a nine a.m. reunion run down the Middlebury River with three other hot boaters, all graduates of Middlebury College, one of whom was a good friend of Matt's, whom he hadn't seen in a year.

"I'll call you back in five," Matt said.

"Well, doll, they're running the gorge in Ripton. Hmm. I'm tempted to change my plans."

"You should. It's closer and you'll be with friends."

"But the Hudson's high, almost a record." Matt sat there mulling things over.

"Well almost doesn't count." Kim did not want her boyfriend paddling a big, ugly river like the Hudson at flood stage. She had rafted the Hudson Gorge at eight feet and it was a cold and scary experience. It wasn't fun.

What she didn't fully realize was that on wider, bigger rivers like the Hudson, there were sneak routes around the rapids. At flood stage sometimes the rapids even washed out. On steep creeks like the Middlebury, however, when the water rose, the rapids just got more bodacious. Usually if conditions got hairy, a paddler's other choice was to take out and portage. But on the Middlebury River, taking out in the gorge wasn't an option.

Matt had run the Middlebury River once before. Not too many boaters ran the Middlebury. It was for experts only. High water covered undercut rocks. The run was narrow and technical, with a series of falls and, below one of them, a must-make move to avoid a recirculating hole - called a keeper. If you were swept into that hole, there was little chance of punching through. All in all, once you started the run, there was no taking out. Fifty-foot sheer walls pressed in from both sides, until in some places the gorge was only ten feet wide - a sluice of raging whitewater. One nasty, class five rapids where the rock walls squeezed closer the higher they rose, was called the birth canal.

Yet the Middlebury run, with the fraternal allure of college buddies, was a challenge that Matt was up to. Certainly paddling solo on the mighty Hudson at thirteen feet would be equally insane. Besides, the others at Middlebury weren't willing to make the long drive to North Creek and set up the shuttle, which together would take most of the day. One of the Middlebury graduates was sponsored by a kayak company. That intrigued Matt. Making a little money from doing what you loved. Matt was dying to see how he compared.

Matt grinned at Kim, pulling her down by her neck, planting a juicy kiss on the nape. Then he grabbed his cell phone, and keyed in his buddy's number. "Joe, you win, I'm going. Yeah, I'll come by tonight."

He clicked off and smiled at Kim. "I'm all set. I might as well leave now. Looks like they'll be five of us. Two of them you know - Tom and Joey. What do you think babe? I'll catch the Hudson another time. I'm off - to Middlebury."

She liked to be called babe. "I love you," she said, as she brushed back the hood on her poncho and got out of the car. She came around to his side and, through the window kissed him good-bye.

She knew from past experience that when he got back would be the best. He would be exhausted, and the sexual animal in him would escape like a freed stallion. She fiddled with the nylon straps hanging from the roof rack, tying down his Wavesport and his Prijon Hurricane.

"Which one are you going to use?" she asked.

"There's no flat water; probably the playboat. I should be back by tomorrow night. Get out of the rain." He turned the key. "I'll call you."

Fourteen

K im trudged up the grassy knoll to her living quarters for the duration of her internship. She would be staying where the tollkeepers used to live. The Essex County Bureau of Tourism occupied the tollhouse office, an adjoining white-shingled building. Her room behind the office was large and nondescript. The only negative was that when the big trucks roared by, the whole building vibrated and the dead cluster flies jiggled and danced on the windowsills. If she had to stay inside all day, she'd go stir-crazy.

A woman named Sally Venne from the Essex County Bureau of Tourism who had interviewed Kim was also assigned to brief her about the bridge and its history. Generally, when it wasn't raining, weekends were the busiest time for the Crown Point Historic Site. So Sally was there at the office.

While sharing tea, Sally mentioned that last summer she met the actor Harrison Ford, who starred in the movie What Lies Beneath. Much of the movie was filmed across the bridge in Vermont, at a mansion built expressly for the movie. The film crew constructed the set at the D.A.R. (Daughters of American Revolution) campground, under the condition that afterwards the house be torn down. Several shots of the bridge appeared in the movie. That was in 1998.

Sally droned on and described the toll buildings, as a place to work, as lonely and windswept. In summer evenings thunder and lightning storms rumbled and flashed through the valley. In early fall remnants of hurricanes and nor'easterns whipped across the lake. During the long months of the dominant winter season, cold winds from Canada blew in heavy snows and ice storms, accumulating ice on the bridge. Toll collectors, who worked the bridge until 1987, felt the cold in their bones. They knew the bridge as an isolated, desolate place.

From her desk, Sally handed Kim a sheet of paper and copies of old newspaper articles. "You can add these to your blue folder," she said.

Kim walked down the hallway and down the stairs, back to her room to go over the information she had been given. After reading the statistics about the building of the bridge, Kim rested her eyes by looking far away out her window. It was still raining. She thought, that's the center span that Jonathan Deed tried to jump from. The same spot, she now knew, a man jumped from, in front of his family, and died. She was feeling a bit blue. If the rain let up, maybe she'd go outside. Kim put down the flyer on the bridge and picked up the folder of newspaper articles.

Finally, Kim carefully tucked the information sheet and the copies of the newspaper articles into her padded tour-guide folder already full of information on the forts and the Champlain monument. The museum had assured her that after a few busy days of questions from tourists, she'd know the contents by heart and wouldn't have to consult her folder.

Kim put one hand on her bedpost and stared out at the bridge, blurry and gray in the steady rain. She placed her folder next to the single bed and meandered to the back window, which had a view of the park. She saw that somebody had started a fire next to a group of people who looked like they were playing cards. One of the men with his back to her was wearing a cowboy shirt like Klocks's. She put her elbow on the chipped windowsill and her chin in her hand and watched.

A dented, brown clunker of a car pulled up. A tallish guy in blue jeans, with a shiny, shaved head and a tattered tweed coat got out carrying a paper bag of something under his arm. He ambled over using a cane, standing for a few moments until someone slid over and made room for him on a bench. Out of the bag, he drew a six pack, turned around and sat down.

I know that guy, Kim thought. That's the guy who was asking all the questions at the Port Henry diner. So this is what a small town is all about. You see the same people over and over. But then again that's comforting. Now she figured she knew two people there, Jonathan, whom she rescued Friday at the bridge and at Barn Rock, and Conway, whom she met at the diner.

She was emboldened to play cards. She pulled her poncho over her head, fumbling through her wallet for bills, scooping some change off the dresser. One thing about college, it had been a good place to learn how to play poker.

Fifteen

"**W**hat's a gal like you doing here on a Saturday night?" drawled one of the players, showing a mischievous grin under his Buffalo Bill's cap.

Before Kim could respond, Klocks shut the guy down. "Easy. She's all right. Her boyfriend will be here later. He's a big jock, you'd like him."

"A big jock, eh?"

Two hanging lanterns lit up the picnic table. Klocks introduced Kim all around.

The only other woman there was a buxom gal named Cindy. She was fingering her plump lower lip, eyeing Kim. "Sit down, sweetie," she said. Cindy's hair was twirled up in a bun on top of her head. She was leaning on the guy next to her.

He was a large fellow with a black goatee and mustache, wearing an embroidered, red leather vest. A motorcycle jacket was draped over his chair. Across from the biker sat the skinny guy in the Bill's cap who had a pack of Marlboros rolled up under the sleeve of his white T-shirt. Next to him, a younger man, maybe seventeen, was sitting hunched over. Kim thought he might have been related to the woman Cindy, maybe her son. His straight blond hair and a gold chain necklace stood out against his shiny, black shirt. Conway, who was still settling in, sat at one end of the bench next to the boy. Across from Conway sat Klocks.

When Kim had been introduced, casually and quickly to Conway, he nodded to her like the others, but that was it. He gave no outward sign that they had spoken the night before at the diner. She thought that was odd.

Kim unfolded a lawn chair that Klocks had gestured to. She could sit at either end of the picnic table, either next to Conway or next to Klocks. Before she gave it much thought, Klocks pointed to the end of the table next to him.

A big tarp, water sliding off it in sheets, protected their poker table. Underneath the tarp, the players and the checkered tablecloth stayed dry. They were as content with their set-up as if they were below deck on one of the fancy Montreal yachts moored in Westport.

The poker game started as a light-hearted, end of the summer game on a hot and rainy Saturday night. The biker, the buxom woman, the thin guy in the Bill's cap, and the boy all appeared to know each other. They had set the tarp up and brought the cards. They were playing nickel, dime, quarter - no poker chips, and just about everyone had a beer in hand, Budweiser or Old Milwaukee.

"You want one?" Klocks gestured to Kim, reaching down to the grass and hard-packed dirt under the table. Klocks was returning to his old self, having survived Barn Rock and starting to feel proud of it, though his shoulder ached and he couldn't rake in pots with both arms.

Kim sipped her beer and was beginning to enjoy herself. She knew most of the games - seven card stud, five card stud, high-low, straight draw poker (ace gets you four cards), and day and night baseball. The biker and his old lady refused to play baseball because of all the wild cards, threes and nines or fives and tens. The only game Kim didn't know was a game Klocks introduced, called Challenge.

The thing to beware of in Challenge was that when you bet, you were betting the pot against an opponent, and before you knew it, you were playing for real money. Pots of fifty dollars were common. The loser, whether going high or low, matched the pot. The other defining aspect of Challenge was that the game took forever, lasting many deals, until one person went unchallenged twice, got two legs, and won the pot.

The first time they played Challenge, Kim sat out and observed, something she liked to do anyway. One thing she knew: like Dorothy in the Wizard of Oz, she wasn't back home in Kansas. This was a different crowd. Conway, in particular, bothered her. Why didn't he recognize her? Or did he, and not want to show it.

Finally at the end of one round of Challenge, while the boy was shuffling, she blurted out, "Remember me from the diner? My boyfriend and I were in there and you asked us a lot of questions."

"I do remember you," Conway said in an even voice, as he was counting his stacks of quarters.

"Well this is the guy we took to Barn Rock."

Conway remained impassive and said nothing.

"The guy with the tattoo," she said.

Klocks stiffened and shot a look to Kim that said shut up.

The big guy in the vest was trying to figure her out. He was stroking his goatee. The intertwined snake and dagger tattooed on his forearm showed clearly.

The boy was dealing the first two cards of Challenge.

"I'm in," Kim said quickly, relieved to have something to concentrate on besides the squinty-eyed looks she was getting from everybody at the table with a tattoo.

"This is for low. The perfect low is ace-two," the boy reminded her with a wink.

"Nope," Conway said, followed by everyone around the table. Kim held a two - five low. She was tempted, but she saw too many dollar bills in the pot.

Conway was sandbagging. He would have won. He had ace-four, and had she gone, would have doubled her. Doubling the pot, making an eighteen-dollar bet, was not what Kim was prepared for in nickel, dime, quarter. Klocks had five-six and said no without any hesitation. He was preoccupied. The rest of the players had high hands and were looking for face cards. Everybody anted a quarter.

Then Conway looked Klocks in the eye. "You all right? The young lady there," as he gestured across the table, "said you got hurt jumping." Conway spoke the words in as sincere a tone as he could muster. Klocks looked down, adjusting his silver money clip around his dollar bills while he collected his change and his thoughts. He was gauging his response.

"This is for high," the boy said.

Klocks decided he had no choice but to play it straight. "Yeah, my left arm is sore. But," he said chuckling, "I lead with my right."

Conway put on a wry smile and shrugged his shoulders. He knew Klocks was sending him a message. Conway slid his third card up off the table and placed it in his hand behind the other two cards. He wasn't ready to look at it yet. "What kind of a tattoo?"

His question stopped all conversation at the table.

"You're asking me?" Klocks said.

Conway peeked at his third card, an ace, and twitched his head slightly while he reached up and ran his hand across his polished head.

Conway nodded a yes to Klocks.

"The good kind," Klocks said.

"Just curious," Conway commented.

"I'm going," Klocks said. He had doubled up on his fives, and was bluffing with a low pair since he was the last to go next to the dealer. Maybe he could sneak in a leg.

The dealer said no.

Conway said, "I double."

Had he caught a second ace? Klocks was tempted to slide his hand across to exchange cards. That's how the game was played, you traded hands in private with whoever challenged you and then paid up at the end of the round of five cards. Conway's question about the tattoo had rattled Klocks. Instead of seeing the double, Klocks counted the pot.

"Nineteen seventy-five," Klocks said. "Make it twenty bucks." He rolled in a quarter. Klocks could either see the double - slide his hand across, face down, and risk losing or winning forty dollars - or fold and pay him the twenty dollars in the pot. Klocks stood up to take a twenty out of his front blue jeans pocket, and tossed it across the table to Conway.

"Thank you, sir," Conway said.

"The name's Jonathan, Jonathan Deed. I go by either Jonathan or Deed." Klocks did not like to be called sir. Sometimes, in Apalachicola, a customer would call him sir. What, did he look older? Maybe it was the beard. Usually though, he figured if someone called him sir, they were covering up an unspoken lowbrow comment with a highbrow "sir."

"Come on, deal," barked the biker, flicking his hand for the dealer to keep the action going.

"This is low," the boy said.

Kim drew a seven. She now had four cards and a seven low. Kim knew that both Conway and Klocks had high hands, so they were eliminated.

When her turn came around, she said, "I'm going."

Everyone else got a shot at her, but they were all "nopes."

"No one's going," the boy said. "You've got a leg. Put a marker up front, in case we forget. A chip or something."

"How's this?" she said pulling out one of those new gold dollar coins.

"That'll do," Klocks said.

"I don't get any money?" Kim asked.

"No money, just a leg. Two legs and you win the pot. You make your money challenging," Klocks said.

"Let's play," the biker snapped. "Last card."

He's eager, thought Klocks. Probably has a good high hand. Klocks drew another five. He now had three of a kind. He figured Conway for two aces.

Klocks said, "I'm in." He tugged on his beard, and glanced at Conway, who was brushing his hand back across the top of his shaved head. That was the exact movement Conway made when he doubled him. What did Conway's subconscious gesture mean? Was it a tell? Maybe it meant he was bluffing. Klocks was thinking, I've gone and paid before. I'm not going to go again unless I have the cards, right?

"I'll see you," Conway said, switching hands with Klocks. Conway had two aces and a king.

Klocks's three fives beat that. Now Klocks suspected that Conway had been bluffing the first time. That he had caught the second ace on the last card.

"Cards in," the dealer called.

"Wait a minute," the biker snapped, "I'll see him." He slid his cards over to Klocks, who wearily slid his own hand over to the biker. The biker had a jack high flush, a great hand, especially with no wild cards.

"Anybody else?" Klocks asked.

"Cards in," the boy repeated. "Pay up."

Klocks turned to Conway, while everybody else including Kim reached for a beer. "Mister, you pay the big fella here. I lost to him." Klocks was transferring his debt to the biker over to Conway.

Klocks didn't like Conway's line of questioning at the Port Henry Diner. At first Klocks felt kind of simpatico with this stranger with a shaved head, who seemed like he too had a troubled past. But now, as he thought about it, his prying, probing manner gnawed at Klocks. Who the hell was he to play detective? What was in it for him?

"Nice hand," Klocks said to the biker.

The others, relieving a little tension, shifted positions on the bench, tilted back in their chairs, or stretched their arms, staring out beyond their makeshift casino towards the bridge, listening to the drizzle and the quiet. This time of night, especially on a weekend, the commercial traffic, the sixteen wheelers, the oil trucks, the flatbeds loaded with crushed cars had already rolled through. The locals and the tourists were already where they wanted to be. (It didn't used to be that way, when the drinking age in New York was eighteen. On a Saturday night Middlebury College kids would drive across the bridge to drink in Port Henry at the Knotty Pine and the Rustic Cellar.)

While the boy was shuffling, one car coming from New York stopped on the approach to the bridge facing Vermont. The car turned on its bright lights, and a couple of doors slammed. Two people ran out in front of the car, bending over, doing something.

While Klocks cut, the boy leaned forward. He was peering out into the darkness. "What are they up to?" he wondered out loud.

"Deal," Klocks said. "We'll find out in the morning."

The two silhouettes got back into the car, which did a U-turn and sped away, back towards New York.

"See, gone already. Probably puking," Klocks said.

Slowly, Klocks was beginning to take command in his renegade sort of way. Klocks was getting back to being Klocks. He needed to persist in the face of uncertainty and now he was determined to do just that. He wasn't about to blow his cover as

Jonathan Deed, but he was intent on breaking out of the murky camouflage that comes from being anonymous.

Maybe his jump from Barn Rock had jarred him back to his old self. Or maybe it was dawning on him that he wasn't accomplishing anything by being indecisive. He firmly believed that a man was judged by what he did, not by what he said. The way he saw things, there were talkers, and then there were doers. Since his harrowing escape from Moriah Shock, he felt he had lost his way, sleeping away the nights and sometimes the days in the bayous of the Apalachicola River.

What he discovered was that when he decided to become anonymous, and take another man's name, he buried his own identity. His personality dulled, his will power waned. He decided that's what the crisis at the bridge was all about, loss of the will to live. The jump from Barn Rock was his first step back to being a man again.

Klocks was worried, suspecting that this guy Conway was on to him. But Conway wasn't the law. Klocks had learned that the prison had a new warden, a woman, whose professional life was not tied to his fate. Klocks's escape from Moriah Shock was history, and the conventional wisdom, at least among the authorities, was that he was dead.

As the game of Challenge wore on the pots kept getting bigger and the anxiety level kept rising. The pssst-snap sound of the pop-tops was as plentiful as the puddles. Kim was afraid to say, "I'll go" fearing somebody would challenge her. Conway and Klocks dueled head to head, each challenging to prevent the other from ending the game. It appeared to Kim like Conway was the big winner and Klocks the big loser, so far.

Klocks, who was ordinarily the taciturn type, started to badger Conway, throwing little pesky jabs at him. "So Conway, how come you wandered down here tonight?" Looking at the biker, Klocks asked, "Do you know him?"

The edges of the biker's mouth turned down, accentuating his Fu Manchu mustache, as he shook his head, no, and then said, "Ain't that too bad." Nobody liked a newcomer coming into a poker game, winning big.

Conway shot right back, "Klocks? Aren't you pressing your luck?"

Suddenly all was quiet, but the plopping of big raindrops onto the macadam. Klocks was as still as the Indian's statue, until a coin slipped from his hand, rolling to the edge of the table, teetering, falling.

Klocks shot out his hand snatching the coin in mid-air.

Kim was transfixed, not fully aware of what was going on, but breathless.

Slowly moving his head, Klocks raised his eyes to Conway, glaring at him, his lower teeth all of sudden visible, like a raccoon with rabies. "Listen mister," Klocks enunciated, exerting tremendous control, "It's Deed, Jonathan Deed." Klocks wasn't going to let some nosey, muckraking stranger ruin his plans.

Conway wasn't cowered. He glared back across the table into Klocks's eyes. "There's this black fellow Damian who works at the Stewart's in Port Henry. He knows you."

Kim saw trouble, thought she should leave. Besides she had to pee and she didn't feel comfortable getting up and pissing on the historic shoreline of Grenadier's redoubt like all the men were doing.

Klocks smiled at Kim, without really looking at her. He stood up, lifting his bottle to his mouth. He had hit guys with bottles before, but in this case, he felt that would be unfair.

The pot in the center of the table was filled with soggy five and ten dollars bills intertwined like a bunch of nightcrawlers. It was five cards for high, and Conway went. He was under the gun, sitting to the left of the dealer, so everyone had a chance to see him, to say, "I'll go."

The biker and his lady friend both said no. They knew this was between Klocks and Conway. Kim said, "I'm leaving," standing up next to Klocks, backing up until the water off the tarp dripped on her.

Klocks was still. Conway was alert, rubbing his hand over his head, a gesture he had made the other times when he had gone.

"I'll double," Klocks said, still standing.

Conway grinned. "I'll redouble."

Klocks rocked back. "No such thing. You can't redouble."

"You can redouble and I'm doing it."

The biker spread his elbows out wide on the table, his lady friend frantically raking their winnings into her purse, her excited eyes darting expectantly from Conway to Klocks.

With a shrug, Klocks turned away as if to leave. Instead, he coiled like a North Country rattlesnake.

Klocks sprang around and unleashed a roundhouse kick, brushing across the broad chest of the biker, knocking over one lantern, before crashing into Conway, who was arching backward trying to avoid what he knew was coming. Conway managed to grab his cane and raise it between Klocks's foot and his own neck as he and his chair were splayed backwards onto the wet ground.

Klocks leaped over the table, clearing it like a hurdler, landing with one foot on top of Conway's chest, knocking the wind out of him.

The boy, who had jumped up out of the way, cocked his head skyward and yelled "Fight! Fight!"

Kim was yards away running.

Klocks had one hand on Conway's neck and the other drawn back in a fist ready to drill Conway's head into the soggy ground. But the big biker stepped in, kicking chairs over, jarring the table aside with his hip, wrapping his arms around Klocks, lifting him off the ground.

"You got him good. No sense killing the guy," the biker huffed. He released his bear hug. "Easy does it," he warned Klocks.

Conway lay on his back in the puddles, dazed but conscious. Between coughs he muttered, "Your signature round-house kick."

Sheets of water spilled off the now-lopsided tarp. Conway stumbled up off the ground and rummaged around on the table, looking for his cards. Conway turned over his hand, three fives and two aces, a full house. He fumbled for Klocks's cards. Three kings, no pair. Conway corralled the pot, picking out the bills, scooping the change into a pile.

Klocks pounced again, grabbing Conway's wrist, turning it, yanking him back, forcing him to release the bills. "No way, Conway. Take what you bet, that's it." Conway winced as he and the coins rolled off the table. Klocks collected half the bills, stuffing them in the side pocket of Conway's jacket.

Conway brazenly scooped the change off the ground into his other pocket. He got up, stumbling backward, dripping wet, his pockets bulging, rubbing his neck. "You broke my cane," he said, trying not to whine, trying to salvage some dignity.

"Better the cane than your neck." The biker guffawed at his own remark. The boy chugged another beer, and was looking this way and that, all juiced up by the jolt of action.

The biker's old lady, showing plenty of loose cleavage leaned back with her hands on her hips and yelled out for all to hear, "It's Saturday night!"

In the shadows, Kim was retreating to her temporary residence turning around every few steps, unable to keeps her eyes off the melee.

Klocks stood feet apart, rubbing his left shoulder, the one that had been dislocated. He kept an eye on Conway fading away in the rain, carrying pieces of his cane, and understood clearly that ex-cop Conway had moved beyond the stage of sniffing around.

"I'm screwed," Klocks muttered. He prayed it wasn't too late to act.

Sixteen

K locks awoke, feeling more like himself than ever. The poker game had energized and reinvigorated him. Psyched him up rather than out. That's right, the Klocks of old, he thought. Turn what could easily have been a negative into a positive.

Sitting up, rubbing his eyes, a blanket up over his shoulders, he was hit by a wave of second, gloomier thoughts. He admitted that Conway knew his real identity. Really, he was screwed.

But he fought off the negative thoughts with one rationalization after another. There wasn't a reward for the body of Wallace Klocks. There wasn't even a warrant out for the arrest of Wallace Klocks. All there was was an escape to the 21 Mine. Which, to everyone else's thinking, was an underwater tomb for a dead body. And you know what? He should be dead.

So be thankful for every day, for every hand of poker, for every piercing glance, for every moment of sleep in the back seat of his Oldsmobile.

He pushed open the car door and for the first time in three days actually saw the sun rising over the Green Mountains, reflecting off the glassy surface of Lake Champlain. The rays were pinwheeling through the sprocket-like steelworks of the bridge that had almost taken his life.

Klocks smiled, and swirled his tongue around his parched mouth, crawling out lengthwise, walking on his hands until his feet dropped to the ground. He got up and relieved himself in the bushes, staring blankly at a well-worn dirt path, now muddy, cutting through the embankment leading down to the water and a makeshift dock. In the middle of the deep path, a flicker of glittering metal caught his eye in early morning sun.

Wearing his boxers and cut-off T-shirt, Klocks stumbled half way down the path, squatted, and with his fingers, dug around the metal object. Nothing he'd rather do than discover treasure - an old coin, maybe, or some relic of a bygone era. He picked up a nearby stick and dug around the object. At first, he thought he was looking at the edge of a gold coin. In a few minutes he held in the palm of his hand a roundish clump of dirt with smooth, worm-like strands of metal all about. Klocks slid on down the path to water's edge, almost falling, paused a moment to collect himself and carefully dipped the object in the water, gently passing it between his open hands. Gradually the caked dirt turned to mud, and dissolved in the lake. At first he panicked, thinking his object was disappearing too. He was left holding a tiny chain that had been crumpled together into a ball of chain links and dirt. He sprinkled some sand into his hand and rubbed the little chain with the sand and water, until the yellowish color of the links started to show.

He wasn't sure what it was, but he was certain it was made of gold and therefore a good omen. The links were still connected, and when he held it between his thumb and forefinger, the chain dangled to a length of about five inches. Klocks shrugged and carried it back up to the car inserting it in the pocket of jeans, thinking that he'd ask that ballsy girl Kim what she thought. He glanced over at the gray shingles of the Essex County Tourist Bureau, two hundred yards away. Hadn't she studied archaeology?

* * * * *

Inside her apartment at the Tourist Bureau, which was within sight of the campgrounds and Klocks's car, Kim was rising for her first full day of work, and she too was happy to see the sun. That meant tourists and work for her, questions to answer and maybe even a tour of His Majesty's Fort.

She looked at her window to the west, the one near her bed, and saw Klocks's car near the picnic table, tarp and chairs all in a pile. Klocks was headed towards the Tourist Bureau. She did not want him knocking on her apartment door, and quickly neatened up, closing the door behind her, climbing the stairs to the office.

She stepped outside onto the landing just as he was about to step up.

Without a word, he cleared his pocket of change before pulling out a tiny, pitted gold chain, holding it eye-level in the morning light, like he had really found something. He reminded her of a kid that way.

"Look what I found, " he said innocently, "over at your redoubt. It's some sort of jewelry. Don't you think?"

He handed it to her and they exchanged looks, as if to say it's better to talk about this than last night. Kim held the chain between her thumb and forefinger, cupping her other hand underneath.

"It could be," she said. "Seems masculine to me, though."

They had a nice civil discussion, and he had seemed genuinely interested in determining what it was and what its history was. Then he said thanks and goodbye and that was that.

Once back inside she watched him get into his car and pull out. Klocks was on his way across the bridge, past the Champlain Marina to the West Addison General Store for coffee and breakfast. She moved back across her room to the window that faced the east and the bridge. Shading her eyes from the sun, she waited for Klocks's car to appear on the bridge. She was still wary yet worried about Klocks, thinking that he was unstable. She was afraid he'd stop again at the top of the bridge.

He did slow when he pulled out onto the approach to the bridge, raising himself slightly in his seat to see what was painted in white across his lane. A big arrow pointed to Vermont with the word "FAGGOTS" spray-painted underneath in capital letters. So that's what those two characters did who stopped their car last night.

Wallace Klocks drove on. He was hungry and he had money. That alone would keep Klocks going. Back in a Troy as a kid, when his mother would bring home another man from Lucky's Tavern, Klocks would climb out his window onto the roof and live on the streets for a few days, or in the cave underneath the Poestenkill waterfall, hungry and with no money. Anything to get away from the sound of ma's creaky bed. As far he was concerned, to be hungry and have money showed he had come a long way.

Klocks drove into Vermont about two miles from the bridge, past the 1896 Bodette Farm, until he came to the West Addison General Store, or WAGS as it was called. Klocks pumped his gas and picked up a local paper on the way in. He bought a quart of orange juice and a dozen Freihofers doughnuts.

He sat in front an array of cigarette cartons on a long table made of wooden planks. The lead story in the Addison Independent was about a Moriah man, age eighty-six, who had won $2.4 million in the megabucks Vermont lottery. The ticket was bought at WAGS and was the single winner in the August 27th drawing. The winner, Sprague, worked for twenty years as the groundskeeper and gravedigger at the Moriah Center cemetery. Klocks bet Spraque would know right off if any of the mausoleums had Tiffany stained glass windows.

After he paid, Klocks asked if there was a stone mason nearby or a place that sold masonry supplies. His granite chimney was falling apart, he said, and it needed to be repaired. The fat and friendly clerk hollered to her mother in the kitchen, who hollered back directions to a place up the road in Vergennes. Before Klocks strolled out, he bought a roll of lottery tickets. As the store clerk rang up the sale she asked if he had bought any fuel, which reminded Klocks of the only thing he didn't like about the place - the lingering smell of diesel.

"Will the masonry place be open on Sunday?" Klocks asked.

From the back, the clerk's mother answered, "He's usually sitting in his rocker on the front porch. He might open up for you."

Klocks left and found Vergennes Masonry easily enough. An old fellow was there, a blue-collar version of the gentleman who had sold him the watch fob and told him about the Rodin sculpture.

They talked about Florida, owing to Klocks's plates, and about gay marriages, owing to Klocks's mention of the white letters he saw this morning spray-painted across the pavement in front of the Champlain Bridge.

The old man got up off his wicker chair under the overhang and sized up Klocks. He flipped off his Holstein's cap and glanced around to see if anyone else was in hearing distance and said, "I'm a native Vermonter, born in Bristol, worked on the dairy farms. But I'll have to tell you," as he drew one foot across the painted porch floor, making a line, "I'm against that legislation. That was the work of outsiders, liberals that moved here from Boston and New York, and now, God damn it, they run the state." He stopped and eyed Klocks questioningly. "Where are you from?"

"I'm from the South. Just passing through. First time in Vermont."

"Well, I'll tell you. I have three sons. One is thirty-two and I've never seen him with a girl. Never. So, I asked him. He lives in the city now, down in New York. He's studying to be a psychiatrist. I asked him, 'Are you gay?' Well, he told me to F-off." The old man paused and shrugged a shoulder. "What are you going do? I still love him. He's my son, right? I still love him. You got to."

"Yes, you do," Klocks said. For him it was no big deal. Klocks had other fish to fry. But then Klocks ventured a question. "Then why are you opposed to the legislation?"

"I'm opposed to outsiders running the state, that's what I'm opposed to."

They moved inside and the man walked around behind the counter. "Listen," Klocks said, "I've got this camp across the bridge in New York, and the chimney's falling apart. I've got to reseat a bronze plaque. It's set in among the stone. I'll probably have to remove the whole thing. I need some tools."

"What do you have, anything? Do you have a masonry hammer?"

"Nope, I have pretty much nothing."

"How is the plaque anchored?"

"Hard to tell. Looks like iron pins." Klocks had done masonry work before. In fact he had pointed up an old chimney before. He had also stolen a stone eagle off the top of a vault from a mausoleum in Schaghticoke. Using a chisel and hammer, he dislodged the eagle without ruining it. So he wasn't a novice.

The old fellow moved from behind the counter around to the display tables and picked out a six-pound sledge, a half dozen chisels and a masonry hammer that cost $36. It was a mash hammer, like a small sledge hammer.

"You get all this, for under a hundred, and you can dismantle the Statue of Liberty, if you have the time."

Klocks lifted the mash hammer. "Too heavy."

The old fellow stood motionless, his slightly hunched back to Klocks, then raised one finger and went and found what Klocks wanted.

Klocks examined the six chisels, then slid three back to the old fellow's side of the counter. "I'll take the hammer, the sledge and these three chisels." Klocks pulled out his silver money clip, with folded dollar bills showing, and slid out the hundred.

"Yeah, that should do you." The old man rang up the sale and gave Klocks a twenty, a five, and change.

Klocks put his hand up. He was visualizing the job. The head of the pins bolted the bust to the stone, would be hard to remove. "Last thing. I need a center punch."

"Yes, we have those." The man returned with two. Klocks inspected the tip of each. He would use the punch to make impressions on the head of the four large pins so that a drill bit would catch. Klocks picked one and slid the twenty across the counter.

While he counted out the change, the old fellow said, "Say, I used to fish off that pier there near the bridge with a couple of guys who own camps in Crown Point. One was Bryant's. You know them?"

Klocks was caressing the tools. He liked the look and feel of the hardened steel of the masonry hammer. The old man's question hadn't registered. Klocks left the change on the counter and was down the steps before he hollered back, "Nope."

Seventeen

I t was time for Klocks to hook up with his one true friend in the Adirondacks, Spike Taylor. He and Klocks grew up poor, south of First Street in Troy. The way Klocks saw it, Taylor owed him from childhood, from scrapes they had gotten into on account of being juvenile delinquents, and then gotten out of, on account of Klocks's street savvy. Klocks's nickname had been "the Owl." To get away from pursuing cops, Klocks flew up buildings and trees and then tracked the "popo" from above like a nocturnal owl. Spike called him Owlie and Klocks called Spike, Spy.

Spy and Owlie had been through a lot of mostly wicked deeds. One time, the elderly owner of a bakery and pizza place threatened Taylor with a knife. The owner was about to cut Taylor, a big guy who made a big target, when Klocks threw a blueberry pie in the owner's face. Spy and Owlie escaped fifty-six dollars richer.

One day a year their nicknames changed. Come Halloween, they'd put on masks. Klocks would climb up onto Taylor's shoulders and sit, and together they'd roam the neighborhood terrorizing South Troy, demanding money. For one day a year they were known as MasterBlaster after the duo-character in the movie Thunder Dome. Klocks was the Master, the brains, and Taylor, who was huge even then, was the Blaster, the muscle.

In his adult years, Taylor straightened out, married and had kids, becoming a correction officer at Moriah Shock, barking instructions at the inmates, making sure they turned on a dime in the mess hall (so much so that individual floor tiles were worn away next to others that looked new).

Klocks, on the other hand, never strayed from his crooked ways. He simply grew more polished in the art of thievery, developing a penchant for stealing art and antiques. He continued without a partner, as a solo artist in the criminal world.

At the tail end of Klocks's escape from Moriah Shock, he had coerced Spike into helping and Spike was four-grand richer for it. Using his boat, Spike delivered Klocks out of Essex County, out of the Adirondacks, south to Troy. Spike got involved after Klocks emerged from a forgotten side-tunnel out of the 21 mine. That was an important distinction for Taylor. For he could rationalize that he had never helped a prisoner escape from the Moriah Shock facility.

* * * * *

Driving back past WAGS to the Champlain Bridge, Klocks looked north across wavy Bulwagga Bay to hilly Port Henry. Taking the road from the bridge was the long way around - four miles west from the Crown Point peninsula to the intersection with routes 9N and 22, and north another four miles alongside the railroad tracks to Port Henry. By boat the trip was only two miles from the bridge to the village and Velez Marina, right where Klocks was heading.

Klocks was counting on Taylor's weekend labor of love still being wooden boats. In particular Klocks was counting on Taylor's one working beauty of a boat; a twenty-four foot, 1933 restored Hacker-Craft. The sleek antique runabout hid a modern beast of an engine - a 454 cubic inch Crusader V8 generating 385 horsepower at 4400 rpms.

On most Sundays, Taylor could be found at Velez Marina polishing the three-quarter inch Honduras mahogany planking of his prized Hacker-Craft, one of only three on the New York side of the lake. At the end of the season, Taylor called in sick, taking a three-day weekend to motor the boat to the southern tip of Lake Champlain, trailer it across to the eastern shore of Lake George, and motor it across the Lake to Morgan's Hacker Boat company in Silver Bay.

A few years ago, before the dot-com bubble burst, Morgan's couldn't make the handcrafted boats fast enough. Especially the twenty-seven foot race boats, which were in demand all over the country. Most of the CEOs who bought them put the NASDAQ four letter symbol of their company on the transom in gold letters. Names like eBay, WIND, and AMZN. Now things were quieter. Many dot-coms had gone under. Conspicuous consumption was no longer in vogue.

At Morgan's, over the winter, Spike's old Hacker-Craft would be refurbished and fine-tuned. The boat was where Spike's overtime went. It was his only excess, his one luxury in the otherwise ordinary life of a prison guard.

Klocks drove through Port Henry and down Convent Hill across the tracks past Finn's snack bar and entered Velez's Marina, where a cluster of ancient wooden boats, each requiring a lifetime of work to restore, lined the entrance to the dilapidated marina.

The year before Klocks had spotted a bulbous, antique fire truck under a ripped blue tarp. But it was gone and not to the Boston Museum, which had offered to restore it for free. The Velez brothers were notoriously finicky about their artifacts. Just didn't care to part with their old boats and motors and stuff. Besides, money didn't mean much to them, so interested buyers left frustrated.

Klocks parked in front of a red, curved Coca-Cola machine that had an art deco look about it and once dispensed the thick, green, seven-ounce, glass bottles. Before he got out, he leaned down to shove the plastic container of oil back under his seat. The engine light was on again, as usual, but his mind was elsewhere.

Klocks walked past the Coke machine on his way to buy a soda from the Pepsi machine inside the office, which was a weather-beaten shack leaning to one side. Klocks chatted with the man in the office who told him Taylor was on his way back from the Westport Marina in his Hacker-Craft.

Klocks strolled out to the end of the dock. It was a glorious Sunday afternoon in late August and he was savoring the warm, breezy weather. He sipped his Pepsi, enjoying the view of the bridge, absentmindedly jiggling the little gold chain in his right hand.

A distant, throaty rumble, a brown speck on the horizon, approaching fast, a meld of stainless steel and epoxy-saturated mahogany planks hydroplaned into view.

My buddy has done all right, thought Klocks, as he watched Spike slice through the waves. For a fleeting moment, Klocks asked himself why was he doing this to Spy, to the Blaster man? Why was he about to bring Spike down? Owlie was tempted to turn and walk away. But hell, no one was going to get hurt, and Spike would just be driving the getaway car.

Taylor was standing behind the wheel of his Hacker-Craft, grinning like a Cheshire cat, purposely creating a playful wake to buffet the few boats that were moored outside Velez's.

At the end of the dock, eyes alert, Klocks stood straight, his legs apart, rubbing his scruffy red beard, his little disguise.

Spike cruised in and Klocks positioned himself to catch the throw of the stern rope. He wound a couple of figure eights around the wooden stanchion.

Spike was docking perfectly. Spike tied off the bow and took off his sunglasses. "You remind me of someone," Spike said, stomping right over to Klocks. He thrust out his mitt of a hand, "Hi, I'm Spike Taylor. What a day!"

"I know who you are . . . Spy."

That stopped Spike. He stared at Klocks's face, and once he recognized Klocks, tilted his head up to the sky, spinning his large body away towards the marina.

"Jeesum crow. What are you doing here?" Spike hissed. "You're supposed to be the bright half." After an exasperated moment of silence and deep breathing, Spike cocked his head, turned and faced Klocks. "Just to tell you, the beard looks dopey. Now what in tarnation are you doing here? I mean this is stupid." Spike immediately began untying the boat. "Get in, and don't say anything. Sound carries over water."

In five minutes, they were out in the middle of the lake squabbling over Klocks's outrageous plan to steal the Rodin sculpture. Klocks was offering money, and finally weighed in with what Spike owed him from their "glory days" in Troy. Spike's debt to his childhood buddy was his Achilles heel, and Klocks leveraged that. Spike responded to Klocks's offer of money by steadily pressing the throttle forward, the blessed rumble drowning out all talk. Klocks was miffed that Spike was resisting buying into his caper.

Surprisingly few Essex County residents realized that an authentic Auguste Rodin sculpture existed outside and unguarded near the Lake Champlain Bridge.

As they approached the Crown Point peninsula and the forts, Spike throttled down and changed the subject, looking off at the British fort. "Hey, a bunch of tourists."

"Spy, it's time I show you a certain monument," Klocks said ignoring Spike's idle comment.

Nothing could deflate Spike's mood on a sunlit summer day out in his glistening Hacker-Craft. Spike was an upbeat, ebullient guy, except when he was working at the prison.

Spike waved his outstretched arm back and forth at the small group of tourists up on the berm around the fort. They waved backed. "People love to wave to boats," Spike said.

"Yeah, everybody loves everybody from a distance," Klocks mused.

Eighteen

U p on the big British fort, Kim and a cluster of tourists were standing on top of a depression marking a bombproof in the rounded, earthen wall. The immense, grass-covered walls of the British fort were made of rows of squared logs and beams, the spaces filled in with soil. Small rooms, called bombproofs, had been constructed deep inside these walls.

Dressed in a white shirt and creased, blue pants, Kim was busy working for the museum, happy the rain had stopped. She was guiding tours to the ruins of the forts, which were across the highway from her room, the campsite and the Champlain monument. The only thing nagging her, in the back of her mind, was that Matt hadn't called. She was hoping he'd just show up, which he was apt to do.

Today she was the guide for two families from New Jersey who were on their way to a dance flurry in Burlington. The museum director had told her to give an abbreviated version of the standard tour.

One man in her group was looking through his binoculars at a pair of large birds high over Bulwagga Bay. "Those might be eagles," he said, almost to himself.

"It's possible," she said.

She explained that a British artillery officer included a bald eagle in the background of his painting of the army's encampment in the summer of 1759, but for more than a century afterwards eagles had disappeared.

"Until," she said, "in 1988 a pair nested on the cliffs above Crown Point and they've returned every year since."

After the man passed around the binoculars, Kim launched into her official tour-guide spiel, slightly nervous, speaking too loudly. She explained that His Majesty's Fort of Crown Point, built in 1759, was the largest British fortress in colonial America, which made it the largest fort in the New World. The outer walls were made of limestone and wood, and stood forty feet high, and, at the base of the wooden crib, thirty feet thick. The walls encompassed a guard house, an armory, a spring well, five acres of barracks - home for thousands of soldiers and, as it turned out, a fatal magazine bastion.

Kim moved to the highest point on the great earthen wall, her blonde hair loosening in the breeze, and pointed a quarter of a mile away down to the shore near the older remains of the French Fort St. Frederic. In comparison its walls had been twenty-four feet high and fifteen feet thick.

As the kids in her group ran back and forth along the grassy top of the berm, the noise of an approaching boat distracted Kim. She pulled out her note cards and continued.

Towards the end of the French and Indian Wars, in 1759, when the British General Jeffery Amherst and twelve thousand soldiers were marching on Fort St. Frederic at Crown Point, the outnumbered French burned the fort and fled. The last two hundred soldiers watched from their bateaux as the entire redoubt burned. They set sail north on Lake Champlain, pulling back to defend Canada.

That fire was the end of the twenty-five year life of the French fort but the beginning of the British fort. On August 4, 1759, with the coals of the burned French fort still warm, General Amherst and his British army marched in and decided to build a new fortress on higher ground. General Amherst observed that, "This is a great post gained, secures entirely all the country behind it, and the situation and country is better than anything I have seen."

But few in Kim's group were listening. They were hearing and watching this loud, shiny wooden boat glide under the bridge by the ruins of the French fort. A large man who was standing in the cockpit steering, waved to their group, and they all waved back, including Kim. She thought she recognized the other man who was sitting in the wooden speedboat.

She finished up as quickly as she could, describing the British fortress as a large pentagon surrounded by a moat-like ditch backed by high ramparts with mounts for a hundred and five guns. She said the fort was capable of housing four thousand soldiers, compared to the smaller French Fort St. Frederic which could only house one hundred and twenty.

Pointing to beneath the Champlain Bridge, she explained that whoever controlled this narrow channel controlled the major waterway and trade route between New York and Montreal. That's why Fort Ticonderoga farther south on the lake and His Majesty's Fort of Crown Point were so important. No roads existed back then. The lakes, the rivers and the canals were the roads.

"We're just about done here," Kim said, looking at her watch, curious about the boat that was docking at the pier in front of the monument.

One of the young girls was flipping her hair around trying to get rid of some tiny black flies around her face. "Did the settlers, the soldiers I mean, did flies bother them?"

"Oh yes," Kim said, happy to be fielding a question. "Usually black flies are gone by now. They're much worse in the spring. And," she continued, "flies did bother the fur traders and the settlers."

She segued into her concluding comments. "The settlers were given land grants by the French and then the British - to build homes. In fact, Crown Point was the first settlement in southern Champlain Valley and the oldest settlement in Essex County."

"What about the Indians?" asked the girl.

Kim blushed. "You're right. The French were the first European settlers. The Indians were here way before them."

"What happened to the Indians?" the girl asked, quite pleased with all the attention she was commanding. Her father, who had his back turned to Kim and had been following the boat with his binoculars, answered.

"We killed them," he said, just as her daughter smacked a fly on her neck.

Kim didn't want to end on that note. "This British Fort," she said, sweeping her hand across the five acres and five chimneys, "was destroyed in 1783 by a huge fire and explosion. What started as a chimney fire spread through the log walls to the powder magazine, ignited one hundred barrels of gunpowder and blew up this magnificent fortress."

Kim's assignment as a tour guide was complete, and except for a few awkward moments she had enjoyed the afternoon. It was great to be working outside in the sun instead of inside as an intern for some brokerage firm in Manhattan.

She removed her historical-site pin and took off her cap, releasing her dirty blonde hair, then jogged down from the rise over the spongy grass toward the monument. She was curious to see the boat, to see if the passenger was, in fact, Jonathan Deed. Before she crossed the road, she darted a look at the museum, which could have served as her sanctuary. But her caution was fleeting. She kept jogging towards the pier, doubling her pace like the athlete she was, exhilarated to be in a flat out run.

Nineteen

S pike gave Klocks a slug in the arm as they hopped off the boat at the end of the pier. Spike had a perturbed look on his face, as though he was in the presence of a naughty child. "You couldn't let well enough alone. You had to come back, didn't you? Just like all the others. Going back to their old neighborhood. Stay too long. The past takes over - smothers them. Bingo, they're back in the joint."

"Maybe, Spy. But you're a man of words, and I'm a man of action. Now let's take a walk to the lighthouse. You're a hundred yards from the greatest sculptor in the world, Auguste Rodin. The Rodin! The Thinker."

They emerged from under the green slate roof covering the pier, and walked heads down into the bright afternoon sun climbing the granite steps to the lighthouse monument. From on high, above the Rodin bust, Samuel de Champlain, La Voyageur and the Indian scout appeared to be watching Klocks's every move.

No tourists were around, except an older couple with folding chairs and fishing rods. Klocks recognized them as recent arrivals to the campground and nodded a silent hello.

To be closer to the water on this beautiful day after a storm, Kim had run a roundabout loop past her lodging and along the shoreline. She slowed to a walk, checking her belt to make sure none of her keys had jiggled loose. She was in good shape and wasn't winded. She expected Matt back this afternoon, and she was upbeat.

She had guessed right, the passenger in the boat was Jonathan Deed. She watched him and the stranger stride up the steps to the monument.

"Jonathan," she called out, half-heartedly. She recalled at the poker game that Conway had taunted him using some other name. She wasn't interested in him, but she was curious, simply because he had come from a whole different way of life. How different, she would eventually find out.

Klocks didn't respond, maybe it was the wind or maybe he had forgotten his latest alias, Jonathan Deed.

Kim paused and leaned against a red maple. She unbuttoned the second button of her tour-guide blouse, and relaxed. She could see the transom of the Hacker-Craft reflecting the sun off the polished wood and thought it would be fun to go for a ride.

Meanwhile, the neighborhood duo from Troy stood beneath the statues. "Can you reach his signature?" Klocks asked Spike, both of who were momentarily struck by this strong, stoic female face. The visage projected six inches from the background plaque of the sculpture. It rested on a pedestal and was bolted into the granite with four large pins. On the lower left corner, above the A. Rodin signature an inch circle cut into the bronze plaque. Visible on the lower right corner, between LA and FRANCE was the same size circle. Klocks could not quite see the upper corners, but he assumed there were two more and that each circle was the head of a large pin or a bronze metal plug covering an iron bolt.

Spike was on the toes of his size fourteen, double D, New Balance sneakers. His head was turned to the side, rubbing on the dedication plaque underneath. "I got it. I can feel the letters. They're engraved."

"I thought so. What about the little circle, can you reach that?"

Spikes shoulder was aching. Keeping your arms above your head was one of the punishments the guards employed at Moriah Shock. "No, Owl, I can't."

The use of Klocks's boyhood nickname triggered an idea. "Jesus," Klocks said, "I'll get up on your shoulders. Get over here, Spy."

Spike was leaning against the monument. Once he realized they were back to their MasterBlaster boyhood roles, he squatted down and Klocks climbed onto his shoulders. With a shudder and a groan, Spike stood up and Klocks was eye to eye with the A. Rodin signature. Klocks broke out of his usual cool demeanor. He was breathless, in awe of the signature. The first time he hadn't been this close. He was genuinely excited to be an eyelash away from the signature of Auguste Rodin.

Once Klocks collected himself, he instructed Spike to move two feet to the right as he inspected the other two corners. His real concern when removing the bolts would be to minimize the damage to the one-piece plaque and bust. From his many dealings with buyers at pawnshops, antique stores and auction houses, he knew, next to authenticity, condition was the key to determining price.

By this time, Kim was smiling, having witnessed two grown men playing piggyback. She walked around the stone steps up across the lawn.

"Having fun, guys," she asked quietly.

Even atop Spike's shoulders, facing away from her voice, Klocks knew immediately who it was, and felt foolish and trapped. He quickly decided the best cover was to play it up.

He whispered to Spike, "Just pretend we're fooling around." Then he said loudly, "Your turn next, Kim. He only charges a dollar."

Klocks attempted to jump off as skillfully as he could, landing on the granite apron. When he jumped, he collided against Kim, almost knocking her over. Whether he did that intentionally or not, even he wasn't sure. Klocks was a "plain Joe" on the outside, but on the inside he was unpredictable.

Spike laughed and said, "Come on, get on. Your turn."

Kim frowned no, but Spike persisted in his jovial manner. Since Kim was always up for a physical challenge, she relented and climbed up on his shoulders. Spike winked at Klocks. There was nothing he liked better than his head between a woman's legs.

"Come on, what do you want to see on the monument?" Spike teased.

"Let's see," she said, playing along. She reached up and touched the bottom of the jutting bow of the canoe. Her head was right in front of a small cross underneath the bow.

Some of the literature the museum staff had given her was about the monument, so her interest had been piqued. "All right," she said, " take me around in front of each one of these stone tablets. There should be six and they're about the same height as this cross."

Carefully, with his arms against the stone, Spike walked around the circular apron, stopping on her command, while Klocks's mind churned with unpleasant consequences from this chance meeting.

"They're coats of arms," she called out. "This one is New France, really Canada, that's Vermont and that's France." The other three were on the North side. "Giddy-up. There's the United States and New York."

She was in front of the sixth and last one. Like the others, the worn writing had been there since 1912, but she couldn't make out the French nor could she remember what the emblem stood for.

Klocks blurted out, "That's Brouage. Champlain's childhood home in France." He knew he should have shut up, but he couldn't resist.

Without warning, Kim jumped off Spike's shoulder, landed squarely and popped up in front of Klocks. She stood there with hands on her hips. "How do you know that?" she demanded.

"The Internet," he said.

"The Internet, huh? All right, Mr. Deed, I'll accept that. But I'm starting to wonder what you're really doing here."

"Listen, Miss Kim, guys like me, once we're out of our twenties, and we're still alive - we're ahead of the game. Anything we do is a bonus. Besides, I didn't go to college, you know. I didn't go to Middlebury College," he said, spitting out the words. "I'm from a low socioeconomic background," he said, enunciating the words. "If you grew up the way I grew up, you might be turning tricks now, my dear."

She was taken aback and a wee bit wary by the tone of his voice, by the mercurial way he changed and went on the attack. Some intuitive defense mechanism within her whispered be careful.

"Don't worry about Owl, here," Spike said with a broad grin and a friendly pat on her back, "he's all talk."

Which was far from the truth. When he was incarcerated at Moriah Shock, the other inmates, most of who were first-time offenders, gave him a wide berth.

"Relax, Jonathan, it is Jonathan, right? I didn't mean any harm. I was just surprised that you knew the name of that flag, that coat of arms," Kim said.

"Yes, it is Jonathan, Jonathan Deed," Klocks said, as he gave Spike a stern look of reproach.

Spike interceded. "Hey, come on now; it's Sunday, my day off. What do you say the three of us go up in the lighthouse and catch the view?" Looking at Kim, Spike said, "They leave it unlocked, don't they in the summer?"

"They're not supposed to. The DEC's in charge, so it's their show. I work for the state office of parks, recreation and historic preservation, to be exact. But I've got a key anyway. So let's go," she said. She couldn't quite control her sassy self. "Maybe Jonathan here can give us a history of the lighthouse, as we climb the sixty original limestone steps," she added in a smug tone.

Klocks was impressed that she hadn't just folded and run. But Kim was an athlete, a basketball player who had been knocked down many times, only to bounce back and make the next shot. She was the new breed of young women that took opportunity for granted. There were no barriers, no glass ceilings, or at least none that she had experienced in the limited job world of a college student.

Unfortunately for her, at this moment, she wasn't operating inside the job world, she was operating outside in the fringe world of a wandering and desperate Wallace Klocks who held some sort of pubescent power over this boyhood giant, Spike Taylor.

On this late afternoon there were no dark thundering clouds, no pouring rain. In the distance the forts, and the bridge, cars and people were visible, though not close by. The older couple was still fishing in the shade of the pier.

The threesome walked around to the metal door of the lighthouse, which faced away from the lake. The lighthouse was built in 1858 to mark the dark narrow channel at Chimney Point. (The early French settlers across the channel burned their homes and fled, rather than be overrun by the British. All that remained were chimneys. Hence the name.) Undoubtedly the lighthouse door wasn't original, but it may have been the 1912 iron door installed when the light station was converted into the Champlain

Monument. Spike pushed on the eight-paneled door and it swung inward.

Spike led, followed by Kim then Klocks. The foundation of the lighthouse was on a terraced rise above the level of the lake. A narrow, unlit cylinder containing the original spiral staircase of damp, slippery limestone led to the watch room at the top.

Inside the stone and brick circular staircase, Klocks's mood darkened. Maybe he was resentful about the breaks in life he hadn't gotten. He had always fought against that bitterness. In the presence of this college girl brimming with opportunity and enthusiasm, an unseen anger was overtaking him.

As the three mounted the spiral steps, Klocks's eyes were level with Kim's rear. Purposefully titillating. Klocks felt challenged. And she was the one at the poker table that blabbered about his tattoo to Conway.

They climbed to the end of the stone steps and the beginning of the blinding white light of daylight. A short wooden ladder led up to the watch room below the lantern balcony. One at a time, the three of them ducked up through the trap door opening onto the watch room platform. Physically, they had handled the climb with surprising ease.

Klocks was quiet as they gingerly walked outside beneath the lantern and its ornamental, copper, conical top. A waist-high parapet stood between them and the drop below. Every four feet the granite wall was topped with a circular ball in line with the massive Doric columns below. It took everyone a few minutes to adjust to the height.

Kim was the first to speak, wanting to fill the precarious silence. She decided to tell the story of Captain Raines. "One of the first keepers of the light station endured a real tragedy here," she said. "There used to be a house, connected out the back, out towards that DEC shed, and the keepers of the light station lived there.

"After the Civil War, Captain James Raines returned to living in the attached dwelling to the lighthouse. Regularly at dusk or in cases of heavy fog, Raines would climb the damp stone steps, remove the thick glass, magnifying globe, and light the oil lamp. This was his main duty as light-keeper, and the light could be seen for fifteen miles, warning boaters of the narrow channel. Often he would look out at the cold lake and the barren landscape, and think happily of his family.

"On March 18, 1868, two of his daughters and an infant grandson wrapped in blankets were crossing the frozen channel in a horse drawn sleigh when the ice began to give way. The new mother thrust her baby to the bottom of the sleigh, and she and her sister jumped out into the icy water. The horse galloped on to the Vermont shore, carrying the baby to safety.

"Captain Raine's two daughters drowned, Anna B. Johnson, age twenty-nine, wife of F. M. Johnson of Addison, Vermont, which is where they were headed with the new baby, and her sister Mary Ellen Raines, age eighteen.

"Captain Raines witnessed this whole thing from the lighthouse and was never the same again. He was in a daze for weeks, until he resigned and moved his family to an inland farm. Naturally he was grief-sticken. During the following weeks, he neglected to climb the steps to light the oil lamp. Yet, mysteriously, every night at dusk the globe glowed from a light within.

"Since Captain Raine's daughters died, some say the lighthouse is haunted. Others say the ice around the narrows is jinxed. As proof they say the ice has claimed one life a year ever since."

Kim stopped her story.

"If you count the ice fishing at The Hole near the bridge," Spike said, pointing, "I bet that's true. At least one pickup goes in each winter. But last year I think only a dog died. I've been out there fishing for smelt when the ice is popping and booming. It's definitely scary."

"Where's that smoke coming from?" Kim asked, circling around back again. Spike followed her while Klocks remained stationary, his body pressed against the wall of the narrower tower. Being this high reminded him of some of the places he had jumped from.

Behind the office and shed of the Department of Environmental Conservation, about a half-mile away, three guys in red sweatshirts were working around a large brush fire.

"I know exactly who they are," Spike said. "Owl, come here, take a look at this. Shock's got them out on a work crew, clearing the field, burning brush."

Spike turned to Kim. "Moriah Shock inmates." He smiled. "That's where I work. But I've got seniority, weekends off."

"Prisoners, eh?" Kim remarked.

"Yep, but those are the good guys. You don't have to worry."

Klocks was standing behind her and Spike, who were leaning out over the wall, their backs to him. Was this his chance? He glanced around at the bridge, and hesitated. He was now standing at the same exact height that the bridge was above water, ninety-two feet. That knowledge spooked him. What was I doing up there? Did she save me? Am I becoming afraid of heights? His sinister moment passed.

Disoriented and dizzy, he placed his right hand on one of the white granite balls (about the size of Spike's head) atop the balustrade. His thumb rubbed against some initials. One set looked like H.S. and reminded him of the story of that Southard gentleman in Apalachicola carving his initials into one of these granite balls. Deep down Klocks envied that kind of innocence. Even as a boy he never had the time or the patience to build gradual relationships.

"Time to go, kids," Spike said. "Time to boogie. I've got some beers in my Hacker. Let's go for a ride."

They kept the same order going down as they had coming up. First Spike then Kim, then Klocks. There wasn't much room at the top of the circular stairs where the ladder stood. Especially with a six four, two hundred and eighty pound guy like Spike, Kim had to wait until he was down the ladder and then down and around the top of the ancient stairs.

Once Spike was out of sight, Kim climbed down the ladder. She heard this odd whistling above her. All of sudden Klocks plopped down next to her. It was as if they were both caught in the same partition of a revolving door. Klocks put his hand on one cheek of her rear, and said. "You've got a nice ass, honey."

Kim was speechless, unprepared. She was five foot ten. He was five foot seven. But she was immobilized with the fear of not knowing what to do.

He spread his legs out across the top steps, blocking her way, and pushed her against the wall. "Take your shirt off, I want to see your tits."

One of his cold hands pressed on her sternum above the buttons on her blouse, ready to rip down. The other pressed against the brick wall behind, keeping his balance.

So this is what it's come down to, thought Kim, shaking, trying to stay cool. She had the presence to see he had no knife, no gun. Should she yell for his buddy? But she didn't even know his name.

Cornered, desperation took over. She jerked up with her knee, caught him in the balls and came around with an elbow to his jaw. She screamed, "Help! Help!"

Her hollering echoed down the concrete and brick cylinder, stopping Spike in his tracks. His guard training kicked in. Immediately he turned around and charged back up.

Klocks was short, but muscular and powerfully built across the chest. And he was a black belt in karate. In a fight of more than thirty seconds, Kim didn't have a chance. But she had surprised him. The knee to his crotch jolted him back to the wall behind him. He partially blocked the blow to his jaw and pivoted off the wall with his back foot and with his other hand ripped open the front of her blouse.

Spike who was back up in a flash, grabbed him by his thighs and pulled him down over the top steps, like a bag of potatoes.

This all happened in less than a minute. That's how it happens, violence. Fast, very fast.

Spike had his full weight against Klocks, flattening him against the cylinder wall. "Come on, miss, get down. Go by us now. Right now! Klocks is sick. He's a sick man. Just go by us and get out of here. Are you all right? You're all right."

Kim was about to break, about to cry. Then she got pissed. She didn't care about being seen in her bra.

"Come on, go. Squeeze by me."

She held her blouse crumpled in her hand.

Spike could see she was about to scream at Klocks. "Don't say anything," he shouted. "Just go. Go!"

She did as she was told and ran down the stairs, holding her blouse together with one hand. She dashed all the way back to where she was staying at the Essex County Tourist office.

The fishing couple passed by the door to the lighthouse. "Are you all right?" the lady asked.

"I don't know," mumbled Kim as she ran away, shaking her head, holding back.

He didn't want to kill her. He just wanted to scare her, to show her who was the boss. At least that's what he told Spike.

When she got into her room, she broke down. She started to call Matt on his cell phone, but then hung up. Instead she dialed a girlfriend back in Middlebury. She needed to talk to somebody, and decided it had to be a woman she could trust.

Everything had happened so fast, in just seconds. She fumbled for a pencil or pen and found one in the drawer. She quickly wrote down one piece of information, proud that she had remembered it. She wrote out C-L-O-C-K. That's what his buddy had called him. Once she got control of herself, she resolved that she would find that poker player Conway, the one from the Port Henry diner who had told Klocks, "I know who you are."

Her girlfriend's line was busy. That was good, that meant she was home. She glimpsed herself in the mirror. She had one red bruise below her neck in the center of her chest, where he had ripped her shirt open. She held up the shirt. All the buttons were gone; airy threads dangled in their place. She would have to get a hold of some matching buttons. The shirt belonged to the Museum. She had one other clean one. Where am I going to get buttons around here?

She was concentrating on the mundane. What had just happened was too painful to absorb. Fixing the shirt was the least of her worries, but in times of crisis people cling to details. When a person is fragile, concentrating on the bigger consequences with no easy solutions only bashes around your insides. Best to wait.

In a fit of anguish, she tore off her bra. Stupid, glorifying apparatus. She stood in front of the mirror naked from the waist up. She didn't get it. What was it about these things? Why were guys so fixated on a woman's tits? Her muscular thighs, she could understand. Her ass, okay. She found both sexy.

These breasts, big enough to count, but not big. Her nipples were small and unintriguing, she thought. It made more sense to her to be like the Polynesians, and when it's warm, go shirtless. After a while, maybe the lure of breasts would be gone. She knew she was still absorbed in the physical transgression, but she wasn't ready to handle the violation, her uninvited loss of self-respect, her loss of innocence. She wasn't a virgin, but she had never been attacked before.

Was there anything she did to deserve this? The guy is a maniac. She should call the police, but she wasn't sure what to do. A lot of confused notions were swirling around inside her head.

As the surge of adrenaline from fighting him off subsided, she found herself on the verge of bawling. The phone rang. It was Matt, but he didn't sound like himself. He had some bad news.

Twenty

"Joey died. He drowned. We still haven't found the body."

Joey was the one Middlebury guy of the five kayakers that she knew. She stood up off the bed, almost yelling. "What do you mean, he's dead?" All she heard was silence. "Matt? Matt, what are you saying?"

Matt was crying, sniffling into the phone. "I was the sweep boat. We got to the take-out, and he wasn't there." Matt took a long breath and closed his eyes. "He was my responsibility."

"He's dead?" she repeated. "Joey's dead?" Her mouth hung open. "Matt?"

In a hollow voice, Matt said, "I'll have to call you back. I'm just not handling this very well. We've found his paddle and his life jacket. His boat's upside down in a whirlpool, below a falls. He might still be inside but no one can get to him. And the river's rising." Matt's voice was empty and distant.

"You're not responsible." I'm responsible, she thought. He wanted to run the Hudson. I should have let him. I should have stayed out of it. Then she heard dial tone. He had hung up.

She needed to talk to someone sensible, with a little wisdom. Should she even tell Matt about what happened in the lighthouse with Klocks? No, she decided, she shouldn't. Not now. He would say she was self-absorbed.

She started to remember Joey. He was a fun guy, with a ready laugh. He graduated a year ago. They had danced together once, at a bar after exams. He had twirled her around and around.

She was crying. Tears rolling down her freckled cheeks. Kim had no blueprint for tragedy. She didn't know how to react. She went to the bathroom, and washed her face in cold water. She got out Joey's number, to see if Matt was there at his apartment.

Fifteen minutes later, she called. Matt answered.

"I figured you'd be there. Tell me what happened," she paused and said gently, "if you want to."

"I'll tell you the same thing I told the police. But the other guys are here and they need to use the phone, too. We can't believe this happened to us. We're supposed to be experts."

"Matt, it was an accident. You always told me kayaking was a dangerous sport."

"We'll see," Matt said, answering some inner question of his own. "Okay, real quick, here's what I know." Matt was trying to work things out in his head and he was having trouble. Even on the phone, she could tell he was drained of energy and confidence.

Through fits and spurts Matt spoke. "The water was high, and it was rising. We didn't realize how fast, until later. Until it was too late. The sponsored guy, Tony, said he'd go first. Usually on a pushy river, the best boater goes first, and the others follow his line. I said I'd be the sweep boat, the guy who's supposed to make sure everyone gets down the river all right."

"But see, Kim," he blurted out, "I was better off running the Hudson alone. I don't care if you're with experts or not. When you kayak, you're alone. It only takes two minutes to drown."

Kim started to feel like now this was her fault. Was he blaming her? He didn't say that. But she had urged him not to paddle the Hudson alone. And now this. In confused silence, she listened.

"It's a classic creek through a gorge. And once you're in there, there's no turning back. And little chance for rescue. We're in line, the five of us. Tony first. And he was good. Joey fourth and me last. Tony and I were the only ones who had run the river before."

"I mean it was technical, with only micro-eddies to catch. But I have run harder rivers. It was like the bottom Moose. You're walled in and there's this last set of falls and this swirling hole at the bottom, a keeper. I punched through, and I swear, I didn't see a boat, I didn't see anyone. We had gotten spread out, which happens. I just assumed they were all around the bend. When we got to the bottom, at the first big eddy above the take-out, there were four boats instead of five. Joey wasn't there."

"We took out, and hiked as far as we could along the banks, upstream. That's when we found his life jacket in an eddy. God, it must have been ripped right off him. Once we reached the cliffs we couldn't go any farther without ropes. We scrambled back to the take-out. Maybe a half-hour later, I don't know. You know we're crazy, praying this thing hadn't happened. We drove and then got out and climbed to the top of the cliffs, to the top of the gorge, and from there we spotted his orange boat shimmering underwater, upside-down right below that hole, that whirlpool, next to what looked like a log. But I swear, when I paddled through, I didn't see any boat. I was in whitewater up to my neck. I almost got sucked back in."

"Honey, it doesn't sound like there was anything you could have done," Kim said. "Do you want me to come over? I could probably get a ride. Or . . ."

"No. His parents are on the way. I have to face them. I don't think there's anything you could do. I'll call you again. I should have followed my instincts and run the Hudson. Alone."

Kim was perplexed and angry at the same time. Was he trying to blame her? He was. He often did that. Looked for scapegoats. But she knew he was hurting, and dare not make it worse for him. He was trying to come to grips with a tragedy.

"It was an accident. You told me the cliffs were undercut. He probably got wedged there," she said, trying to sound calm and rational.

"Yeah, that's what it looks like, like he was pinned. I've got to get off. I'm not leaving here until somebody finds his body. None of us are. I don't know when I'll be back. And right now, I don't ever want to kayak again."

"Remember, I love you," she muttered over her own conflicting thoughts and battered psyche.

After her conversation with Matt, she lay on her bed crying, wiping her eyes, staring blankly at the gray ceiling. She didn't know if the tears were for herself, or Joey.

Then she got up and stood at a window. For some reason, she just did not want to tell her boyfriend. Not yet. She didn't want to tell her boyfriend that the guy they had saved from jumping off the bridge had turned on her, molested her, attacked her. The death of Joey made the decision easy.

Twenty-one

O utside at the covered pier, Spike stood up in the cockpit and pressed the shiny silver button on the dashboard. His Hacker shook to life emanating its manly, cacophonous rumble, which echoed off the undercarriage of the bridge and into Kim's room.

Kim crossed to the other window facing the bridge and caught the boat disappearing behind the riprap bank and bridge abutment. She wanted to see if Klocks was in the boat, but she was too late. All she saw was the stern and the name First Love in gold lettering on the transom.

A shiver of worry, a touch of fright, entered her soul, for fear that Klocks was still at the campsite. She turned and peered out the window into the parking lot looking for his car.

Kim collected herself, phoned her college girlfriend and told her about the death on the river. Then Kim gushed out her news. Her girlfriend spent most of the conversation confiding to Kim about a date at Middlebury who had forced himself on her, something she had never told anyone. She and her date had both been drunk. That was their excuse. In college it wasn't that uncommon - getting drunk and conveniently overlooking that a guy who you thought was your friend had taken advantage of you.

By the time their conversation ended her girlfriend convinced Kim to get some help, to call the police right away. When Kim hung up, she thought of 911, but instead called the Miss Port Henry Diner. Conway wasn't there, but Reginald DeFay was.

Conway was at home on the phone with his New York City connections running a check on Klocks's license plate. If there was anything out of the ordinary about the registration, Conway was going to stop second-guessing himself, and go to the police with suspicions about his identity. Going to the police probably meant the State Troopers in Westport.

When Kim asked the waitress the phone number for the town police, the waitress handed the phone to Reginald, who was on a wooden stool eating a bowl of chili. He was Port Henry's only cop. Without saying anything, Reginald immediately left the diner to go question Kim.

Together they drove back to Port Henry down Convent Hill to the marina, where Reginald was pretty sure the boat would be headed. On the way Kim told Reginald exactly what had happened. "Her version" as Reginald said later. Reginald's mantra was that "there were two sides to every story," so consequently he listened and didn't make an arrest until he was certain a crime had been committed.

For Klocks, who was sitting back in the second cockpit, the whole lighthouse incident was no big deal. I mean he was a convict, he was scaring the broad that was all. Didn't even slap her. Ironically, her status had gone up in his estimation. Having the guts to hit him. He didn't believe it. How could a college girl have had the guts to hit him?

Spike and Klocks kicked back in the Hacker, taking a roundabout way back to Velez's marina. The noise was too loud to talk over, which was fine with Spike. It was dawning on him that Klocks was really screwed up and had nowhere to go. Spike was trying to get the nerve to tell him he wouldn't help. He couldn't help. He'd be tempting fate, having already gotten away with transporting a convicted felon, an escaped convict, out of the Adirondacks. It was a year ago that he had driven Klocks south in his boat past Benson to the tip of Lake Champlain. Only this time Klocks wanted a ride in his Hacker, through the Champlain Canal at Whitehall, down the Hudson, all the way to the Troy Marina.

Spike wasn't a man to fret. He enjoyed the present, and today was a day to be savored - an uplifting gift of nature, a gorgeous late-summer day. Possibly the last hot breeze to sweep across the cooling waters of the lake. The lights of Port Henry glowed against the lavender sky. The temperature had hit seventy-nine. Not a record for the date, but warm nonetheless. The leaves in the mountains and valleys had turned color, signaling that play time was almost over, making the last few days of summer precious, touched with melancholy, ripe with heartache.

In the middle of the lake, Spike cut the engine and let his Hacker drift. Spike tossed Klocks his Marlboros, and as the sun set and the light softened, they smoked. Twenty sweet, silent minutes went by until Spike pressed his favorite button, and his Hacker coughed to life.

Spike gazed north and saw only two sailboats on the water. The lake that Samuel de Champlain, navigator and statesman, discovered and explored in July 1609. Spike was amazed that he had remembered those words on the plaque above the door to the lighthouse. Where had that come from? He hadn't done well in high school and was still embarrassed about his low SAT scores. But that was the guidance counselor's fault, Spike reminded himself.

Another fifteen minutes and Spike could read the huge word GAS painted in black on top of Velez's metal roof. He throttled down as they rounded the Beach Road jetty. His wake washed over the no wake sign, and chuckling, he called back to Klocks. "I always get a kick out of that. How you doing, wild man? You got that out of your system now?"

"No, but I'll leave her alone."

"You better, Owl. That was the move of a rookie, and you're a pro."

As they eased in to tie up, Spike who always stood, observed two people on the end of the dock, waiting. One was Kim, and the other was Reginald, the town cop.

"Look lively, Klocks," Spike called over his shoulder. "You've got visitors."

Twenty-two

Kim crossed her arms. She was determined not to be a victim. As far as she was concerned she was there to kick ass.

As the Hacker eased in sideways to the dock, Klocks stood up in the second cockpit holding the stern line. He looked at Kim fifteen feet away and getting closer, shrugged his shoulders, contorted his face, cocking his head as if to indicate through body language - what can I say?

Kim was in no mood to forgive. She was wearing a Middlebury sweatshirt and the same long blue pants she wore inside the lighthouse.

Reginald, the town cop, caught the bow rope and wrapped it around a rusty cleat attached to a warped plank.

"Reginald, how nice of you to welcome us. But where's the band?" Spike asked.

They knew each other and Reginald cracked a smile. "Hey Spike. How's she running? You taking her south soon?"

"Oh yeah, Morgan needs my money. It's his beer money."

Ordinarily, Klocks knew to shut up, to only answer with a yes or no, and say nothing more. But he knew too, he had to prevent this confrontation from unraveling his plans. He might have to improvise.

Klocks stepped up onto the dock, avoided Reginald, and kissed Kim, as though they were intimate. Kim recoiled and spit, shaking her head from side to side. She was steaming, absolutely bursting with outrage.

Klocks moved back to Reginald, pausing in front of him. But Reginald didn't say a word, so Klocks moved away as if everything was copacetic. He walked down a section of the dock towards the landing and his Oldsmobile. When he brushed by Kim again, he hissed at her, "Shit happens."

Staring at Reginald in disbelief, she spread her arms, and yelled, "Well?"

"Ahem. Mister, I need to talk to you. This woman here,"

"My name is Kim Filkins," interrupted Kim, her patience breaking.

"She's lodged a complaint against you, of ah, attempted rape." Reginald said the last two words very quickly.

Klocks turned around, and walked back towards Reginald and the boat. He would pass Kim again.

Two can play this game, she decided.

"Nope. Nope," Klocks said. "I would like to file a complaint of attempted manslaughter against my girlfriend, for trying to push me down the lighthouse stairs. They're very dangerous and steep. Made of stone."

Right when he said the word "girlfriend," he walked by Kim on the edge of the narrow dock. In a flash she unfurled her arms and shoved Klocks into the lake.

The water was cold and over his head. Neither Reginald nor Spike moved to help him. He bobbed up twice, pushing off the bottom before reaching the dock.

Reginald tugged on his lip. Had he gotten in the middle of a lover's quarrel? They were the worst cases and inevitably dismissed because the complainant would change her mind and refuse to testify.

Reginald glared at Kim. "That wasn't called for," he said sternly.

"You weren't there, I was. If it wasn't for that big lug," she said pointing to Spike, "I could have been raped. For all I know, killed. And I am not his freaking girlfriend!" she yelled, and with that, jammed the heel of her sneaker onto Klocks's fingers as he tried to raise himself onto the dock.

As some of the anger flowed out of her, Kim felt better. Though she felt like kicking him in the face, she resisted. All that Tai-bo training, all those side kicks, and jabs and upper-cuts had made her more physical and accepting of her own broad-shouldered body.

Spike, who was busy fussing with his boat, put his hand over his mouth to cover his smirk. He saw some dark humor in this college girl pushing the hardened Klocks into the water and then stomping on his fingers. But he knew too that Klocks was crafty and had already a planted of seed of doubt in Reginald's head as to whether he and Kim were strangers or lovers.

"This isn't helping your case. Get back," said Reginald to Kim as he pulled Klocks, looking like a clump of milfoil, up onto the dock.

A car drove up to the end of dock. In small towns news travels fast. The driver dropped off one man and drove away. Damian Houser had heard that Klocks had gotten himself in trouble.

Damian walked around the wilting geraniums, happy to be outside and off duty from Stewart's. Damian had told himself that he had come to observe. But he was there on the dock because of a peculiar bond that develops with those who have been on the inside, been sent Upstate.

Now Reginald was trying to figure out what to do with this angry college girl. Politely, he asked her, "Did he have a weapon?"

"No," she said quickly.

"Any witnesses?"

"Well, yes," she said pointing with her chin, "the big guy with the boat."

Klocks was slowly getting up off the dock, soaked. He was looking and acting the part of the drowned rat, knowing it was his turn to play the victim. He took off his shirt and, as he stood shivering, rung it out.

"Here," Spike said, flinging Klocks his blue jean jacket. "Put it on."

Kim caught sight of the tattoo on Klocks's shoulder that she had first seen on Barn Rock. Something else was registering. Something Conway had said at the poker game. The way Conway reacted to Klocks's tattoo. Conway knew something about this guy that she didn't know. For the first time Kim suspected that the man who attacked her had a distinctly shady history.

Reginald eyed Kim warily, trying to read her thoughts. "You touch him again and you'll be arrested, handcuffed. As it is, if he wants to, that fellow you shoved could claim you assaulted him."

Reginald approached Spike who was standing legs apart, elbows out, his back to his boat.

Kim paced, waiting for Reginald to take some action or make some pronouncement.

Damian had ambled out on the dock, sidled up to Klocks, and they were chatting. But underneath Klocks's nonchalance, his mind was racing, calculating how much Kim knew and whether Conway had opened his mouth to her and the cop. Klocks was trying not to show it, but he was rattled. Klocks glanced at Kim, who was glaring at Reginald, waiting.

"All right, Spike, you know I've got to do this. What d'ya see?" Reginald asked.

"What did I see where?" Spike responded with a twinkle in his eye and a playful look on his face. Then he answered, "I heard some noise up the stairs. Maybe somebody had slipped, I don't know. I went back up and they were," he hesitated searching for the right word, "they were together."

"What do you mean, together? Was he attacking her?"

"Not that I could tell."

Kim jumped in the conversation. "He's lying. I was yelling for help, for Christ's sake. That's why he ran back up." She stared pleadingly at Spike. "You saved me. Thank God you were there." She welled up and with the back of her hand wiped tears from her eyes. That was it. That was all the crying she would do.

"Did she yell for help, Spike?"

Spike turned his huge head away from Kim, "If she did, I didn't hear it."

"Goddamn you!" screamed Kim. "Wait a minute. There was an old couple fishing, and when I ran out, with my shirt ripped off, the woman asked me if I was okay."

Damian and Klocks had moved up behind Kim, listening to Reginald's interrogation of Spike.

"If I find that couple, and bring them to you, and they say they heard me yell for help, and saw me running out of the lighthouse holding my shirt, will you believe me? Will you believe me then and arrest him?"

Reginald, the local constable, was center stage. He was searching for the compromise solution that all parties would accept. He knew that if this incident ever went to court, a case like this wasn't going anywhere. This guy wasn't her boss. This wasn't a case of sexual harassment. She wasn't working at the time. And it didn't look like there had been any eyewitness.

In the patrol car on the way to the marina, Kim acknowledged that she hadn't been raped. When Reginald asked sheepishly if she had any bruises, she put her hand to her chest and answered, "Well, no." The red mark below her neck had faded.

If she had actually been raped, he assured himself, he'd have handcuffed him on the spot. The best thing would be to settle it here on the dock, but he could see that wasn't about to happen.

Reginald raised both hands. "All right," he said, "this is what I'm going to do. I'm giving both parties one day. In the meantime," eyeing Klocks, "I'll be doing some investigating of my own."

Reginald didn't believe Klocks's comment that she was his girlfriend. They simply didn't look like they went together. She was taller than he was. She was a college girl. He was older and looked and acted like he'd been around the block. Reginald noted the "I win" tattoo on his shoulder. To Reginald, Klocks seemed to be passing through with no ties to the area. Reginald figured if he gave him a day, maybe he'd be gone, and become somebody else's problem.

Reginald took out a pad of paper and a blue pen from his breast pocket. "Kim, I've got your name and address."

Kim was preoccupied, her hand in her pocket feeling for a crumpled paper. After she ran from the lighthouse, she had written a name on that scrap of paper.

Looking past Kim at Klocks, Reginald said, "Mister, I need yours."

"Jonathan Deed," Klocks said, nodding his head approvingly.

Kim squeezed her eyes shut and vigorously shook her head no. She had remembered the name Conway had called him.

"I'm staying at the Crown Point campground. I'm paid up for another week. That's my car over there, the Oldsmobile."

"The one with Florida plates?"

"Yes."

"And you've got no other address?"

"Not at present, sir,"

"What's your plate number?"

Klocks tensed inside, but answered breezily, "I don't know it, sir." A computer search of the license plate number could be touchy. Events were tightening. Circumstances were closing in, all on account of an over aggressive college bitch. He barely touched her, for Christ's sake.

"All right, I'll read the plate on my way out." Reginald checked his watch. "Both parties meet me at my office. Up on Main Street at the village office, between the church and the bank - the one that keeps changing names. Meet me there at five o'clock tomorrow evening. Kim, if you find the fishing couple, bring them with you. That's it, go home."

Reginald reached out and touched Kim on the arm, as the others filed off the dock ahead of her. "I believe you," he said quietly. "But there's nothing I can do right now. He has a witness and you don't. I need more information."

Shaking her head, pursing her lips, she turned around and faced Reginald. Finally she exhaled and announced, "He is not who he says he is."

Twenty-three

C onway sat in his armchair twirling his back-up cane, waiting for a return phone call. He begrudgingly admired this fellow Klocks, who had crawled for three days to find his way out of a blackened maze of shafts and tunnels. A feat that would have confounded and killed most mortals.

On Kim's insistence, Reginald drove her to Conway's house on Mill Street. As the town cop, Conway didn't have much faith in Reginald. Conway had once asked him for assistance in evicting a woman who for three months hadn't paid her rent. Instead of helping, Reginald rattled off the rights of a tenant. When, against his better judgment, Conway served the eviction notice himself, she slammed the door on his foot.

Reginald, Kim and Conway held a confab in Conway's grungy house. To Conway's surprise, Reginald was coherent and decisive, unrolling a plan of action that started with verifying the registration of Klocks's license plate and ended with calling in the state police. They agreed to reconvene at the village offices tomorrow at five o'clock. Reginald was doubtful Klocks would show, particularly after listening to Conway, who concluded, "I say he's the same guy who escaped from Moriah Shock."

Conway offered Kim a ride back to her room at the tollhouse and Kim accepted. He and Kim didn't say much on the way back, but Conway got to thinking as they drove the lonely four-mile straightaway out to the bridge. He got to thinking that life is a two way street, and that he might be in danger. After all he was the one who had accused Klocks of being Klocks. But being nervous didn't suit Conway.

"If this guy really and truly is Wallace Klocks, and I think he is, are you sure you want to stay there tonight? Sunday night - not too many others around."

She remained silent.

"Mind you. He's not an idiot. He's back here for a reason. I don't know what it is. But for sure he doesn't want his identity revealed. And that's where this thing is leading. Especially if you find that couple. Then, he'll be charged. And that means he'll be fingerprinted. Probably take twelve hours to run the prints through the database, unless the village office is wired into the FBI's system."

"You know, I just don't feel like running," Kim said.

"Is there a phone in your room?" Conway asked.

"Yeah."

"Is there someone who could stay with you?"

"There is, or was - my boyfriend. He's got the car. But he went kayaking, and there's been an accident, a drowning. I don't know when he's coming back."

Driving slowly, Conway was lighting his pipe, passing Champ's Deli and Market on the right. "Did you know the kayaker?"

"Yeah, I did, sort of."

"Here, here's my home phone number. It's unlisted. Steer for a minute." Listlessly, she reached over and grabbed the wheel while he scrawled his number on a piece of paper. She was tired. "If your boyfriend doesn't show, call me, I'll come pick you up, and you can sleep in my son's room," he said tapping his pipe into the ashtray. "I'll make sure he cleans it up."

Kim was about to put her faith in another older man. Then her gut spoke to her head. Hello? What just happened? Conway had been helpful, for sure, but she didn't know much more about him than she knew about Klocks. She knew he lived in Port Henry. He wasn't a drifter. He had kids. Or at least he said he did. Never mentioned a wife. No way she was going to spend the night at his house.

She picked up the paper with his number, and mumbled a "thanks" as he pulled into the parking lot. All she wanted to do was go to sleep. At least for now the anger was gone.

"I haven't finished poking around. We'll be in touch." As an afterthought, he called out, "Lock the door."

Conway didn't drive away until he saw her close the door. Kim flicked the switch for her room light and stood motionless, thinking. She sighed. She turned and walked back outside toward the trailer of the older couple parked near the woods.

Their lights were on and she saw the greenish tint of a TV. She felt a little odd, knocking in the drizzling dark. Inside, a man called out, "Who is it?" He spoke in a gruff voice, disguising his fear.

"It's your neighbor. I live in the tollhouse. I work for the Museum."

"What do you want?" he asked. In a fainter voice, Kim heard the woman say, "Let her in Harold."

The metal door swung open, and the couple stood there, the woman holding a black cat. Kim started right in, making eye contact with the woman.

"Remember you saw me running out of the lighthouse, and you asked if everything was all right? Well, everything's not all right, and I need your help."

Harold turned to his wife. "I told you. I knew those two were trouble." And then back to Kim. "But we're not getting involved. We're too old."

"It's not me so much. I just need you to say you saw me running out of the lighthouse," then in a different, lower voice, looking away, she said "clutching my shirt. He ripped my shirt off."

Now the woman stepped forward. "We are sorry. But we go from camp to camp, and there's a lot of this, this kind of trouble. We don't get involved. We're just here to fish. My husband has a heart problem."

"I understand," Kim said, giving in. She looked at the yellow eyes of the black cat and left. This is not my lucky day, she thought.

As she walked back to the only light in the tollhouse, Conway was three miles west driving up over the railroad tracks. He turned north on 9N and 22 and a bank of clouds blocked his view of the stars over the Green Mountains of Vermont.

Conway loved storms. The first drops of rain fell on his windshield. Conway waited until he could hardly see out, then turned on his wipers. The winding road bordering the swamps of Bulwagga Bay turned up and away from the railroad tracks. An old car with lots of chrome drove towards him. Two people were in the front seat. As the car disappeared in his rear view mirror, Conway glimpsed a Florida license plate.

"Shit," he hissed, thinking the car could have been Klocks's Oldsmobile 88. He wasn't positive. He ran his hand over his shaved head. One mile later in the pouring rain Conway drove past Wheelock's car dealership and chugged up the hill into Port Henry.

He pulled into Stewart's to see if Damian was there. He wasn't. He stood in the rain biting his nails. He had a pistol at home, but not with him. He jumped in the car and gunned his Plymouth back down the hill. He had no idea what he would do if he caught up with them.

Conway was doing this for her, for Kim. After all, Klocks was an escaped convict and Damian an ex-convict. As far as he was concerned Kim was in danger.

It was a slick, rainy night, and no one else was on the road. He passed Emil's hot dog stand where he had first seen the

Oldsmobile. He wished he had spent some of his income from rent on new tires, but he hadn't. He rubbed his hand over his wet head.

He was coming up on the hard left turn for the Crown Point Bridge to Vermont. He fishtailed around the turn, leaning back pressing down hard on the accelerator. He wanted to intercept them before they got to the campsite and Kim.

He raced along at eighty-five. But no red, rear lights shone ahead in the rain. He concentrated, steering with both hands, afraid of hydroplaning. The Bridge Deli sign glowed a blurry yellow through the rain and the thwack, thwack of his wipers. The deli must be open. A car was pulling out. Conway braked, skidded sideways, regaining control.

It looked like them. He flashed his bright lights to be sure. It was an Oldsmobile 88. It was them. Conway roared up to the rear bumper. The car had Florida plates.

"What's that guy doing?" Klocks yelled. "Get off my tail."

Damian turned around, a cigarette between his lips. "Some jerk, forget about him."

Conway was driving too fast. His Plymouth smacked their bumper.

The Oldsmobile lurched forward, jolting Damian and Klocks. "What the . . .! Is it a cop?" Klocks shouted, squinting into his rear view mirror.

Damian strained his eyes, rolling down his window, shoving himself out into the rain. Klocks floored it. Damian was half sitting on the window, holding on to the inside of the door, getting pummeled by the wind and rain.

"It's Conway. Goddamn it! I know his car," he yelled.

Pulling himself in, like he was doing the limbo, he repeated, "It's Conway. Do you believe it?"

Klocks was silent, grinding his teeth, eyes on the long sweeping stretch of highway ahead. He pulled away from Conway.

Conway didn't have a plan. He knew the campsite was fast approaching, in two miles. Conway backed off, hadn't actually meant to bump Klocks. He had skidded into him, he told himself.

"Hold on," Klocks warned. The needle on his speedometer touched fifty.

Instinctively Conway hit his brakes, slowing to the speed limit as he watched Klocks's red lights disappear into the darkness.

Klocks slammed on his brakes, jerking the steering wheel all the way to the left. His Rocket 88 skidded down the highway, sideways. Telephone poles flew by. The car tilted up on two wheels. Damian flung himself to the floor, crouched in a ball.

A moment of black, and then in a blink, Conway was squinting at two tiny white lights, staring at headlights growing bigger and bigger - zeroing in on him. Conway's eyes froze wide open, and his head snapped back. He became fully aware that he was the target.

"Oh yeah, oh yeah," Klocks screamed, "you want to know who I am? This is who I am." Klocks sped straight ahead, riveted on Conway's headlights. His powerful 324 cubic inch V-8 engine sounded like it was going to explode.

One hundred yards and closing. Klocks was doing sixty, Conway thirty.

In a field off the road sat a brown, weather-beaten barn, bales of hay sticking out of the open loft, two delicate white birches framing the corners. It was the kind of lonesome country sight that passersby stopped to photograph.

Klocks bore down, his bony hands grasping the steering wheel in tight fists. Damian squeezed tighter, his elbows and arms wrapped around his head.

Conway reacted. He needed to be a faster-moving target. In a frenzy, he stomped on the gas pedal. Within seconds, his car swerved off the road, careening up off a roadside ditch, soaring into the stormy night, into the field, airborne. As he landed the front tires blew, the hood popped open, and he plowed through the barn door, bales tumbling from the loft.

Klocks eyes emitted a wicked gleam. He laughed the diabolical laugh of a demented contestant, winning one game, victory in hand.

Twenty-four

Damian's hand shook as he tried to light a cigarette. "Is he dead?"

"Don't know, don't care. It's not my fault," Klocks said. "He drove off the road."

"But," began Damian, still frazzled.

"But what? I never touched him," Klocks said, as he executed a proper broken U-turn.

"True, true," Damian said, bobbing his head between puffs.

Klocks had a plan and he was going to stick to it, even if he had sabotaged himself by groping Kim, and before that, by jumping off Barn Rock. Everyone's entitled to personality changes, he thought, rotating his sore left shoulder. He was multifaceted, that's all, showing different sides of his personality to different people. A chameleon, changing colors, changing character.

Nobody's perfect, and he was far from it. But now he was fooling himself. The problem was his past bad deeds were starting to bother various facets of his personality, surfacing in weird ways, affecting his behavior. That's the only way he could account for coming close to raping the girl and close to jumping off the bridge.

This incident with Conway was another matter. Conway chased after him and deserved what he got. Klocks was fending off, that's all. Driving through the rain, back to the campsite, Klocks repeated aloud, "Stick to the plan. Stick to the plan."

Damian lit another cigarette and finally sat back. He had heard it before. He was used to hearing Klocks utter phrases out of nowhere, directed at no one. Anyone who had been incarcerated could relate. After a while everybody starting talking to themselves. Damian was twirling the radio dial trying to get one station in clearly, a station that played hip-hop or jazz. He couldn't believe he was starting to like jazz.

It rained harder and Klocks drove slower, leaning forward, cracking the driver's side window to get a little air flowing, rubbing the inside of the windshield with the side of his fist.

Ever since Klocks's ma died, Klocks thought about death. It's part of the reason he pulled off his escape. He was afraid he would die in prison, afraid he would waste away or be knocked off. Dying in prison was the dread of all prisoners. No one wanted to die in prison.

Klocks knew he would never go back. He had a will that had pulled through before. "One hell of a will," he reminded himself.

In the rain and his fogged windshield, he almost missed the right turn for the campsite.

"How come you're out here? There's nothing out here," Damian said.

"Oh yes there is," Klocks said. "Turn that up."

The National Weather Service had interrupted the radio station's regular broadcast to announce a flood watch for southern Vermont.

That's not us, thought Damian. Ever since he had taken his job at Stewart's, he was compelled to learn about the weather. It was the number one topic of conversation, the number one icebreaker in the North Country.

Damian said, "That's a watch, Klocks. Not a warning."

"What's the difference?"

"A warning means we're going to get clobbered. A big storm is definitely headed our way. A watch means maybe. It means don't go out and stock up on flashlights and canned goods yet. Stay tuned."

"The rain might help me. Might be a good cover." Klocks turned his head to look at Damian. "You know what to do, right?"

"Right, captain. Ditch the car. Remove the plates and bury them, so they can never be found. Let's see, and how much am I going to get?"

"Two thousand dollars within the month. You know my word is good. That's all I have left in this life. That and my reputation. This job will make me a legend."

"What are you doing, cutting the bridge in half? Let me guess, you found buried treasure?"

"In a way I did." Klocks turned off his lights, and his Rocket 88 crawled through the parking lot into the campsite. "We're here. By the way, what are you going to do with the car?"

First Damian had thought about driving it into the lake, then he thought about ditching it up in Mineville in a shaft filled with water. But Republic Steel had erected a steel mesh fence topped with barbed wire around all the open shafts including the 21 pit. He could demolish it, take it to a junkyard, but then someone else would know. Can't burn it.

"Whatever you do with it, it can't be found for, I don't know, for at least two months. They've got to think I drove out of here. By late tomorrow they'll find out the car is not registered to Jonathan Deed, and they'll put an APB out for it as a stolen car. That's what I want. I want the cops on the lookout for that car. So it absolutely can not be found, Damian. Don't screw up."

Klocks and Damian agreed that the less Damian knew about this job the better it was. Klocks assured him that no one would be hurt. In fact he assured him that no one really owned what he was going to steal. It was the perfect crime for Klocks.

It was a crime with no victim, and that's the kind of caper the public loved. The public never got upset with daring heists of fabulously expensive jewels or renowned impressionistic paintings. The original artist had died, usually decades ago. The owners had donated the painting to a museum and had already received their tax write-off. The museum had insurance. If the heist was clever, and appealed to the public's imagination, many times it spawned a movie, like Topkapi, or The Thomas Crown Affair.

Damian hesitated. "Klocks, I need to ask you a question. You know the painting of the tiger and the nude, by Chantal's mother? Do you still have it?"

"What makes you think I stole it?"

"Come on Klocks, give me a break."

"Yeah, I still have it. It's down in Florida. A bunch of reprobates are staring at it behind some bar."

Damian took a chance. "Where in Florida?"

Klocks laughed. "I like that painting. Tell Chantal, I'll give the painting back to you in my will."

Klocks leaned over and rummaged through the crap in his glove compartment. "Move over, Damian. Get in the back."

"It's pouring out."

"Just climb over the seat. You're going to be back there all night anyway. What I have to do is going to take me till dawn."

Klocks threw him a crumpled pack of Camels.

Damian flicked his Zippo lighter, which was like a torch. "Whatever," he said in disgust as he took a drag, and rolled down a back window. He opened a chrome ashtray on the back of the front seat. "I'm comfortable. Wake me up when you want me to leave."

"Dream of a deep, dark place for this car," Klocks deadpanned.

Klocks was scraping the stuff out of his glove compartment. He didn't bother saving the nickels and pennies, except for one piece of metal that caught his eye, the links of a gold chain that he had found nearby over the bank. He examined it for a moment, his head filling with blood, down near the floor, his feet up on the seat next to the steering wheel. He raised himself and slid the precious chain into his little pocket sewn inside the regular front right pocket of his jeans. That motion of slipping the chain into the watch pocket triggered his memory. It came to him what the chain was used for. It was the chain to a pocket watch. A simpler version of the fancier fob the old man in Apalachicola had sold him.

Certainly the corroded fob was an omen, and Klocks was given to superstition. The question was, was it a good omen or a bad one?

Damian was lying across the back seat holding his cell phone. "Busy again," he said, dropping the phone back into a side pocket on his cargo pants. Damian did not go anywhere without his cell phone. He was staring at the car floor when he noticed a glint. He lit his Zippo again so he could see.

"What are these?" Damian asked.

"They're the tools, idiot. Give them to me." Quick as a darting lizard, he grabbed Damian by his shirt knocking his cigarette to the floor. "Do you understand, I'm the man. Only I could pull this off. Understand that."

Klocks tossed the keys in the ashtray below the radio, and then scraped them back out to open the trunk. He took a deep breath before opening the car door and stepping out into the downpour. He stood at the open trunk and gathered two separate coils of rope, one a braided nylon climbing-type and one a thicker, old-fashioned hemp rope. He had rigged a webbed bo'sun's seat out of the hemp rope, coupled with a rudimentary pulley system. He slammed the trunk and trudged off in the direction of the lighthouse monument, trailing rope behind him.

It was the darkest night since he had camped there. He had counted on all the campers being gone, and they were, except for one Airstream at the other end of the park, with a night light on. He suspected it might be the trailer of the retired couple. But on a night like this nothing would get them outside.

Klocks dropped the ropes at the base of the monument. "Grrrr," he growled, reacting to the canines in Heber's sculpture, who were above his head. They were like sphinxes, watching and guarding. He met their penetrating eyes. He must keep his spirits up. He calculated it was going to take six hours to get this baby down. "Without a scratch," he said aloud.

He jogged through the growing puddles back to the car and leaned in the front door, wiping the water from his eyes. "You got a hat?"

Damian was one of these guys who could sleep anywhere, anytime. He treasured sleep. He sat bolt upright, having already fallen asleep. "Yeah, yeah. Here, take it. It's my Giant's cap."

Klocks pulled the hat down, closed the car door, splashed around to the trunk, and turned the key. He reached in and hauled out a satchel full of tools and the battery-powered drill that Damian had rented. Klocks left the keys sticking out of the trunk, purposely, knowing he'd have to get back in there.

Klocks opened the back door, where Damian was prone again. "You're sure the battery works, right?" Klocks asked.

"The guy turned it on for me, in the store."

"You know where I got the hang of using it?" Klocks said. "Up at the prison workshop. Wish me luck."

Damian was ready to fall back asleep, but was having difficulty as it dawned on him that he was an accomplice.

As Klocks plodded back to the monument, he took a brief look in the other direction towards the toll booth buildings. One light was on downstairs, showing dimly through the rain. It could have been Kim's light.

That was a dumb thing I did, Klocks thought. But I am who I am. I don't know why I went after her; I don't.

For the first time, Klocks heard distant thunder. Lightning lit up the sky, illuminating his tools. He was soaked, but didn't care. One time he had spent an entire night of thunderstorms stealing Tiffany windows from a mausoleum.

Klocks was remembering incidents like that to psyche himself up for a long night's work. As he reached the granite terrace apron around the monument, he stopped and looked back. Water pounded down and lightning flashed closer, revealing an empty parking lot, except for an Oldsmobile and an Airstream.

Twenty-five

K locks's leather satchel hung from his shoulder like a wine pouch, spilling over with tools. The rope rigging lay on the granite apron. He felt around with his feet and hands to get his bearings, to get a sense of where things were. He tapped his shirt pocket to see if the penlight was there. In his satchel he kept a battered, waterproof flashlight as backup.

The Champlain Monument was bathed in darkness, but not the utter blackness he had known under the earth for three days in the 21 Mine. Down there you could cover your eyes with your hands and not see a difference.

Outside at the monument his eyes were adjusting to the darkness. The lightning flashes helped. In four minutes Klocks gained his night vision. It was like he had infrared capabilities, seeing and sensing the contours of the bust of Rodin's mistress.

Time was his enemy and by morning, he must be done and gone. Klocks tossed the half-inch thick hemp rope up over the upturned prow of the canoe. He ran one hand through his makeshift pulley that was attached above the webbed seat under his crotch, and pulled the remainder of the rope through. He took the loose end, wound the rope in loops for a lasso, flinging it back over the prow with one hand as he let go of the slack with the other. He grabbed the dangling end and tied a monkey's fist.

Given the weight of the tools, especially the drill and the sledge, hoisting himself up would require all his strength. He wedged the end of the rope between his feet, stood on the knot, and tensing arms and legs, pulled on the rope, hauling himself up, until, inch by inch, he was swinging eye to eye with his prized Rodin.

He was breathing hard, but his rigging was functioning. He tied a bowline knot, fastening the rope around the bow of the canoe. There he sat, hanging in the air directly in front of the twenty-five by twenty-two inch bas-relief, his face brushing the bronze hair of Camille.

"I'm going to do my best not to hurt you. I can't afford to. You're too precious," he whispered.

After a reverential pause, Klocks proceeded. First like an old-fashioned safe cracker, who channeled all his senses to his fingertips, he rubbed the lower corners of the plaque locating the outline of the heads of two of the four circular pins that locked the bust in place. With the fingers of his left hand, he felt the cherished signature of A. Rodin. An inch or two above the priceless signature, was the head of one pin. But he didn't want to start with that pin. He hadn't perfected the knack of dislodging pins, and he dare not mar the signature. Better to make his first try on the lower right corner. To the right of the word "LA" and above "FRANCE" lay the circular head. He traced the one inch circle with the fingernail of his right index finger. He would start there.

He removed the pen light from his pocket and placed it in his mouth. From within his satchel he felt for the center punch, holding it in his left hand. With his right he grabbed the sawed-off handle of the six-pound sledge.

His outstretched legs kept his web chair stationary so that his torso was even with the lower right corner. Holding the light with his teeth and lips, pressing with his tongue, he switched it on. He placed the punch exactly in the center of the head of the pin, and tapped it with his sledge. It made an impression, an indentation, something for the drill bit to grab onto.

A blast of lightning, a roll of thunder, a burst of rain. This is hard core, thought Klocks. The first phase of his plan was to drill out each of the four pins. He reached into his satchel for the battery-powered drill. "This frigging thing better work," he muttered. He was surprised he had been allowed to operate a drill in prison, but he had. He was surprised about a lot of things at Moriah Shock. Overall it hadn't been that bad.

He pulled the trigger, and the bit whirred in the air. Keeping a perfect right angle and steady pressure, he lodged the bit into the indentation made by the punch, and applied pressure. The drill chewed up the head of the pin. Strips of dirty metal coiled around the bit.

In seconds he was into the shank of the bolt-like pin. The plaque itself was three-eighths to a half-inch thick. After half an hour of drilling, he disintegrated an inch of the bolt. More than enough, he figured.

Klocks repositioned his rope seat, pushing himself with his right leg to the left of the stone pedestal. He positioned himself in front of the lower left pin, near the treasured signature. Using the same procedure, he tapped the center punch to indent the head of the pin and then drilled. The bit grew hot to the touch. Again he ripped apart the head of the pin. Klocks kept pushing hard, boring out the bolt. Two bolts down, two to go. An hour and a half had passed. Klocks estimated freeing the Rodin would take five hours.

The storm was a good cover. Klocks loosened his knots and laboriously raised his seat two feet. He tied off the rigging with a bowline knot, gave it a test tug and felt secure. The pins in the top corners were harder to locate. The heads had melded into the bronze of the plaque. He found himself looking down at a rough tangle of hair on Camille's head and was able to take the pen light out of his mouth and rest it in the bronze folds of her hair.

He sat suspended in the dark, close to the canines and the bow of the canoe. That put him beneath the larger statues of Champlain, the Voyageur and the Indian, which on this night shielded him from the rain. To Klocks, the stone canines poised on furs in the canoe were now guarding him too.

In an hour he was able to disintegrate the top two bolts using the same technique. But his satisfaction from drilling out the bolts was premature. The one-piece plaque and bust, the bas-relief, had been so tightly set in stone that it would not budge. The rough, uneven stone blocks held the plaque in place. Klocks suspected that the original stone masons had been directed to cut and fit the granite stone around the bronze plaque, rather than recess the plaque in existing stone. The four-inch inset narrowed toward the face of the monument, making it impossible to pry out the plaque.

Klocks wavered. Gingerly, he put all his tools away, except his sawed-off sledge. He took out his gloves. The metal bust was jammed on the protruding stone pedestal, which, Klocks decided, would have to go. The lightning lit up the sky behind him to the east across the channel to Chimney Point.

One of his favorite movies was The Shawshank Redemption. Klocks, who was rooted in brutal reality, had found part of the escape scene hard to believe: beneath the prison infrastructure, the prisoner, gripping a rock, pounded open a hole on a sewer pipe in concert with the muffling thunder.

Yet Klocks was doing the same thing, waiting for the lightning, raising his mash hammer and smashing down on the pedestal. Two blows of his sledge in synch with two crashes of thunder and he broke off a large chunk of the supporting granite pedestal.

A smaller fragment hit his leg. Klocks shook and rubbed his leg, which was already numb from being in one position and now bruised from the falling stone.

After breaking the pedestal, he wedged his pry bar up behind the base of the bust, and pried the bust away from the granite. He moved the bottom slightly, but the sides and the top were still stuck where they had been since 1912.

Frustrated, Klocks lay the pry bar in his lap, and reached again for his masonry hammer. Klocks chipped away more stone, cringing lest he slip with his chisel and mar the priceless Rodin. He concentrated on chipping back the edges of the granite blocks surrounding the bust. With one gloved hand he shielded his eyes from the flying chips.

While Klocks guarded his eyes, Kim opened hers.

Twenty-six

Kim was sitting on the bed by the window, watching the storm and waiting. She had seen the inside light of a parked car go on and off a few times. She was waiting for Matt, and by the time he showed up, twenty minutes later, she was convinced the other car belonged to Klocks.

She just needed to be comforted and held. Matt, too, having driven in the storm with time to think, was feeling alone. When he arrived, she unlocked the tourist office door turning out the lobby lights as she led him by the hand down the stairs to her room.

They made wonderful, soft love and slept arm in arm. Kim hadn't whispered a word about the incident in the lighthouse stairwell. She'd tell Matt in the morning, or maybe she wouldn't tell him at all. She believed in sharing, but what was the benefit of sharing that indignity, that violation, with your boyfriend?

While they slept, Klocks worked.

Kim woke chilled and lay under the sheet with her leg touching Matt's. When she thought she heard distant tapping, she quietly slid out of bed and grabbed the quilt. Kim wiped the steam from the window and cupped her hands around the damp pane to look outside.

She couldn't see much through the rain, but in the background she heard something. She waited and watched. She wasn't sure of the exact origin of the sound. Lightning flashed. She saw a glint at the monument. She didn't know that it was Klocks raising his hammer, chipping the granite.

She woke Matt. She was hesitant, but the reality of being attacked in the stairwell had made her paranoid.

"Matt, come here. Tell me if you see anybody out there."

"Out where?" he mumbled into the pillow.

"Outside. Here," she gently led him to the window. "Look."

Groggy and naked, Matt crouched over the window and dutifully peered out. "All I see is rain."

"Wait for the lightning."

"I'm not going to wait for lightning. Why don't we wait for dawn." He rolled back into the bed. In resignation, she threw the quilt over Matt, who fell fast asleep.

No way she was going back to sleep. Now, the only person she had confidence in was herself. After her less than satisfactory meeting with Reginald, she wasn't willing to call the police on a hunch. And the fishing couple hadn't been willing to verify her story. When she was certain, then she'd call.

She put on her blue jeans and tucked in her nightshirt. She found her yellow slicker and hood, but no flashlight. Just so Matt wouldn't be worried, she scribbled a quick note saying that she went outside to check out the noise at the monument.

Kim was fearful, though not yet frightened. She was cautious, creeping only a few yards at a time in the direction of the bust of Camille. She saw the one other car in the parking lot, and it looked like Klocks's Oldsmobile. To be sure she'd have to see a Florida license plate.

As Kim crept closer, Klocks wedged his pry bar under the right side, and was able to nudge the side of the bust half an inch outward. It was a start. The beginning of the end of what was becoming an ordeal. He retrieved the climbing rope that he left coiled on the terrace. He would use the thinner nylon rope to slip under the plaque to prevent it from falling, and ultimately, to lower it to the ground. He guessed the sculpture weighed two hundred pounds. In preparation for dislodging the entire bas-relief, he put the pry bar and the hammer back in the satchel, and focused on letting his rigging down a few inches at a time. He took one glove off and held it in his mouth while he struggled to loosen his wet bowline knot. Slowly, using two hands and his makeshift pulley, he lowered himself down to the terrace.

His bag of tools clanked to the ground. Kim clearly heard that. Now she was scared. Someone or something was out there at the monument in the pouring rain.

The fishing couple nestled in their Airstream on the far side of the lot was oblivious to nocturnal noises. Parked under a dead elm, their only worry was being hit by a falling branch in the storm.

The lightning flashed and Kim froze. She saw a man bent over in front of the monument beneath the fierce figures of Champlain, the Voyageur, and the Huron. The Rodin bust was lost in the surreal montage.

Thus far, Klocks and Damian were unaware of Kim's approach. Klocks was pacing, stretching his sore leg, before hoisting himself back up carrying the climbing rope. Soaked and chilled from the night rain, he resisted going back to the car, to warm up. It was four in the morning. In an hour, the sun would lighten the sky. By that time he should be long gone. He gazed east, beyond the tourist house where Kim was staying, in the direction of sunrise. He noticed her apartment light was off. That was a good sign. But then he witnessed the light go on. That was bad, because it meant somebody was up.

Kim had just returned and was shaking Matt awake, telling him someone was out at the monument. It looked like that thug Klocks, defacing the statue of Champlain. Now, she said, they should call the cops.

Klocks didn't know what was happening inside Kim's apartment, but he figured Matt was back, and Klocks naturally assumed Kim had told Matt about the special attention Klocks gave her in the lighthouse. And he knew how jealous boyfriends reacted.

Klocks's hardened alter ego surged forward. His intuition spoke to him. There was no turning back. He wasn't one for harming innocent bystanders and he disdained using a weapon. He didn't even own a gun, and had no respect for punks who shot people, though he had once succumbed to that himself. Maybe that was part of his problem, he couldn't live up to his own rules. Maybe that's why his behavior was so schizophrenic.

Klocks stepped out of the rigging, grabbed his masonry hammer and ran back to his car. He woke up Damian who was perfectly comfortable in fetal position on the back seat.

"Damian. I need your help. Right now! See that car over there?"

"Where?" Damian sat up.

Klocks was getting agitated. He took Damian's head between his hands and pointed it outside. "There. The only other car in the lot! I need you to go out there and slash the tires. All four of them. I think I've been spotted. Right now. Just run out and do it."

"What, you want to make it so they can't drive?"

"Yes, that's the idea."

"I'll take off the distributor cap," Damian said.

Klocks ran to the corner of the tourist building nearest the telephone pole. "Okay," he called back, "do that then."

Kim was inside dialing the local police number Reginald had given her, while Matt hurriedly dressed. She got a recording referring callers to the state police in Westport.

"Nobody's there. Shall I call the state police?"

Klocks scurried up the pole in three seconds, like he lived there, splitting the phone line with the chisel end of his hammer.

If Kim and her boyfriend were on to him, now they were isolated. He had until sunrise. As did they.

"Yep, call them." Matt's tune had changed. When she had announced breathlessly that Klocks was outside in front of the monument, extracting something, she blurted out about her incident with Klocks on the lighthouse stairs.

She keyed in the number, 962-823. . . and the line went dead. She stared at Matt with her mouth hanging open. "The line went dead," she whispered.

Matt lunged across the bed and switched off the light.

Twenty-seven

K locks strode back to his Oldsmobile. He was on a mission, his red beard dripping, his pace quickening.

"Damian, I've got an hour's more work, and then I'll need you to back the car up, right onto the slab."

"Whatever you say, old buddy," drawled Damian who was standing in the rain tossing the distributor cap from hand to hand, cables dangling like octopus arms. Underneath his nonchalance, Damian was questioning the pact of loyalty he had made with Klocks at Moriah Shock.

Klocks splashed through the puddles on the pavement, imprinting his footprints on the spongy grass, stomping across the granite apron - all the while eyeing the tourist bureau building.

A truck from Vermont roared over the bridge, reminding him that Monday morning would soon be upon him. Klocks squeezed into his bo'sun's chair, slung his satchel over one shoulder, his coiled three-eighths inch nylon rope over the other. He untangled his pulley system and using his arm strength, hoisted himself back up to his cramped position in front of the bust of Camille.

The right side of the sculpture was angled out. Klocks's task was to patiently pry out the bust until he could fish the nylon climbing rope up behind it. Using his hammer and pry bar, he chipped more granite away and pried underneath the bust, edging it out. At last, the lower corners were exposed, one sticking out farther than the other. Only the friction from the upper corners held the bust in place.

Klocks tied a double slip knot and slid the harness up behind the bottom third of the plaque. He tossed the other end up over the ear of dog, over the jutting canoe bow, and let it fall loosely to the ground. He gathered up the slack, coiling it in his lap. He was no longer cold. Sweating and thirsty, he opened his mouth to catch a trickle of water falling off the bow of the canoe.

He took the untied end of the rope and looped it around the remaining jagged piece of pedestal. He yanked down on the final half hitch to make sure it held. He would need Damian's help to lower this baby down.

Another truck rumbled over the dark bridge. Come daybreak, Klocks and Damian couldn't be out there dismantling the Champlain monument. Maybe drivers would assume they were park workers cleaning the statues. But Klocks doubted that.

Klocks lowered himself down and hopped out of his webbed seat. He ran over to the car. "Damian, Damian, get out here. Come on."

Quickly Damian tied the laces on his running shoes before trotting close behind Klocks, who was in nocturnal mode, at home in the dark.

Klocks straightened out his rigging and got back into his bo'sun's seat. "Grab this rope, right here, where it's touching the ground. Run it around the corner. Use the friction of the stones."

Klocks reset his pulley and raised himself, exhausted and intense. He drove his pry bar behind the upper right corner and with the feel of a skilled stone mason, jimmied the bust loose. The entire bust was sticking out at an extreme angle, and now the lower left corner was jammed on the broken pedestal, caught against the rope.

"Just in case my knots don't hold, be ready, Damian."

Klocks stopped and again speculated on how much it weighed. The bust wasn't that big, about two feet by two feet, but there was a lot of bronze in it. He revised his first guess upward to a solid two hundred and fifty pounds.

"Here goes," Klocks warned. With his hammer, he tapped the inside edge of the bust until it slipped off the broken pedestal and jerked the rope tight. Klocks kicked back away from the stone wall.

He glanced up at the dogs. He glared at Kim's building. No lights that he could see. The sculpture hung free eight feet off the ground.

"Damian, this is it! Hold for fifteen seconds. I'll be down."

Klocks undid his half hitches and unwound the first two of three loops of rope around the broken pedestal. "Ready? I'm going to slowly let the rope out."

Braced with two legs pushing against where the bust was once embedded, holding the rope with two arms, he unwound the last loop. The bust lurched downward. Klocks's slack was gone, along with the palms of his gloves. The bas-relief swayed four feet off the ground.

"Hold on. I'll be there." Klocks uttered these words while he furiously untangled and lowered.

Damian was afraid to answer. Even the energy required to talk might take away his concentration. His black face was turning red. He pulled tightly against the stone corner. The rope stretched in the air like a tightrope. Klocks dashed around the corner and grabbed hold.

Behind them a thunderous roar - not from the storm, but from an engine.

They were startled, but there was no turning away from the task at hand. "Move around the corner. Use your legs," Klocks commanded.

The stone terrace was covered in two inches of water, and they both slipped. Damian managed to grab the stone corner as they slid, while Klocks regained his feet. The Rodin now swung a smidgen above the rainwater.

For five hours Klocks had been struggling with Rodin's bust. Klocks exhaled in relief. "I did it." They let it drop down.

Immediately Damian turned around to where the noise had come from. He didn't see anything. That was the problem. Except for the white Subaru with the kayaks and without the distributor cap, there was nothing.

"Your car! Where's your car?"

Klocks was kneeling over the bust of Camille, rubbing his hand over the gnarled mass of bronze on top of her head. He swiveled around in time to see orange taillights turn left out of the campgrounds onto the road to Port Henry.

Klocks shook his head in disbelief. "Damn her. That broad stole my car. Can you believe it?" Klocks stood up and slumped over, leaning on the large dedication plaque beneath where the Rodin had once reigned. "Damn it! Damn it! Damn it!" he cursed, each time pounding the stone monument with his fist.

Twenty-eight

K im and Matt sped towards the Miss Port Henry Diner. She would have her all-American revenge. "I'm going to nail him," she said. "Matt, he'll probably smash your windows, whoever he is."

Matt forced an uneasy laugh. "We'll know who he is soon enough," he said. "Just as long as he leaves the kayaks alone. Then again maybe I'm through with that sport."

Kim was driving. The picturesque barn wasn't visible in the dark. The engine and oil lights glowed red. She turned right, north on route 22. The engine was overheating. She drove to the edge of town, as far as the green and white Champ sign listing the sightings of the Lake Champlain monster. There, the engine seized and the Oldsmobile came to a jarring stop.

She got out and slammed the door. It was five thirty in the morning. She knew the diner opened at six. "Let's walk. It's not far," she said.

In their harried state, the simmering engine seemed to hiss at them, like a mechanical minion loyal to Master Klocks. His habit of neglecting to add oil had bought him some precious time.

Kim and Matt marched off to the diner in search of Conway and the police. Matt did his best to keep up with Kim, who seemed energized by the intrusion of Klocks into her life. Half an hour later, past Witherbee-Sherman's ornate French building which served as the town hall, past the gas pumps for Stewart's, across the Grand Union parking lot, they reached the steps to the diner. Their brisk pace dissipated their anger, somewhat. They were beginning to worry that maybe they had gone too far by stealing the car.

Usually Kim radiated a friendly openness, which was sometimes misread as a come-on. She was starting to be self-conscious about her tomboyish tendencies to show skin in a rough and tumble, athletic sort of way. Kim pulled her hair back in a pony-tail and her sweatshirt down. Underneath, she wore a halter-top. Outwardly she wore a scowl. This morning, she was beset by the doubts of a woman who has been accosted by a man.

Just before she pulled open the diner door Kim turned and asked in a low voice, "Was it my fault, Matt?"

With a straightened arm, Matt kept the door shut. "Get that notion out of your head. The guy is an ex-con. He's trouble. You're totally in the right."

Matt seemed to care. He was usually so laid back about feelings. She felt strong again, and at least temporarily, discarded her second thoughts.

Matt patted her behind as they entered the early morning tribunal of the local cohorts.

Reginald was inside. Before Kim and Matt had a chance to sit on the stools, Reginald corralled the two of them back outside onto the concrete steps.

Quietly, he filled them in on who he suspected this drifter was. Jonathan Deed was an alias. Reginald described Klocks's Moriah Shock background, which was sobering. Kim and Matt were relieved they hadn't confronted him.

"Listen, I've done a little research on this guy, Klocks." Reginald said. "And it is Klocks, by the way. Don't forget the tattoo. He's a 'show me the money' kind of guy. That's why he's here. He thinks he's untouchable, here in Moriah. This is the place he pulled off his greatest act, disappearing down the 21 Mine. And now he's back for a reason. But I don't know why."

The two of them were silent, absorbing Reginald's speech. A loaded logging truck lumbered by shaking the foundation of the Miss Port Henry Diner. Kim realized she had underestimated Reginald, at first labeling him as the town buffoon. Now she was certain the man at the bridge was Klocks.

Reginald was hesitant to drive to the campsite without some sort of backup. He decided the three of them weren't going there without the protection of the state police. Reginald, Kim and Matt reentered the diner.

"Where's Conway?" Kim asked.

Reginald shook his head from side to side. "You'd think he'd be here."

Reginald removed the saucer from atop his cup, swallowed his warm coffee, and paid. The three of them walked across Main Street to the village office. There, Reginald showed Kim and Matt the fax confirming that the license plates belonged to an eighty-year old gentleman named Harry Southard who lived in Apalachicola, Franklin County, Florida. The plates were not registered to a Jonathan Deed or a Wallace Klocks, and Klocks's Oldsmobile did not look like Southard's Cadillac.

"Why didn't he steal the Caddy?" Reginald wondered. "Ahh, then he probably would have been pulled over on the way up from Florida."

The three of them stood outside Reginald's minuscule office contemplating their next step. Maps of Essex County, Lake Champlain, Moriah and the Adirondack State Park covered the pink walls of the village office.

"Just out of curiosity, did you talk to the old couple?" Reginald asked Kim.

She hung her head. "I did. They don't want to get involved. The husband said if I was hurt, maybe. Who knows? I didn't press it."

"What was Klocks doing in front of the monument last night?" Matt asked.

Reginald was mulling things over. "Most people around here are going to find it hard to believe that the guy who escaped into the 21 Mine is still alive. I find it hard to believe."

"Fine, it's freaking hard to believe," Kim said impatiently.

Matt put his arm around Kim. "Kim. What about the monument?" He could see she was caught between thinking clearly and getting upset.

"Well, I do have to work tomorrow. I should know this stuff." She took a minute, sniffled and grew quiet. The monument wasn't in the museum's historical site jurisdiction, but museum officials included it in tours because of its history as a windmill, a working light station, and as the Champlain Memorial. "Guess what, boys," she smiled, "there's a Rodin sculpture there, in the stone."

Matt tilted his head back and laughed in disbelief. "Klocks is something, isn't he?"

After a moment of stunned silence, Reginald drew a deep breath while recalling that a priceless work of art, a Rodin, was located in the sticks at the Champlain Monument.

Matt contorted his face. "This is his curtain call, stealing a Rodin sculpture. I guarantee you it's the single most valuable thing within a hundred miles of us. I'm sure it's worth millions. Millions. He's something, man." Matt spun around in a circle as he spoke.

"All right," Reginald said, "I'm calling the troopers. I don't think the Crown Point station is open. I'm calling Westport. If we're going down there, we're going in force." Reginald added, "Conway should be here. He's the one that put me onto Klocks."

Twenty-nine

K locks pulled himself back from the edge of despair and brushed off the loss of his car. The only thing he had the time for was to hurdle each obstacle.

"I worked hard for this and no one's going to take it away from me. Not without handing over a lot of money. So there, take that. I've got resources and then I've got resources. Bamm!" he shouted. "Damian, you got your cell phone?"

"I do."

"You're the man."

"I ain't the man, but here's the phone."

Klocks talked as he keyed in Spike's number. "Damian, I don't think anybody knows you're here. They probably couldn't see over here when they hijacked my wheels. That broad . . ."

Klocks broke off his conversation with Damian to speak to Spike. "Here's the deal, no change, but . . ."

Klocks finished his instructions to Spike and tossed the phone back to Damian. "Call Chantal. Have her pick you up. Like pronto. Or get someone else who can keep their mouth shut."

"That narrows it down to . . . nobody!" Damian remembered one of Klocks's mantras. A secret is only a secret if you didn't tell anybody else. Once two people knew, it was no longer a secret. Reluctantly, Damian left a terse message for Chantal on her cell phone.

Klocks barked at him. "Get over here. We have to move my Rodin."

"His Rodin," Damian groused.

* * * * *

So far Spike had done nothing wrong. He hadn't stolen anything. All he knew was that Klocks desperately needed a ride in his boat. Spike understood that at some level he was employing the rationalizations of the inmates he guarded. But so what? Klocks was his only childhood friend from Troy. Short of breaking the law (that is, short of getting caught), if he could help, he would. After all he had helped before.

Spike had already called in sick. Klocks's phone call just moved up the schedule a few hours. Spike's last words were, "You should have kept your hands off her. You should have left her alone."

Spike drove his Bronco south on route 22 from Westport to Port Henry, the same route he took to work. Except he didn't veer right up onto the Pelfershire Road cut-off to Mineville. Instead, he sped south to the Velez Marina. At the same time Reginald was phoning the Westport trooper barracks at exit 31 off the Northway.

Spike knew almost every trooper, and he occasionally got stopped, but never got a ticket. Correction officers and state troopers pledged the same law enforcement fraternity, and troopers seldom wrote tickets except for egregious violations. Guards had a shortened life expectancy similar to that of cops in New York City. Troopers felt prison guards were in the same line of work and had the tougher job.

Spike made a left turn at the base of Convent Hill, crossed the D & H tracks and made another left into Velez's, passing by a long open shed containing the remaining wooden Lymans and Chris Crafts which hadn't turned to rot. No one was at the marina early on a Monday morning. Spike was tempted to hide his

Bronco, but instead parked it where he always did, close to his Hacker-Craft.

Before unsnapping the canvas cover on his mahogany decking, he jiggled the pooled water away. Each time he looked at his precious wooden boat he repeated to himself, it's worth the money, it's worth the money. Since the bubble burst in the stock market, his mutual funds had tanked, Amazon.com had gotten clobbered, and he was feeling considerably poorer. His new outlook, born of necessity, was that he was a long-term investor.

The rising sun was peeking over the Green Mountains after what had been a rainy night. Spike tossed his dry-bag into the cockpit, turned the pumps on and, using two fingers, simultaneously pressed the silver choke and electric starter buttons. The sweet rumble was like the voice of an old girlfriend, full of nostalgia and good times. His spirits brightened and he forgot about the money.

He maneuvered away from the dock and roared out of the marina, once again drenching the "no wake" sign. It was about this time each year that he drove his boat to South Bay just northwest of Whitehall and the Champlain canal. So, he reasoned, he wasn't doing anything out of the ordinary.

* * * * *

Klocks was petrified that every car driving to the bridge from the New York side was coming after him. In a feverish state, he stopped to listen for the bellowing of Spike's getaway boat, barking out conflicting orders to Damian, at the same time advising him that if a cop showed up, to run away along the wooded shoreline.

Damian grumbled, seeing that he was back in the thick of things. After he had turned his life around up here. Man, he shook his head, now he was doing something he shouldn't be doing. "Just get here before the cops, Chantal," he mumbled to himself.

"Take these tools down there, put them right next to the water. Spike knows not to dock at the pier."

Damian dutifully jogged by with the satchel overloaded with tools.

"I thought you were through with Chantal?" Klocks said.

"Yeah, well, she's kind of been there for me, you know what I mean. She's going to flip-out if she sees you."

"We don't have time for that. When she comes, run out there. And then keep driving over the bridge to Vermont. They might be stopping cars in New York. You'll be safe for the day in Vermont. Maybe you'll get lucky."

"Shut up Klocks, I don't need your crap. I'm helping you, aren't I?"

"You are, Damian, and if I make it, I owe you big time. And if I don't, I'll say a prayer for you," Klocks said.

"Wait a minute. You owe me two grand. Remember?"

Klocks was silent.

"You do remember?" Damian repeated with nervous intensity.

"I'll pay you, I'll pay you," Klocks said wearily, looking away.

Just don't come back, Damian thought to himself, praying for his own salvation. Damian was having an internal monologue, lecturing himself, whipping himself with words, doing penance. Another terrible lack of judgment on his part. He vowed if he got out of this, never again would he do anything this stupid, this wrong. He was pleading for a small break, not to be caught, not to be implicated in any way. He hadn't done anything really wrong had he? As the sun came up, he stood on the bank cursing himself.

The rays struck Klocks like light on a vampire, sending him into a frenzied retreat into the shoreline forest. "Where's the damn boat?" Klocks demanded of the horizon.

The way Klocks saw it, it was a race between Spike and whomever Kim and her boyfriend rustled up. Klocks was counting on Spike's boat. He knew Kim was paying him back for his friendly ways on the lighthouse stairs. He didn't have time to peer in her window for confirmation that she was gone. He understood payback. She had stolen his car to go round up a posse.

While they waited for either savior or captor, Klocks and Damian had one last Herculean task - to lift the Rodin bust up off the marble foundation and carry it down over the shoulder of Grenadier's Redoubt to the edge of the Lake. Klocks rotated his shoulder, sore from Barn Rock. None of his elaborate rigging would help and Klocks, sleepless and exhausted, needed help.

Legs apart, he and Damian positioned themselves to attempt to lift it when they heard a vehicle. They froze, staring at each other. It was a Dodge King Cab, and it was coming directly at them. Once Klocks made out what was printed on the driver's side door - Bog Pond Ranch, he knew who it was.

"Get going," Klocks said as he slipped a hundred-dollar bill into Damian's shirt pocket. "Toss the distributor cap on the hood of that college boy's car. Run." Klocks mumbled, "I'm getting soft."

Damian ran, snapped a wiper blade over the distributor's cables, and kept running, jumping onto the running board of Chantal's truck. She rolled on through, as if this was how she always picked him up.

Thirty

The first phone call, at 7:45 a.m., was from Reginald to the trooper barracks in Westport. The second call was from Westport to the sub-station at Crown Point, notifying that outpost of a complaint of a possible stolen car along with some shenanigans at the Crown Point Campsite.

The seldom-manned Crown Point State Police sub-station personified the boonies. It was difficult to find, located at the end of a hardscrabble road. An abandoned railroad station with orange, sun-streaked boards, too far gone for even the Preservation Society to be interested, leaned nearby. At the dead end, a cluster of camps at the Monitor Bay Campsite rented for $7.00 per day to non-residents and $4.00 per day to residents - according to the hand-painted, wooden sign. Off to the left, next to a Quonset hut on a dirt and gravel turnaround, shuttered by sheds and trailers, sat an unassuming yellow wooden structure. Inside, in a room barely big enough for one oak desk, was the improbable site of the New York State Police Sub-station at Crown Point.

The phone rang at the Crown Point sub-station just as Damian and Chantal were crossing the Lake Champlain Bridge in Chantal's purple pick-up. Sergeants Baker and Forks were there at the station each with a squad car. The presence of two officers was unusual; the result of another North Country emergency they were wrapping up, and it wasn't even 9:00 a.m.

A pack of dogs had chased a doe and a fawn into the lake, and, unless the troopers could save them, it looked like the dogs would kill them both. The Essex County's Sheriff's Department boat was out of commission with a cracked hull. The troopers thought about calling the Coast Guard in Burlington, but they'd be too far away to respond in time, as would Plattsburgh. So the troopers crossed the field from the sub-station to the Monitor Bay Campsite and commandeered a Boston Whaler with a Mercury outboard. They could see and hear a pack of wild dogs on the Vermont shore, agitated, barking.

By the time Troopers Baker and Forks arrived offshore in the boat, the dogs had dragged the fawn to shallow water and it was dying a miserable death. Three of the pack of five dogs had tags. Trooper Baker took out his gun and shot the fawn.

After much thrashing and eye-bulging terror on the doe's part, the troopers roped and lashed her to the side of the Whaler and brought her over to the New York shore. Once untangled she stumbled and ran across the field. Before entering the cover of the pines, she turned her head, gazing across the shore at her ravaged fawn and the howling pack of dogs that had brought her down.

Forks docked the Whaler and looked around for someone to thank, but no one showed. The boat probably belonged to somebody renting one of the Monitor Bay cabins. Baker had to drive south to Ticonderoga and he and Forks agreed to meet afterwards for lunch in Jan's Diner, on 9N and 22 just north of the hamlet of Crown Point. Baker had heard that it was under new management.

When the phone rang Forks was reloading his weapon, a rare experience. Most troopers went months, even years, without firing their gun in the line of duty. The message from Westport was to drive towards the Crown Point Bridge, investigate an accident on the spur road, and then see what was up at the campsite. Forks said he'd go.

He knew the terrain of the shoreline there, and would have liked nothing more than chasing a crook over the ledges and cedars. He was in training to run the New York City Marathon. In preparation, he had run the annual Elizabethtown to Westport Nine-Mile Mini-marathon, and had even run the 30K Fort-to-Fort race, which started at the bridge near the monument. (The run followed route 22 south over rolling hills and ended 18.6 miles later inside Fort Ticonderoga after a grueling run up Benny's Hill, named after Benedict Arnold.)

Thirty-one

Daybreak was upon Klocks as he watched the rear blinkers of Chantal's truck to see which direction they'd turn, right towards Vermont or left to New York. They went right, and Klocks glimpsed the purple pickup through the poplar and maples across the bridge, a brief, wistful look on his face, as if he'd like to change places.

His moment of reverie was broken by a thundering sound as Spike's Hacker-Craft careened around the ruins of the two forts, banked under the bridge, full throttle, skidding sideways, correcting and taking dead aim at the Champlain Monument. Klocks scrambled down over the hill to where he had piled his ropes and tools and waved Spike in. Together, they secured the boat to some saplings, and Spike jumped ashore, landing in water up to his knees.

Immediately Klocks realized they had a problem. It was too shallow to pull the boat closer. They wouldn't be able to lift the sculpture into the boat. "Get back in, Spy. You're going to have to move to the pier. The hell with being seen."

With the stern rope, Klocks was able to hold the boat close enough so that Spike could climb back in. "Hand me that crap," Spike said. "Hurry."

Klocks handed Spike the satchel of tools and chucked the ropes in the back cockpit. He threw Spike the stern line, and ran along the shoreline down to the pier. In a few seconds Spike docked the boat, leaving the engine running, as Klocks whipped the stern and bow ropes around the stanchions.

Together they jogged back up to the monument, bounding up the slippery steps, skidding to a stop ten feet from the Rodin.

"What happened here?" asked an old woman. She put down her pail and looked up. It was the fishing couple from the Airstream. She was standing over the Rodin on the marble terrace amid the debris of torn-out grout and pieces of granite. "Did this happen in the storm?" she asked, looking at her husband.

Her husband, fishing rod in hand, was caught staring directly at Klocks and Spike. The husband sized up the situation, as did they. "Could have," he said with a nonplussed look on his face. "Could have, yep," he said as if trying to reassure the two men poised at the top of the steps.

"Definitely was the storm," Klocks said clearly and loudly.

"Come on, hon," the old man said taking her hand, "I forgot the bait." The woman gave her husband a quizzical look as they turned around and padded back to their trailer under the trees.

Klocks and Spike didn't have time to calculate the consequences of this unforeseen run-in with the elderly couple, who seemed to hang around like trained detectives.

"Watch the edges," Klocks warned, but Spike had already sliced a finger. They propped the statue up on the edge that had rested on the pedestal, and, using their bulk, jerked it up like weightlifters. "It's not too bad," Spike huffed. "We'll go down step by step, sideways."

Daylight ushered in the morning construction traffic. Through the mist rising off the lake, two empty dump trucks rattled over the bridge towards Vermont, one right on the tail of the other. Early morning fog was a natural occurrence on the Crown Point peninsula.

"Jesus," Klocks quipped, "if the cops aren't here by now. Maybe they're not coming."

Spike concentrated on where he placed his feet. "What," he said, "makes you think the cops are on the way?"

"That college girl Kim. I got a bad feeling."

"Hey, maybe the troopers are busy. Could be a jackknife on the Northway. Besides they have to make it here from Westport." Spiked eyed the boat, gauging how to heave the Rodin into his boat without scratching the epoxy finish.

"Ready," Spike said. "No wait, put it down."

"Shit, let's go, let's go," Klocks said.

Klocks had no choice but to follow Spike's lead. They placed the bas-relief on the edge of the pier beside the boat. From a compartment under the deck Spike grabbed a towel, then untangled Klocks's rope, creating a cushion on the floor below his dark green upholstery.

"There, we can rest it on that," Spike said.

The Hacker was sputtering up smoke and water through its dual exhausts. "Be careful of the deck," Spike said straining his outstretched arms making sure the bust cleared the polished mahogany.

Klocks was grimacing, straining from the effort of a night of work. "Careful of my Rodin," he mouthed back at Spike. Their lower backs tightening, they eased the treasure into the second cockpit, angling the sculpture onto the ropes, its side resting on towels protecting the upholstery.

Klocks stood straight and twitched his head like an owl. He thought he heard a distant siren. "Go, go," he yelled, as he frantically unwound the rope from the stanchions.

Spike was at the throttle. He reached back with his huge hand and pulled Klocks aboard as they launched. "I'm on, I'm on," Klocks yelled, over the thunderous noise of the engine.

"Watch the stern," Spike yelled back. Klocks turned in time to kick off the dock giving the boat the extra few inches of clearance it needed. "Flip up the fenders. If we're going to be spotted, we might as well look good. After all, I didn't steal this woman's head, right Owlie?"

"Right Spy. I mean what are friends for." Klocks and Spike were behaving just like they used to when they raided homes years ago in Troy. The tighter the situation the more the bantering.

"Where to, Owl?"

"South, baby, all the way to Sotheby's."

Seconds counted and that's how Klocks liked it. That was living. As they roared away, showering the water behind them in a rooster tail of spray, they were in a race against Kim and the cops.

"Faster, faster," Klocks implored, thumping the dashboard with his fists. Spike slowly pushed the throttle all the way forward. The Hacker plowed ahead. In a heartbeat, they reached the deep channel in the middle of the lake.

Things started to plunge over the side. Item by item, Klocks dumped all his rigging, his tools, his sledge, his chisel and hammer, even the aged mortar and bits of stone that clung to Camille. When he finished, he tucked the towel around his prized Rodin.

In the fishing couple's Airstream, the old man put down his binoculars and said to his wife, "I've seen enough." Ten minutes later the silver bullet crept out of the parking lot, turning left towards Port Henry.

Thirty-two

T he Port Henry patrol car rose up over the railroad overpass as a freight train rounded the turn, wheels squealing against the burnished rails, flushing up a pair of wood ducks from the marsh of Bulwagga Bay.

Reginald and two civilians in the back seat were in the car on the spur road headed for the campsite and the monument. In the opposite direction, an ambulance whizzed by. Reginald turned on the scanner. The Westport station had dispatched a trooper to an accident on route 903, the spur road, with instructions to continue on to the monument. Along the long straightaway Reginald pulled over at the site of the accident. Trooper Forks was parked next to a hay field. A tow truck was bumping across the field towards a barn.

Forks approached Reginald.

"What's up?" Reginald asked.

"Hard to say," Forks said as he surveyed Kim and Matt.

Reginald read Forks's eyes and explained, "We're headed to the campsite at the monument. Somebody's stealing something. They're witnesses. They're okay."

Forks nodded, then answered Reginald. "I don't know if he fell asleep, or was drunk or what. No skid marks."

Kim was watching the tow truck connect its hooks to the rear bumper of a crumpled Oldsmobile sticking out of the barn.

"Matt," she gasped, grabbing his forearm, "that's Conway's car."

Forks looked at Kim and said, "He was unconscious for a long time, but he should live. They're bypassing E'town, taking him straight to Plattsburgh."

Reginald ran his hand across his chin. "How did it happen?"

The radio in the trooper's car squawked, and Forks walked away, opened the car door, reaching in to snatch the mike, stretching the cable. Reginald got out of his patrol car and followed.

He listened as Trooper Forks received orders from headquarters to proceed immediately to the Crown Point Bridge. A man and wife fishing at the campground had just called the Westport station confirming that a statue at the lighthouse memorial was either being damaged or stolen. In a reflex action, Forks and Reginald patted their holstered weapons in anticipation. Eyewitnesses had corroborated Kim's report. Forks and Reginald would be investigating grand larceny.

Reginald filled Forks in about the identity of their probable suspect, Klocks, and insisted Forks call for backup. Reginald hopped into his car. They both sped off. Forks, in the lead, flicked on his flashing light. Reginald in the sheriff's car could barely keep up. Forks was quickly doing eighty-five on the windblown flats. This was more like what Forks wanted police work to be - putting down a fawn, investigating a bizarre accident and now this.

Forks whipped into the parking lot aiming directly for the monument, his siren blaring. No sense hiding anything now. From the end of the covered pier, a boat pulled away. Forks jumped from his cruiser and ran to the monument. He saw the debris and stepped back, mindful that he was at a crime scene.

The howl of a boat at full throttle echoed off the undercarriage of the bridge. Forks wheeled around and ran down the granite steps, taking them three at a time, racing to the end of the pier. The boat was too far out to recognize. All he could see through the fog was a plume of water and the outline of a shimmering transom.

Reginald, breathing hard, walkie-talkie in hand, caught up with him.

"Can you patch me through to the Westport office?" Forks asked.

Reginald pressed the tuning button to the right frequency and gave the handset to Forks.

"Hello, who's this? It's Forks. I'm at the Crown Point campground, at the pier, beneath the bridge, and I want an APB on a boat heading south at a high rate of speed. I want it stopped and boarded. Possible suspect in the theft of a statue from the Champlain Monument."

His chest heaving, Forks jogged the length of the pier, his footsteps echoing off the roof, up the stairs to the monument. The big statues, Champlain, the Huron Indian and the French Voyageur, appeared to be untouched. Where the bust had been was obvious; though in its absence, Forks and Reginald would have been hard pressed to say what it looked like. A grimy, rectangular dark space, like the entrance to a cave, was all that was left - above a smaller plaque which read "Samuel Champlain, Intrepid Navigator, Scholarly Explorer, Christian Pioneer."

Conway and Kim hustled over to Forks and Reginald. "I told you he was up to something," Kim exclaimed.

When the dispatcher asked Forks to describe the statue, Forks looked to her for information. "What kind of statue?"

"It's the plaque of the head of a woman." Self-consciously, Kim blurted out "It's a bust, about two feet by a foot and a half of a woman's head with inscription around it. It's a bas-relief by Auguste Rodin, the most famous sculptor in the world."

"Are you hearing this?" Forks asked into the mouthpiece. He listened while the others gathered closer. "They're sending for the Coast Guard but that's going to take two hours," Forks said. He turned to Kim. "Miss, there's another trooper on the way to cordon off the crime scene. If you would, I'd like you to wait here and fill out a report."

Kim was about to protest when they both heard a siren, and the second trooper fishtailed through a puddle in the parking lot, splashing water on the only other car there, Matt's Subaru. The trooper got out carrying his roll of tape for marking off the crime scene.

Kim slapped a granite block with her hand, marveling at the heist that had been pulled off, slowly walking beneath the gaping hole underneath the statues.

Matt walked over after trying to reconnect his distributor, and said he'd jog to the museum and tell them what was going on. "They're going to want to know all about this. This is big. You wait and see. Every government agency you can think of will be up here, not to mention the press."

Aware of precious time passing, Forks said, "We've got to get creative here. Reginald, do you have a boat?"

"A bass fishing boat, that's it."

They all stood staring out over the lake at the only boat receding on the horizon. Reginald heard the throaty rumble of the engine and had a pretty good inkling of whose boat it was.

Forks spoke, sketching a possible scenario. "This guy Klocks could have had somebody coming by in a truck or something. The boat, though, was pulling away just as we got here. That's all I have to go on." He paused. "Listen Reginald, for now I need you to drive back up to Port Henry and get your boat and head south on the lake. I'm driving to Crown Point. I've got access to an outboard, a Boston Whaler. It's not much but it works. It will get me out on the lake. And in the meantime I'll call headquarters to send down the chopper." Jerking his head out towards the lake, he said, "If that boat has this bust, and we don't get them in the next half hour, they're gone. So let's roll."

Reginald raced off in his sheriff's car headed back north to the Velez Marina. Trooper Forks briefed his backup before he too hopped in his car and squealed out of the lot back to the Crown Point Sub-station, on the chance that by launching from Monitor Bay he could intercept Klocks.

Thirty-three

At a crisp fifty miles per hour, early on a mild Monday morning, First Love planed over the unbroken surface of the deserted lake. Spike looked ahead at the narrowing body of water and lined her up between Five Mile Point on the Vermont side and Stony Point on the New York side. There, south of Crown Point, the tracks of the Delaware and Hudson carved through the rocky shoreline cliffs, brushing the water.

Spike recognized the outflow of Putt's Creek as they sped southward. Just beyond the creek, Spike spied a single boat tied up to the dock at Monitor Bay. Only ten minutes had passed since they had roared away from the pier at the monument.

Klocks's eyes darted back and forth searching for pursuers. So far, he felt he had a chance to pull this off, the last and biggest job of his career. This was his winning lottery ticket. That's what he told himself. He had worked hard to achieve this prize, depriving himself to bring lady luck his way. He knocked on wood, which unlike in prison, was everywhere.

"This day, and this day only," Spike yelled above the roar of the Crusader V8 engine. "That's all I have, Owlie. Take the wheel."

"What?" Klocks was incredulous. He wasn't the driver. Spike was always the driver.

"Take the wheel. Keep it steady. Stay in the center of the Narrows."

As Spike let go of the wheel, Klocks had no choice but to grab it.

Between the twin cockpits, underneath the deck and above the place where Spike kept his clean white towels, was a hidden compartment. Spike contorted his arm and nudged a section of the wall until it tilted open. He reached in and pulled out a gun - a big heavy, cowboy-like 357 magnum.

He slid the gun onto the dashboard.

Klocks was caught off guard and eyeballed Spike.

The Hacker's throaty rumble drowned out normal conversation. Spike motioned for them to again change places. Spike put one arm around Klocks, pulled him closer, leaned down and yelled into his ear, "I'm here for you, but I'm not going down with you."

Klocks continued to eye him suspiciously, glancing every few seconds at the gun. The gun was creeping around on the vibrating dashboard, as if it was on a Ouija board with a will of its own. First the barrel pointed at Spike and then it jiggled its way over to Klocks.

Klocks despised guns and the way they gave power to punks. He had done some bad deeds with a gun, but only to fellow thieves who were about to rat on him.

Spike said, "If we get caught, if the cops come, hold this baby up to my head, as if I'm a hostage. That's the only way I can get out of this." And then he cradled Klocks closer and planted a kiss on Klocks's forehead.

Klocks felt emotions that he had suppressed his whole life, emotions of trust and love for another man. But, along with the spray on his head, he wiped those deeper feelings away. In the past he would have throttled a man for kissing him, no matter how honorable his intentions. But loneliness and desperate moments made Klocks a little unsure of himself.

"No problem, Spy. Is it loaded?"

Spike chewed his lip before he spoke, knowing that Klocks was a mercurial guy, capable of split-second personality changes. "Yes, my friend, it's loaded."

Klocks was preoccupied, concocting the nuances of their escape. He yelled to Spike, "Take your shirt off."

"Fine, I will." Spike flung his shirt off and his hairy gut hung over his belt. As big and powerful as he was, he never could get rid of that gut. Never really tried. It was a manly symbol up in the North Country. Spike loved it when Rulon Gardner, the farm boy from Wyoming, upset the Russian super-heavyweight in wrestling to win the gold medal in the Olympics. The American had a gut and he had beaten the evil empire's unbeatable.

As Klocks spoke he gladly took off his own filthy, smelly T-shirt. From the stern he dragged the shirts, kicking up off the slick water until they were soaked, tied them in a ball and threw them overboard to sink. He wanted to do away with any telltale stains of dirt and grout and lead from hacking away at the Rodin, and he wanted to show two guys out on the lake catching the last rays of summer.

Taking a moment to collect himself, he carefully placed another white towel over the Rodin, tucking in the edges. His dame Camille was totally covered.

Usually it was the other way around. But, because of the thunderous and beloved bellowing of wooden boats, Klocks saw it before he heard it. In the sky behind them, he zeroed in on a shiny object. A helicopter was flying fast and low, gaining every second.

Klocks yelled forward. "Shit! A chopper is coming. We're having a good time working on our tan. You have any beer?"

"Check the cooler."

Frighteningly fast, the thing was upon them. "Vroompppph," the helicopter whipped over, right on top of them, followed instantly by a rush of wind.

"Stay cool," Klocks said. "They're trying to rattle us." He raised his empty beer can in salute to the state police chopper maneuvering for its next buzz cut.

Two troopers in crew cuts and headphones were at the controls. On the second pass the copilot leaned way out of the cockpit bubble.

"Just wave," Klocks said grinning. The chopper looped around and whizzed over their speeding bow. Ducking, Klocks yelled, "Hide the gun! Hide the gun!"

With his elbow, Spike knocked the gun onto the floor and kicked it up underneath the bow next to the anchor. He didn't know if the troopers in the chopper had seen the gun or not.

"Don't change direction, " Klocks yelled. "We haven't done anything wrong. We're out for a joy ride, headed for the canal."

"You're right. I haven't done anything wrong. Remember that," Spike shot back. "I probably know the pilots."

"Yeah, I know them too," Klocks cackled. "They're the same imbeciles who flew down into the pit of the 21 Mine. I was watching. Here they come again."

On the first two passes the pilots were stirring up their quarry. This third time they were flying by standard procedure, hovering directly over the Hacker, matching the helicopter's air speed to the boat's water speed.

Spike was trying not to panic. He clutched his Giants cap, and yanked it down over his head, hoping not to be recognized.

Klocks continued to grin while draping his legs protectively over the white towels covering the bust. Looking up, he exaggerated his smile and raised the beer in a toast. He saw little black wheels and landing skids. It dawned on him that the chopper didn't have pontoons, couldn't land on water.

About fifty feet above the Rodin, the copilot leaned out and barked through a megaphone. "This is the New York State

Police. You must pull over immediately. I repeat. Pull over to the shore."

Spike was praying for a tunnel, like in the movies, but there was no tunnel.

Klocks cupped his ears and shrugged his shoulders as if he couldn't hear them, which was close to the truth.

The wash from the rotors was kicking up the spray around the boat, creating a whirlwind of water and air, pulling at Spike's cap. He and Klocks were caught in a vortex of noise, wind and water churned up by the meeting and mating of a metal bird of prey with a wooden flying fish. Things were chaotic. Spike was catatonic, frozen at the wheel, never once looking up at the chopper pummeling him with noise and wind. Stony Point and the railroad tracks were fast approaching.

Klocks needed to come up with an instant plan. Klocks was at his best when he was cornered. He didn't think. He reacted. The gun, that's all he saw. That big western gun, up on the floorboards. But that would be sealing his fate.

"Pull over now," the copilot commanded, flying out to the side nearly skimming the water, the rotor blades dangerously close to the boat.

"Ikey, is there a bridge ahead?"

"Nope," Spy called back banging the deck with his big fist. "We're in deep."

"Amen," Klocks said.

"You have thirty seconds to pull over," the copilot blared through his megaphone.

"Or what?" Klocks said out loud to himself, clenching his jaw. "You start shooting? That would be a mistake my friend."

Klocks started to whistle, louder and louder.

Through the whirling chaos, Spike heard the simple whistle, heard the warning. "No! Klocks, no!"

Spike unclenched his two hands from the wheel and lunged below for the gun, but Klocks had sprung first, and had his hands on the 357.

Using all his weight, just like that American farm boy wrestler, Spike pancaked Klocks, smothering him with his 280 pounds, while he tried to rip the gun from the gasping Klocks.

"Get off me! Get off!" Klocks moaned.

The boat zigzagged then swerved towards the New York shoreline, closing in on Stony Point.

The engineer of a north bound freight train, seeing the boat veering straight at the tracks, was repeatedly and desperately blowing its whistle trying to warn the boat away.

The blast of a train whistle and Spike's love of his runaway boat changed his priorities and he burst straight up off the floorboards.

The pilots, witnessing the struggle beneath the bow, broke off, fearing a collision between the boat and the train.

A great spray of water splattered the tracks as Spike wrenched the wheel to the left away from the tracks.

The helicopter peeled off, its tail rotor barely clearing the cedars on the rock cliff above the freight train.

Holding the gun, Klocks scrambled to the back cockpit, as Spike knocked the throttle back to neutral and cut the engine.

"Spy, please, quick. I can't lift it alone," Klocks pleaded, dropping the gun.

Spike spun around looking up in the air. He heard the whosh-whomp thumping of the helicopter but the bird was out of sight behind the cedars of Stony Point.

The Hacker was close enough to the screeching freight train that Spike could see the wheels throw tiny sparks into the lake. Leaping into the rear cockpit, Spike grabbed an edge of the Rodin, actually tore it away from Klocks in a big bear hug, and dumped it over the side, just as the yellow caboose rattled by.

Klocks watched the Rodin careen downward, fluttering side to side, sinking out of sight into an underwater crevice in the side of the cliff. His dream was drowning, buried in the lake. He scanned the shore for a landmark, to remember always where she lay beneath Lake Champlain.

Above the tracks on the blasted-out cliffs, in white paint, was some faded graffiti - a girl's name, Helen, scrawled inside the dim outline of a heart. Klocks's mother's name was Helen. That would be his marker - at a right angle, ten feet out from the shoreline.

Blood dripping from one hand, Spike jumped back over the mahogany deck and snatched the eight-foot gaff, pushing the boat away from the rocks. A southerly breeze aided his efforts, moving the boat away from the sunken Rodin.

Spike cocked his head, incredulous. "I don't hear the chopper."

From beyond the tracks two men hollered, "Freeze!" They both had their guns drawn, leveled at the two of them in the boat. The pilots had landed their helicopter and scrambled through the sumac and saplings over the point.

Spike and Klocks slowly and carefully raised their hands. Klocks, as coolly as he could muster, said, "You never gave us a chance to pull over. We've got to get this boat to Lake George by tonight."

"Shut up. Don't move," one pilot said. The pilots approached as far as the railroad ties, guns pointed.

In the distance a Boston Whaler and a bass fishing boat were closing in.

Under his breath, Klocks whispered, "Let the boat drift."

"It is," Spike said through clenched teeth.

Arms up, Spike stared straight ahead at the state police pilots, thinking as fast and as clearly as he could. He had never been much at school, but he managed to do fine in life. Gainfully

206

employed, married with two little girls, a beautiful blond wife, Spike wasn't taking a rap for his buddy. Not this time. The gun was a problem. Had the pilots spotted the gun when they were dive bombing the boat? Was it still a way out for Spike? Did they know that's what Klocks and Spike were struggling over?

"Where's the gun?" Spike asked, without moving his lips.

Klocks tapped the gun with his toe, inching it to the side, until it was between his feet.

Spike had learned that Klocks, when cornered, could be diabolically clever. Spike feared for what he would do next.

The boat drifted out beyond the slabs, floating along the shoreline, parallel to the tracks. Spike stood behind the wheel, hands up. Klocks was standing in the stern cockpit.

The pilots were on land thirty feet away with no safe way of apprehending their suspects. The younger copilot assumed a firing position on one knee, his pistol grasped in two hands, bracing with an elbow, eyes and hands steady. The pilot moved along between the rails, the crunching sound of crushed stone accenting each step. In the background the lapping of water, suddenly distinct.

The pilot walking stopped. No one moved. No one spoke. Ripple by ripple, wave by wave, the boat was drifting farther away from shore and farther down from where they had dumped the Rodin.

The silence unnerved Spike.

The pilot took two more steps off the railroad ties to the water's edge, planting his feet. He was now as close as he could get without falling into the lake. The depth increased dramatically only a few feet from the railroad bed that had been carved out of the ancient, granite cliffs.

The crescendoing whine of two small outboard engines pierced the standoff.

"Don't move, keep your arms up," the pilot commanded.

Spike turned his head a smidgen so that only Klocks could hear him. "Whatever happens, I won't rat on Camille."

"Shut up," snapped the pilot. They were nervously waiting the imminent arrival of Trooper Forks and Reginald DeFay.

"Jesus," Klocks grumbled, "this is torture. Why all the fuss?"

"Keep 'em up, just a few more moments, boys."

The Whaler and the bass boat were closing, as were Klocks's options. Shoot two cops and disappear into the woods to be tracked and hunted like a stray wolf. Klocks didn't like the looks of the copilot who hadn't moved or spoken. He was the one kneeling and he was young. Rookies could be trigger-happy.

Spike had to do what he had to do. Pointing at Klocks, Spike yelled to the pilots, "He's got a gun," and dove sideways into the water, rocking the boat.

Instinctively, Klocks collapsed down into the rear cockpit as the copilot fired, grazing Klocks on his right shoulder.

Klocks screamed out, "I've been shot! I've been shot! You've shot an unarmed man!" Klocks had never, ever taken a bullet and couldn't believe that he'd been shot.

Klocks kicked the gun as far away as he could.

Spike swam to shore seeking the protection of the pilots.

Forks zoomed up in his Boston Whaler, having unbuckled his holster so he could draw his weapon. He smashed into the transom of "First Love" and was practically hurtled into the rear cockpit, landing with his gun barrel pointed at the upturned blathering face of Klocks.

"I got him! I got him!" Forks hollered to the pilots on shore.

On shore, Spike lay face down, motionless, his body half in the water, his hands behind his head, a nine-millimeter Glock 17 trained on him.

"I'm a hostage. He held me hostage the whole time," Spike sputtered.

"He did, huh?" the copilot said, kicking him in his ribs. "I'll bet he did. Turn over."

Spike rolled over.

The pilot took a look at his face. "I know you. You're a C.O."

The copilot whipped his gun back over towards Klocks who was now splayed over the stern deck, handcuffed, blood dripping from his shoulder onto the stenciled lettering of Spike's damaged transom.

The pilot thought for a moment. "Taylor. Spike Taylor. You're from Westport. Yeah, I know you. I played for E'town. I played against you in the Toilet Bowl on New Year's Day. You chipped my tooth."

"Yeah, but you had the ball and you were about to score. I can explain all of this. I thought we were going for a joy ride. This guy blindsided me, kidnapped me really, put a gun to my head. I was a hostage."

The pilot snapped back to the present. Cold and steady, he regarded Taylor. "We'll see," he said.

Thirty-four

T he immediate buzz in the Adirondacks was of an escape artist, who, thought to be dead somewhere in the bowels of the 21 Mine, resurfaced one year later to steal the single most valuable piece of art in the North Country.

Three weeks after Klocks was nabbed, the Essex County District Attorney, a big guy with a crew cut, delivered an airtight case. The Rodin sculpture was gone, and the D.A.'s office had two pairs of witnesses, Kim and Matt, and the fishing couple, all of whom would testify they saw Klocks at the scene dismantling part of the monument on the night it was stolen.

Investigators found tiny bits of granite and one shard of bronze in the stern cockpit. A geologist examined the granite and confirmed that the granite came from the Fox Island quarry in Maine, the quarry that ninety-three years ago supplied the granite for the Champlain Monument. Circumstantial evidence alone was mounting for a conviction.

The D.A.'s office was forced to go to trial because no matter what the district attorney offered Klocks in the way of a plea bargain, Klocks wouldn't admit to stealing the Rodin, and he wouldn't tell where it was. At E'town's Arsenal Inn, Hap's in Crown Point, McQueen's in Westport, and the Miss Port Henry Diner, the question was how and where had Klocks hidden the Rodin?

In a sworn deposition taken from the fisherman, he stated that with the aid of his binoculars he had seen Klocks dump "all sorts of stuff" off the stern of the boat. Guided by the fisherman's recollection, state police scuba divers spent a week in wet suits underwater south of the Crown Point Bridge at depths of from sixty to ninety feet. Among other things, they recovered a mash hammer that the Vermont store-owner acknowledged he had sold to Klocks. Finding the hammer just intensified the search and the speculation that the bas-relief, as the locals learned to call it, was buried there in the muck in the channel south of the bridge.

After three more days of intense but frustrating searching, the divers found Klocks's leather satchel and his webbed bo'sun's seat, but no sculpture. Again the detectives interviewed the helicopter pilots, and then had the divers relocate to the waters off Stony Point where Klocks and Spike had been apprehended. The copilot seemed to recall seeing, from the air, a large object covered in towels lying in the stern cockpit. The pilots pinpointed where the boat was when Trooper Forks rammed the Hacker with the Boston Whaler. What the pilots didn't realize was the boat had drifted a considerable distance from where Spike, unseen by them, had heaved the Rodin overboard, close to the shore.

The divers widened their search, but they never thought to search farther up and closer to the shoreline in the crevices of the cliff below the railroad bed. Their instinct, reinforced by their equipment of fins, masks, air tanks and diving suits, was to dive deeper, farther out from shore, where others couldn't go. Moreover, most of the divers were convinced the Rodin had been hidden or dumped in the vicinity of the Crown Point Bridge.

* * * * *

National museums were concerned that a priceless bas-relief made by a world-renowned sculptor was lost forever. The curator of the Metropolitan Museum of Art embarked on a seven-hour train trip on Amtrak, from Manhattan's Penn Station to the Westport Depot Station, spending Tuesday night at the Deer's

Head Inn in Elizabethtown, to meet with Klocks early Wednesday at the Essex County jail.

She came to plead with this man Klocks to reveal the location of the Rodin sculpture for the sake of the art world, for the sake of antiquity. In return she promised to petition the court for leniency. Klocks was actually impressed that this refined lady would travel all the way up to the sticks just to see him.

Turning on his charm, Klocks asked her about the train ride, remarking how the trees were changing colors. She commented she had taken the train rather than fly because she had heard the trip along the shores of the Hudson River and Lake Champlain was a scenic one.

"The lake is beautiful this time of year, so lonely and secretive," she said.

He raised his eyebrows, fixing his piercing blue eyes on her face, her high cheekbones and her thin, patrician lips.

In response to his stare, she raised her carriage even straighter, knowing that the authorities had assumed he had dropped it somewhere in the lake. "Who knows what lies beneath?" she asked.

"It's not what lies beneath, it's where?" he said, challenging her.

The sheriff's deputy's slouching posture belied his acute listening ability. Klocks was in a playful mood and the deputy was all ears.

"Tell me," Klocks asked, "does bronze corrode in fresh water, or will it last for centuries?"

"It will last, but not for centuries. For decades," she said, "to the best of my knowledge." She sweetened her offer, trying to soften him up. "You know, even the French government, whose representatives brought the bas-relief across the Atlantic, is concerned. Perhaps they would pay a small reward," she added quickly, "to a charity of your choosing."

That information had an effect on Klocks. He was an international art thief now. He had a reputation. He was somebody. Everybody wanted to talk to him. The networks wanted to interview him. But he knew, as well as he knew the dimensions of the bars on his cell, that as soon as he divulged the location of his Camille, he was toast, history, a goner to be locked up and forgotten forever. He preferred his present state of notoriety.

To think that two months ago he was sleeping on a decrepit houseboat on the backwater bayous of the alligator-infested Apalachicola River. And now the French government was concerned about him. An aged lady from the Metropolitan, with a diamond the likes of which he had never seen, had traveled seven hours on a train to beg him to give up the whereabouts of the treasured Rodin.

The Essex County inmates watched the TV news showing state police divers in wet suits and oxygen tanks searching off the end of the pier, under the Champlain Bridge, and at Stony Point - near the tracks where the Hacker almost skipped off the lake and smacked into the freight train.

Klocks didn't breathe during that footage, scanning the background for clues as to where precisely the divers were looking. He saw the cliffs in the background above the tracks, but no Helen painted on them by a wayward North Country boyfriend.

Klocks's suspicious nature got the best of him and he worried that Spike would go skin-diving and retrieve the Rodin. He tried to guess what Spike would do with it. Klocks figured Spike fully understood that if he retrieved the Rodin without Klocks's permission, he was a dead man - if Klocks ever got out of jail.

Klocks was rubbing his forehead in consternation over Spike's release on bail. He tried not to be resentful, and was even in admiration of the stunt Spike had pulled off. "He's got a gun." Klocks shook his head in disbelief.

In the process of searching the boat from bow to stern, the State Police had of course found the gun on the floor of the cockpit. It was registered to Spike, who as a correction officer was legally allowed to carry a concealed weapon, but the fingerprints were all Klocks's.

Spike was indicted for harboring and abetting a fugitive, an escaped felon. Spike's charge was a gift, based on the fact that he was viewed as a fellow law enforcement officer, in the same line of work as the troopers who arrested him. Spike was well respected at Moriah Shock. The D.A., under pressure from the New York State Correction Officers Association, refused to prosecute the more serious charge of accessory to grand theft. Spike might have pulled off his assertion he was a hostage, except the word got out that he and Klocks had been friends in the past.

Regardless, Spike claimed he stopped by the pier and was showing off his Hacker-Craft, when Klocks snatched his gun and commandeered him and his boat. The authorities didn't believe him, but Spike persisted anyway. Spike's lawyer, Scott Jones, negotiated a plea bargain to a lesser charge. Jones who had been Westport's quarterback in the annual Toilet Bowl never asked Spike, in the confidence of the lawyer-client relationship, if he did it. He never asked, "Did you help Klocks steal the Rodin? Yes or no?" Spike was so puzzled by this omission, that he finally asked Jones, "Why didn't you ask me if I did it?"

Jones said, "Because then I would know. And I don't want to know. It's easier that way. Easier for me to fight the righteous fight." At first Spike wasn't sure how he felt about that answer. But then he thought whatever it takes to get somebody off. That's what lawyers do.

One thing Spike did know, from hanging around Klocks: Don't waver. Devise a plan and then stick to it; no matter what stick to it. (His stockbroker had told him that too. That's why he still held some worthless dot-com companies. But he held eBay. He still held a winner.) So from the beginning, every time they interrogated Spike, his story was the same.

The state police investigators rolled their eyes in disgust each time they heard his version of what happened. But that's the way the law was. Tough to convict Spike without a body, or in this case, a bust.

Thirty-five

T he more the reporters dug up, the more the saga of Wallace Klocks unfolded on the front pages, day after day. His alias of Jonathan Deed was long forgotten. Even Klocks started to refer to himself as Klocks. From national media to the local rag, he was the talk of the town.

The New York Times covered the story from the perspective of an easily accessible Rodin sculpture that few in the North Country even knew existed. The Times carried a front page story in the Sunday Arts and Leisure section on the lonely, desolate outpost in Crown Point that showcased the work of the world's great sculptors. The article highlighted the American sculptor Carl Heber who created the dynamic statuary in the Champlain Monument - the heroic and adventuresome trio of La Voyageur, Samuel de Champlain, and the Huron Indian. The Times reporter felt Heber's work overshadowed and dominated the La France bas-relief by Rodin. But the reporter acknowledged that Heber's statues would have been difficult to steal and worth far less than the Rodin bust.

The national magazine ARTnews focused on the recent scandal in the art world alleging that hundreds of the Rodin sculptures were fakes, promulgated by the French mastermind Guy Hain. In June of 2001, Hain was convicted by a French court but failed to appear for his sentencing and subsequently disappeared. The associate director of the Rodin Museum in Paris said, "The quality of the Guy Hain bronzes was so high that everyone was fooled." The independent expert the court hired to examine the sculptures declared that, "Fakes of Rodin sculptures are now in collections of some major museums throughout the world." That same year the MacLaren Art Centre in Ontario, bought fifty-five works by Auguste Rodin valued at forty million dollars Canadian. The director of the Rodin Museum in Paris wrote a letter publicizing his belief that many were not authentic.

The uncovering of the proliferation of these fake Rodins had the effect of making the La France bas-relief even more valuable. It had been a part of the Champlain Monument since 1912, five years before Rodin died and fifty years before the forger Guy Hain began his scheme of creating Rodins from the original artist's plasters.

The Troy Record and the Albany Times Union focused on Klocks the individual because he had grown up in Troy. He had committed crimes there, escaped from the Rensselaer County jail and been recaptured on the ledge of the library, enhancing his reputation as a daring outlaw.

In his youth Klocks had been the leader of a gang stealing from a suburban neighborhood of big white houses in the hills above Troy. Without any trace of recrimination, one mother reminisced about Klocks, recalling that when her family went on vacation, Klocks's gang of juvenile delinquents broke into their home and stole an ATM card, a stereo, a gun and money.

Among the poor in Troy some folks glorified Klocks as a modern day Robin Hood, taking from the suburbs in the hills above Troy, giving back to the city poor below. Klocks did give money and loot away to a few of his friends, particularly women; those who had a certain fascination for him. One of his two probation officers, a divorced woman from Albany, remembered him fondly "in his blue jeans, muscle T-shirt and piercing blue eyes." She noted, "He was always prompt and polite."

After reading about Klocks and the Rodin on the front page of the Burlington Free Press, a dealer in rare books representing the Shelburne Museum in Vermont visited Klocks in jail. He didn't care about the whereabouts of the Rodin. But the dealer did inquire about the whereabouts of a signed, first edition book of original Audubon lithographs called Birds of America. Klocks had been accused of stealing the book several years ago from the Shelburne Museum in Vermont. But he was never arraigned.

All the Rodin publicity was finally pushing Klocks's Vermont case to the forefront. A few days after the visit from the Vermont dealer, Klocks was informed that he was to be transported by federal marshals to appear in state court in Montpelier.

The weekly Valley News had two consecutive front pages dedicated to the theft, and their reporter Susie McKnight, who lived in Westport, became friendly with Kim, and once or twice they jogged together. Kim's job of tourist guide for the Crown Point Historic Site suddenly had a new and exciting dimension to it. She had escorted the Times reporter and his photographer to the site, and even posed below the cavity in the Monument where the Rodin had been embedded.

A curator of the Rodin Museum in Philadelphia phoned Kim asking for articles and pictures of the stolen Rodin. Once Kim adjusted to her dual role of witness to the Rodin episode and guide to the Rodin exhibit, she conceded that she liked the attention of the press. On the days when she was told ahead of time that a TV or print reporter was doing a story, she started to wear a bit of make-up and eyeliner.

Her boyfriend Matt, on the other hand, didn't want any part of the brouhaha surrounding the stolen Rodin, or answer any reporter's questions about what he might have seen as he dashed out to steal Klocks's car. That was all a blur, as was everything in the weeks following the drowning of the kayaker. Instead, he was drawn back to Middlebury, to the tragedy on the creek, determined to work through second-guessing his own actions, fighting to keep intact the carefree memories of his college days.

Kim's preoccupation with Klocks and his theft of the Rodin continued to bother Matt. He was no longer the focus of her attention and he resented that. Kim understood where Matt was coming from. For her this was the summer she learned that persons like Klocks and Conway and even Matt were not all neatly packaged and presentable. There were loose ends, complexities that she reluctantly grew to accept and even desire.

Klocks's background story was getting seamier. Investigative reporters revealed detectives from Rensselaer and Albany Counties had used Klocks as an informant, a snitch, on other petty criminals in the area. Whenever a burglary was committed involving art or antiques, detectives had sought out Klocks to finger the culprits - in return for favors, like a reduced sentence for his own involvement.

One detective for the state police, who had dealt with Klocks years before, and who had miscalculated before, now viewed him as a hardened reprobate. After the theft of the Rodin, Detective Roy Duntley traveled from the state police headquarters in Albany two hours north to the Elizabethtown-Westport Exit 31 on the Northway for an interview with Klocks in the Essex County jail.

Duntley hammered away at Klocks, letting him know that regardless of whether he told where the Rodin was or not, with his record, he was looking at a minimum of twenty years in prison. After Duntley left, Klocks brooded over that. He did not want to go back inside. He did not want to spend twenty years Upstate in Dannemora in a cell next to Son of Sam.

Klocks made a basic and vital decision that people make every day. Each day people decide to live. An infinitesimal few decide to die. Klocks accepted the prospect of death. Twenty years was too long. He would embrace life even if it meant death.

He didn't care. In his mind, he had decided. He devised a clever plan - a plan unique to a man like Wallace Klocks.

Thirty-six

When the story broke in the newspapers about Klocks's extensive background as a thief, Kim was beside herself. Seeing it in print, in writing, had drilled it home to her. She had played poker with a convict? Who was presumed dead and drowned in a mine; infamous for a miraculous escape. She just couldn't believe it. Yes, he was, well, different. She had witnessed him speak with his feet and his fists. This was the guy who had attacked her on the stairs of the lighthouse. The guy she thought she had fought off, or had he just changed his mind? By the time she put the article down her hands were shaking. She needed to talk to somebody. Maybe she should visit Conway in the hospital. But she was worried that she had misread him too.

She had to speak to somebody. She was trying to forget about Klocks, but she couldn't. Klocks was still in her life, speaking to her through newsprint, mesmerizing her by his compulsive criminal behavior and his aura of invincibility. Even though, Kim reminded herself, she had probably saved his life twice, once at the bridge and once, with the help of Matt, at Barn Rock.

Matt, who was back at Middlebury College struggling to get on with his carefree life of adventure sports, just wanted to forget about the summer. He was trying to snap out of his doldrums and he was not quite as willing to come running.

It was never quite the same between Kim and Matt. He did come back, but as the days crept by, and Kim was determined to keep working, she understood that now she was basically alone. The drowning of the kayaker and the attack in the lighthouse separated Matt from Kim, and cut chunks out of their armor.

He exhibited a new resolve and after graduation planned to move to Colorado as an Outward Bound instructor. She had wanted to keep him as a friend, but saw that slipping away.

She phoned Matt and said she'd like to see him. So he came, for one last visit to the Miss Port Henry Diner. They parked in the Grand Union parking lot and turned the volume back up. The song was Marvin Gaye's "Sexual Healing." After a moment of awkward silence, Matt turned the radio off.

They got out and walked to the diner, observing that the clock on top had stopped, and the spinning wheel on the bottom no longer spun. "Those aren't good signs," Matt commented.

Kim smiled and remained silent. They took one of the two booths in the right corner. The waitress plunked down Matt's black coffee, while Kim ordered tomato juice with a lemon.

She started to talk about Klocks again.

"Can we talk about something else?" Matt said, rubbing his forehead.

"All right, I'll talk about an object. That little gold chain that you-know-who had me research. It's an historical artifact, nearly two hundred years old. It's a tiny chain for a gentleman's pocket watch. It's called a fob." Kim twirled her tomato juice with a metal spoon. "We'd know more if he'd found the watch," she said, jiggling the ice in her empty glass. "You know what," she said hesitantly, "even crooks like to be liked."

After an uneasy silence, Matt asked, "Have you visited him?"

"What? So he can molest me, attack me again? Nah."

Matt took in the dreary day outside. He put his fist over his mouth, and got the nerve to sneak a look into Kim's eyes. He detected uncertainty.

"Do not visit him," Matt said, grabbing her forearm to get her attention, then self-consciously letting go. Using his finger, he lectured her. "Klocks is a serious, a dangerous criminal. Do not underestimate him. You visit him - he'll take you hostage and walk out to the tune of bullhorns and clicking cameras. The press, my God, they love him. Don't even think about it."

Matt had read her right and she hung her head, glad that she had talked to him.

"Thanks, Matt. Take me back."

"I'll take you back, back to the bridge," Matt said, surprised that he wasn't leaping at the chance of reuniting.

Both of them left feeling better, somewhat relieved, but somewhat puzzled why they didn't feel exactly the same way they used to feel towards each other.

Kim was amazed and distressed at herself that she had actually contemplated visiting Klocks. Maybe because she had seen him at his weakest on the bridge and at Barn Rock.

Matt drove, turning the radio off, while Kim lay down with her head in his lap. With his hand he brushed her hair while she closed her eyes for the ride to the ancient and barren Crown Point peninsula.

Thirty-seven

T he state police finally located the proper owner of Klocks's stolen Florida plates, a certain aged gentleman named Harry Southard living on Avenue B in one of the brick, Victorian houses of Apalachicola, Florida. On the phone he seemed to know all about what happened to the license plates for his Cadillac Coupe De Ville, what happened to the Rodin, and Klocks. Old man Southard said he had been following the story in the weekly Valley News, which was mailed to him on Thursdays. He told the investigator he felt partially to blame, that he knew Klocks was damaged goods from the start; that as an antique dealer Klocks's had succumbed to his criminal nature in the old man's presence.

Southard told the state police bureau of criminal investigations that his Cadillac was on its last legs, and that against his granddaughter's advice, he planned to drive it up north to the Adirondacks, to his home town, to give it away to his grandson. The thing Southard fretted about was the Rodin. He lamented, "Why haven't they found it?"

The investigating detective didn't speculate.

Harry Southard was ruminating. "I'll be up. I can help." His last words, barely audible, before he hung up with the investigator, were, "You'll find it. It's in the water."

The investigator thought no news there, but duly noted the old man's comments on his report, which he inserted into the ever-bulging file of the wily Wallace Klocks.

* * * * *

The knowledge of where the Rodin was weighed heavily on Spike. He'd even lost weight. Inside he was knotted up, torn between a promise to a childhood friend and a desire to return Rodin's La France back to her seat below the lighthouse.

Spike didn't make promises idly. In the business he was in, that of guarding convicted criminals, the guards and the criminals operated under certain unspoken codes of behavior - which under their severe surroundings became codes of survival. A broken promise in the outside world usually meant disappointment or embarrassment. In the inside world of prison a broken promise could mean a longer sentence, imminent retaliations, and even death. Promises were not made nor taken lightly.

Spike was of that ilk. As long as Klocks was alive he couldn't conceive of giving it up on Klocks. That's what he finally decided. Spike wasn't going to rat on Klocks as long as he was alive.

It seemed as though the state police had dredged the entire lake, retracing the path the Hacker from the tracks on Stony Point back to the pier. Spike reckoned that when Camille twirled down into the deep she must have slipped behind a blasted out heap of jagged rocks carved out the bed for the tracks of the D&H.

Thirty-eight

A s the star prisoner Klocks was adjusting to the county jail, granting interviews, soaking up his notoriety. Klocks envisioned spending the maximum allowable sentence of one year at the Essex County Jail, before the District Attorney ordered him transferred to one of the other nineteen prisons within the Adirondack State Park.

That gave him a lot of time to ponder his failings, to plot his escape and to practice push-ups. He got so he could do seventy-three consecutive, full push-ups, where he touched the floor with his chest and straightened his arms on each one.

After Klocks physically exhausted himself, he would project, as he liked to call it. He would try to picture a way out of his final demise. Like all men, inside he wavered. He recognized the secret to success was to persevere in the face of uncertainty. If he waited until every fiber of his soul and body was certain of every decision, he'd be catatonic, caught in a permanent state of indecision. One of the other inmates told him that General George S. Patton's motto was, "A good plan executed violently today is better than a perfect plan executed at some indefinite point in the future."

Now that Klocks was back in custody, no way he was staying. Death would be better. He had already courted death in the cold blackness of the mines. Maybe he had one more manic escape within him. The guards were scared of him. Maybe they sensed something. Or maybe they knew more of his background than he realized. Maybe Detective Duntley had been doing a little marketing work advertising the disappearances of two other petty criminals, both associates of Klocks.

Klocks clenched his fist, banged a cell bar once, then ran his fingers through his thinning hair. He was in the throes of an internal monologue with himself. "That's right they were all criminals. Just like me. Damn it, just like me," he repeated to himself.

On the one hand he wanted his freedom, but on the other hand he wanted control over his fate. He wanted control over his own life, even at the risk of death. He had risked all, and survived. He had successfully disappeared only to discover, even as an avowed loner, he could not sustain being anonymous.

Now he had to think. He had to focus and that was his specialty. The power of concentrated thought born out of a clear-cut and attainable goal. Klocks had no illusions. Escaping from a minimum security prison like Moriah Shock was one thing, escaping from an up-to-date maximum security facility where he was ultimately headed, was another.

Maximums had closed circuit TV monitoring every doorway, every entrance, every possible exit. They had touch-screen computer technology that enabled a clerk in front of a screen to lock down any and all doors in a millisecond. Outside the electrified fences were rows upon rows of circular razor wire. Buried ground sensors activated an alarm if anything heavier than a crow landed on them. Escape was nearly impossible. If he was going to escape it had to be now or when he was being transported.

Klocks calculated the odds of suicide versus escape. Guards did not carry guns, because if they did, sooner or later prisoners would grab them and hold them hostage. The only time guards carried guns was when they were transporting a prisoner from one location to another, be it from minimum Moriah Shock to maximum Dannemora, or from the Essex County Jail to the Montpelier Court House.

Statistically, the highest incidences of escape attempts occurred when prisoners were being transported. The guards were forced to contend with outside variables over which they had no control, compared to the fixed routine and lock-down of a prison.

Yet, when a correction officer or a federal marshal was transporting a prisoner, he was not accustomed to shooting first; he was not primed to fire his weapon. Drawing a gun and shooting is not a reflex action. It's really the last thing they're taught to do, ready to do, or want to do. Firing a gun invariably generates an investigation into proper police procedures, where the cop becomes the suspect. Most cops, and the vast majority of correction officers, retire without ever having fired their weapon in the line of duty.

Klocks's best chance of escape was during transportation from one facility to another. All kinds of accidents happened to vehicles transporting prisoners. Sedans developed flat tires; vans skidded down steep banks; buses ran off the road; vehicles got rammed. All these so-called accidents had happened as part of escape attempts.

If Klocks could finagle some outside help, like Spike or Damian, maybe he could pull something off. But their help was doubtful at best, having already paid their debts to Klocks. Klocks concluded he'd have to go it alone.

Klocks calculated that if he could get himself in a situation where the transporting officers thought he was going to die anyway, they would be doubly hesitant to fire at a fleeing prisoner. How could Klocks make it appear as though, in desperation to escape, he was about to die or commit suicide? Then human nature being what it was, no guard would fire at him.

Klocks was aware that Vermont wanted to extradite him. Lionel Hatlinger, his court-appointed attorney, told him that. Hatlinger was from Willsboro, an Essex County town farther north on the lake, and was an expert at the tactics required to delay a trial and extradition. Hatlinger was a questionable character in his own right, but by Essex County standards a genuine heavyweight whose operative policy on behalf of his client was to stall, and as a last recourse, to lie. Hatlinger had gained a bit of local notoriety by his colorful defense of a North Hudson paramour who had stabbed her aged lover's wife to death.

Hatlinger admitted that he had run out of delaying tactics for Klocks and within two months his client would have to comply with Vermont's federal court order to appear in state supreme court in Montpelier. It was now October.

Two ways to escape, two tickets to paradise stuck out as possible scenarios for Klocks. One involved a train and one involved a bridge. If he were being transported east from Elizabethtown to Montpelier, he had to pass both.

Klocks used his dormant power of proximity to visualize anything he had seen along the route, much like a photographic memory. He tried to envision how his captors would react to a set of circumstances, to see what others planned to do. In his mind he "saw" the tracks; where they crossed the road at Westport on down to the cutoff for the Crown Point Bridge.

Entering Westport route 9N dipped under the Amtrak passenger line, which D & H freight also ran on. Then south of Westport near the town boundary with Moriah was a second underpass. The route they would take to Montpelier crossed the tracks one last time at the overpass just after the left turn to the Crown Point peninsula.

In his mind he saw the tracks above him, the Westport overpass at the Depot Theatre. South of Port Henry Klocks recalled that the tracks ran close to the road along Bulwagga Bay near a tavern. Klocks's mind was telescoping. Let's say he somehow got himself standing on the railroad tracks, still handcuffed and shackled. Would the marshals shoot if he were running away, hobbling down the tracks? Probably. Would they shoot if a train was bearing down on him and he was about to be crushed? Probably not. Maybe they'd hesitate just long enough to give him a chance.

The insurmountable problem was coordinating his transportation to the exact time of the passing of a train. That was beyond even the wily Wallace Klocks. The freight trains kept their own schedules and Amtrak was always late. No way he could even know when a train was coming. And even if he knew, he had no control over the timing of the prison van.

Klocks couldn't visualize an opportunity at Bulwagga Bay or any of the three railroad crossings. He discarded the train idea, but not the overall concept of making it appear as though he was about to die. In time, he switched his ability to visualize to the bridge, a permanent structure with no arrival and departure schedules.

Klocks took a break from his mental gymnastics, standing up on his toes and gripping the bars of his small, square, second-floor window, raising himself up to the outside. A monarch butterfly caught his eye. What was a butterfly doing up so high? Its brief, fluttering, three-day life was about to end

I've already lived a thousand times longer than that precious insect, Klocks thought. Just like butterflies, we all die. If he didn't plan his own escape he was doomed to do endless time. If he escaped, whether he survived or died, he was destined to live in infamy, to have called his own final shot - immortality in Upstate New York.

Thirty-nine

I n the next two months the furor surrounding Klocks died down, except for one visitor in early December - an old man from Florida named Harry Southard. He had finally made it up from Apalachicola to Crown Point, prepared to give away his Cadillac, talk to Klocks, and then fly back to Tallahassee.

Southard was accompanied by his grandson who was wearing a wool toque, gloves and a running suit. Southard wore his tweed suit. They drove up from Crown Point, through Port Henry and Westport, west on route 9N, slowing down past the Black River Cemetery where a few of Southard's more prosperous childhood acquaintances lay. He drove over the Boquet River past the historic Hand House into E'town, making a left at the blinking stoplight up Pumpkin Hill onto Court Street. Southard parked his vinyl-top Cadillac directly in front of the Essex County Jail which was conveniently located a few pillared buildings away from the department of motor vehicles. He wanted Klocks to be able to see the Caddy from the jail, while he took care of the necessary paper work. Southard soon discovered that in New York State, even to give a car away, there were forms to fill out and fees to pay.

At the motor vehicle department Southard mentioned that the odometer reading of 140,022 miles might not be correct. He anticipated a time-consuming rigmarole about the validity of the title he was gifting. But the clerk informed him that reporting the mileage on the title of a car more than ten years old was not necessary.

Southard smiled and checked the time of his pocket watch that hung from his vest on an ornate pearl and gold fob. Shaking slightly he walked on the sidewalk back to his Caddy and placed the green and yellow forms onto the seat and then decided he should restart the engine to warm it up. Early that morning, the temperature had been in the single digits, a foreshadowing of what was to come, and Southard's Caddy wouldn't start right away. Again the engine wouldn't turn over.

A state trooper, who had just escorted a man to the county jail, was parked nearby. The trooper opened his trunk, got out his cables and was kind enough to jump-start the Cadillac. He was the trooper who sat in the copilot's seat of the helicopter that chased Klocks on the lake.

Southard engaged the trooper in a conversation about the lost Rodin. Old Southard was genuinely curious, but he also had an ulterior motive - location. Southard was a keen listener, and he took in all the details of the trooper's story about capturing Klocks but not the Rodin. Southard could picture the shoreline from Monitor Bay to Stony Point because he grew up fishing the shoreline. While the car warmed up, Southard sat on the passenger's side, collecting himself, with the door open to the sidewalk.

During this stay in the North Country, undoubtedly his last, he was doing some research at the Hammond Library on his family tree and Crown Point's history. (Most everybody felt the town should have been called Hammondville after Civil War hero and father of the iron ore industry, General Hammond.) In his old age Southard was growing nostalgic, even weepy, about his childhood years in Crown Point.

Shrugging off the past, for now, Southard was ready to confront and confound Klocks. His grandson helped him up out of his seat and assisted him inside the jail. Then the boy left on a nine-mile jog back to Westport, where his grandfather would pick him up at Ernie's grocery store.

Seldom was Klocks surprised, but Southard's visit startled him. He recognized the old man right away. In Klocks's mind he was the sorcerer who had got the best of him. Since Klocks left Apalachicola on his pilgrimage to the Adirondacks, he had often wondered, in hindsight, if Southard hadn't conjured up this whole escapade with the Rodin, and then manipulated Klocks to carry it out. Klocks wasn't bitter, but he was wary. They stood across from each other on either side of a wooden table in a small room with walls of concrete blocks painted institutional green. A guard, burly and seemingly bored, slouched in the corner.

Southard wanted Klocks to be able to see a particular piece of old-fashioned jewelry hanging from the side pocket of his waistcoat. Before Southard sat he deliberately checked his pocket watch so Klocks would get a good look at his fob.

"How did you get that back, old man?"

"I stopped in Saratoga on the way up."

"But how did you know where to look?"

"Same way I'm going to know where to look for the Rodin."

At the mention of the Rodin, the guard stiffened slightly, listening intently, but trying not to show it. The local, regional and state law enforcement agencies were feeling the pressure and puzzlement from the public over their inability to recover the prized statue, which all of Essex County suddenly deemed the most important and worthy treasure to grace their rural county - even though ninety percent of the thirty-seven thousand residents had never laid eyes on the Rodin.

Klocks treated Southard with bemusement, unsure of what to make of him. Klocks rattled on about the posse that pursued him, while trying to figure out if Southard was serious about looking for the Rodin.

Southard peered at Klocks beneath his bushy eyebrows. "Did you spot those initials I carved in stone on the lighthouse?"

Klocks's mind was elsewhere and he didn't respond.

"H. S. and H. S. for Harry Southard and Helen Speers," Southard said.

Klocks actually gulped at the mentioned of the word Helen. He remembered Helen was the name of the old man's girlfriend. Klocks stopped talking. He was spooked. Helen was his secret marker for finding the Rodin.

Twenty minutes later, Southard left with the smug feeling that, with a little luck, he would best the wily Klocks.

Forty

After the inauspicious visit from Southard, Klocks nodded his head knowingly. A day of reckoning was coming, for both of them. Winter had set in early. Six inches of snow on Thanksgiving, games of broom-ball on frozen ponds the first week in December, followed by six days of cold, windless nights. Klocks figured he had forty-eight hours until the feds came to take him to Vermont.

The Essex County sheriff had been there, almost two years ago, on the lip of the crater above the 21 Mine, when the climbers returned, ragged, from following Klocks's trail. The searchers were certain he had fallen down a water-filled shaft and drowned. The sheriff was still in disbelief that somehow Klocks had escaped from that hole. The sheriff was determined that Klocks would not escape from the county jail on his watch. And the easiest way to do that and foil an escape artist was to transfer him to another facility. Interstate transport of convicted criminals was handled by federal marshals and the Essex County sheriff was anxious to make Klocks the fed's responsibility.

When the papers arrived confirming the exact time of the transfer from the county jail to the federal marshals, the sheriff was relieved. The various state and federal agencies had finally acquiesced to the sheriff's stance that Klocks was too much of an escape risk, to remain in a county jail. After the court hearing in Montpelier, the marshals agreed to transport him south to Comstock, a maximum-security facility where Klocks would await trial on the theft of the Rodin.

* * * * *

The pugnacious lawyer, Hatlinger, walked by the visitor's room, disregarded the deputies and marched into the sheriff's office. He removed the sheriff's cowboy hat from a chair and sat. Half an hour later he had the information he wanted. In two days his client, Wallace Klocks, was being transported to an arraignment hearing in federal court in Montpelier, Vermont, and then on to maximum-security Comstock. One hour later Hatlinger conveyed that information to Klocks.

Once Klocks digested that news, he dictated his will to Hatlinger. He gave any and all of his earthly possessions in Essex County to Spike Taylor of Westport, New York. Klocks bequeathed the option to repurchase the painting of the nude lady and the tiger to Damian Houser of Port Henry. All of his other Apalachicola possessions, including the lease on his antique store, its unsold contents and whatever grungy items remained at the house boat on Bonatee Creek, he bequeathed to the antique dealer near the only stop light in Franklin County, Florida. Hatlinger scribbled away on his notepad.

The next day Hatlinger returned with a properly typed, legal will for Klocks to sign. Hatlinger handed the pages to Klocks, who, as he signed, casually removed the paper clip, which made signing easier. Hatlinger signed as a witness, and was about to call in a guard for the second witness when Klocks waved him off. Hatlinger indicated he'd take care of the second signature later.

Sitting on his cell bunk Klocks wrote a final note in scratchy longhand to be opened by his attorney Hatlinger in the event Klocks failed to return for his Essex County trial date. Klocks was silent, squashing uncertainty, resurrecting his primal mode of solemnly calling the shots.

During lunch, the sheriff paid Klocks a visit, and announced that the federal marshals would arrive tomorrow morning to transport him to Vermont. The sheriff took out a folded newspaper article from his back pocket. "My wife asked me to have you sign this." The sheriff handed Klocks a ball point pen. The headline read, "Klocks, The Escape Artist," above a photo of Klocks in front of the jail being transferred from the state troopers to the custody of the sheriff. The sheriff's wife seldom left her house and lived vicariously by gossiping on the phone, watching TV and reading the newspapers.

"What's her name?" Klocks asked.

"Carol."

Klocks signed on an angle across the lower corner of the photo. "To the Sheriff's wife, Carol - All the Best, Wallace Klocks." The sheriff made sure he got the ball point pen back, shook Klocks's hand and left, somewhat sheepishly. The Sheriff grudgingly admired Klocks's spunk behind bars.

Klocks leaned back and took a long breath, puffing out his cheeks. He wasn't hungry, but he ate to keep up his strength. He found concentrating on a daily activity like eating to be restful and reassuring.

While Klocks ate potatoes, macaroni and cheese, the Sheriff retreated to his paneled office, and phoned the federal marshals in Albany to pinpoint the exact time the vehicles would arrive to transport Klocks to Vermont. During the conversation, the Albany administrator regaled the sheriff with the story of how Klocks had escaped from the Rensselaer County Jail, before being recaptured on the ledge of the Troy library.

For the first time since his election four years ago, the sheriff unlocked the small desk drawer on the right of his desk, reached into the back and slid out his Colt revolver. The revolver was already loaded and he clicked the lock off, carefully placing it back in the front of the drawer, leaving the drawer open an inch.

You can never be too careful, he thought. With that caution in mind, and time to kill, he practiced reaching for the gun - sliding the door open with his right hand and grabbing the gun with the same hand without hitting his knuckles. He then gave the order for the guards involved in the transfer of the prisoner to be issued weapons.

Klocks too was mulling things over, trying to prepare for every contingency. But one person troubled him. Had he been played by the old sorcerer? Had he been set up? Was he the sorcerer's pawn? Klocks was paranoid Southard was after the Rodin.

Once those doubts set in, that's when Klocks decided to give Spike the go-ahead. That afternoon Klocks phoned Spike and persuaded him to visit, telling Spike he was leaving and had something to give him. Reluctantly, out of some perverse obligation, Spike showed up, scowling. His last gift from Owl had been plea-bargained down to probation, and he was lucky at that.

It turned out for Spike it may have been a worthwhile visit, at least for Spy's loyal conscience. In the spirit of settling his estate, so to speak, Owl gave Spike permission to locate the bust of his girlfriend, Camille.

"Ikey, she's yours. Camille is yours. If I go, cash in. Remember where she is?"

Spike shot a concerned look at the guard in the corner. "No, I do not know where she is."

Klocks leaned close and whispered. "Directly across the tracks from Helen. I'd say eight feet from shore."

Spike snickered and raised his eyebrows as if everything Klocks was saying was a joke. "Where are you going, Owl?"

"I'm crossing the bridge, sometime Wednesday, and I'm not coming back. I got the word. They're nervous. They're sending me to max." He paused to let that sink in. "Why don't you go fishing near the piers and wave to me?" Klocks tilted back his chair, balancing on two legs, and laughed.

Spike, who was in uniform, glanced at the guard and shook his head, frowning. "The Hacker's stuffed safely away in Lake George. Anyway they'll be ice fishing out there soon. Might be already."

"Times up," the guard said.

Klocks popped up and moved around the table towards Spike, who was momentarily confused, pushed his chair back and stood up. But then Klocks hugged him, something he had never done before. Klocks took a step back and holding Spike at the elbows looking up at him. The guard had moved in behind Klocks.

In a distant voice, Klocks spoke. "I'm going where stars surround me and peace and love are mine. Canis Minor and a beautiful blue moon. I'll be smiling," Klocks said.

Spike had never seen Klocks's eyes glossed over and focused far away. He had heard him speak that way, poetic-like about the stars. He knew that Canis Minor, the lesser dog, was Klocks's favorite constellation.

Being a thief who usually operated at night, and moving around from place to place the way Klocks did, he had developed a special relationship with the night sky and the stars. He even studied them a bit, going to the Schenectady Planetarium to see their shows.

Spike walked away thinking that something was up. Either way he guessed he might never see him again, and selfishly, Spike thought that was the best thing that could happen.

Forty minutes later, a few minutes before five, a second visitor showed, also at Klocks's behest. The guard thought the visitor was there to be admitted, but the sheriff informed him that Damian Houser was here to visit Wallace Klocks.

The same guard that had witnessed the conversations and interactions between Klocks and Spike witnessed the conversations between Klocks and Damian. It was the end of his ten-hour shift, and he was a little less vigilant and a little more distracted. Damian, a little jittery, not liking to go anywhere near a jail, unbuttoned his sport coat and sat in the only other chair in the room, the same seat Spike had sat in.

In his own peculiar dialect of code words, Klocks thanked Damian for helping out with Camille, and told Damian he had written him into the will.

Damian clapped his hands together and leaned forward across the table. "What do I get?"

"You get my silence," Klocks said his eyes glazing over. Then he got up and crossed over to Damian. This time the guard didn't move, waiting for the expected hug, which took place as Klocks spoke.

"I'm onto a better place now. Peace and love are mine."

As Klocks hugged Damian he slipped his hand in Damian's coat pocket out of view of the guard, and pulled out some folded Kleenex. On the way back to his chair, Klocks appeared to sniffle, covering and wiping his nose with the Kleenex. Then he wadded up the tissue and shot it into the corner wastebasket. The guard thought nothing of it, and escorted the sniffling Klocks back to his cell.

Forty-one

S unday and Monday, while Klocks was turning inward, meditating, steeling himself for what he was preparing, a cold front blew in and hung over the lake. For forty-eight hours the temperature was in the teens, and most importantly, the air was still - no wind.

In early winter, the hardy residents of the former mining town of Port Henry played one particular game of daring that sometimes cost a life. Who would be the first person to take his shanty out on the thin ice?

For the foolhardy few who wanted to be the first out, or the last off, it was a game of chicken with the elements. Each year a truck went through the ice. Each year someone died or almost died. Each year the locals spent days of shivering work raising a pickup or snowmobile from the bottom of the lake.

Shanties were shacks on runners with one or two holes in the floor for ice fishing. Some five holes were fancier and bigger with one hole in each corner and one in the center. But generally ice shanties were pretty small, and could fit across the bed of a pickup. Or a shanty could be dragged out on the ice by a couple of four-wheelers.

Over the hundred and ten-mile length of Lake Champlain, the collection of ice shanties beneath the Crown Point Bridge was the best known. The Hole, as it was called, was where Port Henry set up its village. The higher the unemployment in Crown Point and Port Henry the more sightings of Champ in the summer and the more shanties on the ice in the winter.

The shantytown was always a poetic sight in the winter - a cluster of colorful child-like houses out on the blue and white ice with the sparkling bridge in the background. Something Adirondack folk artist Edna West Teall might have painted.

This winter Wayne Parker and John Striker, sons of miners, decided theirs would be the first shanty on the ice. Parker even allowed his oldest boy, Bobby, to stay home from school and go with them on their first attempt. The ice was four inches thick, but it wasn't frozen all the way across the lake. Off the boat launch at the bottom of Convent Hill, the three of them crept out on the ice in their Dodge Ram pickup. They followed a winding four-mile path, sometimes with open water visible on both sides, to out near the bridge, parking dead center over The Hole. As long as there was no wind they felt they were safe.

They slid the shanty off right there and drove back the exact way they had come, hardly a word spoken each way. When they climbed back up onto land, Bobby's dad raised a fist in triumph. He parked the truck and took a deep breath.

"We did it," he said, shaking Striker's hand and patting his son on the back.

"As long as it stays cold and still," Striker agreed.

And it did stay cold and still. The next day, Wednesday, they drove back out, the three of them, Bobby missing his second straight day of school as a senior at Moriah Central School. Bobby had assured his father he was graduating, whether he went ice fishing or not. At 7:30 a.m., a bit more relaxed, Parker broke into salt and vinegar potato chips while still in the cab, to go with his morning cup of coffee.

Ice fishing was fun if you were catching fish. You were inside an igloo of sorts, absorbed in your own world, concentrating on the tiniest of tugs against your forefinger. But if you weren't catching, three hours of jigging for smelt could be an eternity. It required a certain stoic constitution. A few brought portable TVs, but Parker disdained watching TV in a shanty. It wasn't right, he always said.

They came prepared with a gas heater, a bunch of dried maple wood already split and plenty of Vermont cheddar cheese, hot sausage, and a big pot to boil water and cook the hot dogs, and of course plenty of Genesee and Old Milwaukee beer. Once he stepped down from the truck, Parker slid a six-pack from underneath the coils of rope, and cracked open a Genny.

First with an auger then with the ice-saw, they cut two holes in the ice, positioning the shanties over them. In the glittering sunlight, they smiled as they saw the reflection off the windshields of two more trucks making their way towards them across the ice, shanties teetering on top.

The three of them waited outside for the new arrivals, the ones they had blazed the trail for. One side of the channel remained open water, over near Fort St. Frederic. Well into last season, using their ropes, Parker had rescued a father and son who had gone through the ice on two snowmobiles close to the Fort.

The men in the other pickups arrived, unloading cases of beer, and a couple of chairs. They kidded Parker and Striker in a congratulatory sort of way, and Bobby felt like for once he was an equal, not just Parker's son.

Time to fish. They brought shiners as bait. They sat on boxes or stools and set their lines. Parker was busy thawing the frozen chili. He loved ice fishing, eating chili and drinking beer. And talking. And he liked to listen too - to listen to the ice talk. Bobby too knew about the sounds the ice makes, but it always startled him. The expanding and contracting ice popped like rolling thunder. Sometimes the ice would groan and creak and pop, and a crack would appear running through the middle of the shanties. That always generated a few jittery wisecracks.

After a half-hour they had caught two smelts, both number 2s, eight inches long. Striker started in. "Ain't no fish left in this lake. It's the lake trout and lamprey. Every time we mess with nature, we mess it up." But he didn't say these words with any true resentment. It was shanty talk.

With Parker's boy there, Striker didn't feel quite as free to talk about women. At least not women they had known. Occasionally women did come out to the shanty village at The Hole, but few wives came. Just as well. When Ti Mill wasn't hiring and the men weren't working, it was better to be away from each other during the day.

"This used to be one of the best lakes for walleye," Striker continued between sips of beer and slurps of chili. "Then they put the lake trout in. That was a money thing. That just spoiled it."

Parker was jigging his stick. "Got one," he said, taking his line in hand over hand, standing up.

"Not a bad size," Striker said.

Parker tossed the smelt in a pail. That made three in an hour. Not exactly record breaking. "Maybe we won't make it to Norm's today." Parker turned to Bobby. "He pays four dollars a pound. Ships them all over."

Both Striker and Parker were hoping Bobby would catch one, being he was missing school and they were the first ones out on the ice and all. And later, he did catch one, a big one.

Forty-two

On Wednesday, December 13th, at 9:45 a.m., a black Chevrolet Astro van and a blue Ford Expedition slowly and silently pulled up behind the county jail. Two deputy marshals descended from each vehicle, their breath blending with the white exhaust, clouding the cold air.

The Sheriff told a guard to open the rear door to the marshal's vehicle that Klocks would be sitting in. A wire mesh cage separated the front seat from the back. The guard opened the rear door as if it were red hot, reaching with his outstretched arm, pressing the button quickly, backing away in an instant.

"Johnny, Klocks is not in there yet," the sheriff said with a nervous chuckle.

Two minutes passed. Chanting erupted in the main cellblock. Louder and louder, to a primal rhythm, inmates chanted, "Klocks! Klocks!" The steel gates burst open and a phalanx of guards escorted Klocks across ten feet of pavement into the back seat. Aside from the rear door of the van, there were no doors to the back seat.

Two guards more or less lifted the shuffling Klocks into the back seat of the Astro. Klocks's feet were shackled, wrapped in heavy chains, and he was handcuffed to a chain around his belly. The handcuffs, however, did not have a clamp over the keyhole.

The federal marshals made one other mistake. Generally when a prisoner was being transported it was the responsibility of the police agency picking up the prisoner to do a strip search. In this a case the federal marshals had incorrectly assumed that the county guards had searched him.

Once in the van, the mix of the metal and locks, the protective grate between himself and the two federal marshals who would be in the front seat made an immediate impact on Klocks. He looked out his side windows and saw one good thing, no bars. He looked inward. His eyes were changing from dazzling to dull. He was falling into a trance, akin to the state of a religious fanatic on a suicide mission.

In the cage of the back seat handcuffed and shackled was the indomitable Wallace Klocks, outwardly serene, inwardly calculating, his mind working with the focus and desperation of a quiz-show contestant. Outside two guards stood six feet away on either side of the Chevrolet van, each aiming a shotgun at the back windows, safeties off.

The sheriff was chatting with the two deputy marshals who would be in the Ford Expedition behind Klocks. Both of the deputies were enjoying their last smoke before the caravan pulled out. The sheriff told them about an escaped ostrich that was gallivanting around a field along their route. Two other county deputies who had escorted Klocks to the van, and had been down in the 21 Mine searching for Klocks, stared at Klocks. He had grown a beard; but they just found it hard to believe that he had actually escaped from that black hole of a mine. They, of course, were making the erroneous assumption that Klocks had gone down into those deepest mines; that the blood, the footsteps, the one boot led to the shaft where he had disappeared.

Klocks was impressed with the new respect they were giving him. No one even dared get close to him for fear his handcuffs and leg irons would pop off and the guards' weapons would fly into his waiting hands.

No guard would be riding next to him in the cage. He wanted to bring his fingers to his face but he couldn't without tucking way down, and right now, he couldn't afford to miss anything. He thought maybe there'd be a third vehicle, but there wasn't. Made no difference.

The deputies climbed up into the van. The one in the passenger seat turned around and stared at Klocks for a brief moment.

"You're from Troy right?"

"Yep, the Collar City." Klocks smiled. Anything he could do to maintain an air of civility and routine. Everything's normal. This is going to be another normal, everyday job of transporting a prisoner from one facility to another. That's the mood Klocks intended to convey.

The driver turned the ignition and Klocks felt his pulse race, felt a tingling in his shoulders and hands. Too soon for that. When the time came, he needed to explode like a terrorist's bomb, like a coiled snake.

After they drove down Court Street, and turned right at the blinking light at the bottom of the hill, heading for Westport, the deputy unscrewed the cap on a steel thermos and poured himself some coffee. It was 11:00 a.m. on a clear and cold December morning.

Klocks had said his good-byes. Was he trying to escape or commit suicide? The answer was, for Klocks, he was trying not to lose. If he died escaping, that was fine. Dying outside of prison, choosing the time and the place, calling his shots, that was acceptable. He was only a loser if he stayed in prison. He wanted to be thought of as a master criminal, an antique thief, a cad who stole the million-dollar Rodin. If he died in prison he was an anonymous loser.

The black Astro and the blue Expedition picked up speed at Camp Dudley road, roaring by the defunct Airport Inn entering the long straight away. Klocks felt the surge of speed and got down to business. He whispered a good-bye to Spy, apologizing for dragging him back down so late in life.

Up front, the drivers were passing the time in idle conversation looking out into the fields trying to spot the ostrich the sheriff had told them about. The deputy in the passenger seat picked up his walkie-talkie and alerted the Expedition to look to their left for the ostrich.

Klocks bent way down at the waist and blew out his nose, one nostril at a time. Among the gobs of mucous and traces of blood, he picked out a key. A paper clip slid right out falling on the floor, pinging off his shackles. Klocks shifted his right foot an inch and covered it with his boot. The key he held in the folds of his skin between thumb and forefinger, gradually rubbing away the slime.

Klocks had stuck a paper clip up his left nostril and a key up his right. He had pilfered the paper clip from the three-page will that his attorney had typed up, and had snorted the key to the handcuffs in the middle of the Kleenex that Damian had passed him.

The two car caravan sped under the railroad bridge separating the summer folk of Westport from the year round workers of Moriah. Klocks eyed the right side of his cage seeing if he could he could push off and pivot from there and still slam through the left door window with his two feet wrapped in a metal chain.

They were in the rolling farm hills above the lake now. Out the window Klocks saw the blue of the lake and farther south, in Bulwagga Bay and out towards the Champlain Bridge, which he couldn't see yet, a grayish color. It didn't register with Klocks, but that portion of the lake had frozen over in the last few nights of still air.

Odd thoughts entered his mind now. The gall of Southard to wear that fob, his mother making noise in bed with another man. He banished those distractions and meditated on his precious night sky, and all the TV coverage and newspaper articles. Then he searched deeper in his mind. He was trying to find his zone of peace and power. He needed to harness the energy from both. And most of all, he must not hesitate, he must not give into temptation. He must not sabotage his own plans. He must persist in the face of uncertainty.

The van slowed, and he glimpsed the silvery bridge on the horizon. The van swerved slightly heading down hill to the tracks again, past the entrance to Velez Marina, up Convent Hill and then very slowly through town past the Miss Port Henry Diner. The deputy picked up his walkie-talkie, and alerted the expedition behind to be on the lookout for any "babes."

From his several trips between the diner and the bust, Klocks had memorized the road from the old Grand Union parking lot south to the turn for the bridge. He had no regrets. He had done what he could do. As one prison psychiatrist had told him, "We do the best we can."

I did the best I can, he thought. He was feeling the peace and now the power. Necessity and shrinking time demanded his complete animal attention. He reached for the power.

The vans followed the dark, snake-like route wedged between the cliffs and the bay. They followed the tracks. A freight train roared by, squealing. As it did Klocks felt the train was calling to him, saying good-bye. Leaning over, the key between his teeth, tasting the metal, his head down near his knees, he used the groaning and creaking of the train to mask the small noise of inserting the key into the cuffs. The cuffs clicked open just as the caboose clacked by and their van slowed for the left-hand turn onto the bridge to Vermont. Four miles to go.

Klocks kept the cuffs on. At a glance he still looked as though he were handcuffed. Klocks examined the window again, saw the safety glass and the thin wires imbedded in it, sure he could break the window if he got off one solid side kick with both feet. Inch by inch he slid away from the window. He found the power zone and began to whistle. The deputy turned around. Klocks shut up, blankly looking up at him, hiding the Zen.

"This is where you took the sculpture right, the Rodin?" said the driver, speaking to Klocks for the first time.

"That's what the papers said," the deputy added.

"Right," some robotic voice for Klocks answered.

"And you're not telling, right?"

"Right," Klocks said through his clenched teeth, while he screamed inside for him to shut up. Fortunately, the deputy was taking in the sights, looking from the lighthouse to the ruins of the forts. Klocks sidled closer to the right window. He couldn't help but see the monument, where he had camped and played poker with that college girl, and nailed Conway. But what his eyes were seeing, his mind was blocking out. He was totally absorbed in his mission.

Klocks was in position. He started to count to himself. The driver couldn't see over the crest of the bridge. The driver and the deputy were looking at the view as they rose upward and onward toward the center span of the bridge.

"What's that?" asked the driver.

"It's an ice shanty. Boy that's early. There's still water over there," the deputy said.

Klocks didn't hear them. He was counting down. When he got to three he thrust himself across the back seat, coiling up with his knees ready to unleash a two-footed karate kick. His chest was heaving. He was about to explode. At the thump of the last heartbeat, he rammed both feet and shackles through the back left window, popping the spider-webbed glass onto the pavement. Instantly he hurled his body headfirst out the jagged opening.

The deputy yelled, "My God, stop!"

The driver slammed on the brakes. The van swerved into the oncoming lane. The deputy behind them slammed on his brakes, nearly ramming the Astro.

Klocks was dangling from the outside of the car window his waist chain caught on the broken glass. When the Astro skidded to a stop, his momentum flung him forward, twirling onto the pavement.

A pickup from the opposite direction screeched to a halt to avoid hitting a man rolling towards him, the man's arms covering his head.

Klocks scrambled up and hopped to the edge of the bridge, vaulting the waist high barrier. The four deputies clamored out of their vehicles, guns drawn. Another car swung sideways to a stop.

Klocks turned his head, his eyes popping wide, focused inward. He spun his body around facing the marshals, facing the four guns. "I win," he crowed.

They didn't fire as he plunged headfirst over the rail. He dropped ninety feet, howling in a dark voice, "I winnnnnnn."

The weight of Klocks's shackles cartwheeled his feet around, in slow motion, like a daring trapeze act. Beneath the bridge, on this still December day, one inch of black ice had formed. After long seconds, he crashed through feet first.

Four deputies, one lady in a car, and a carpenter, froze high on the center span of bridge. Then the carpenter ran back to his pickup, grabbed his cell phone, dialing 911. The marshal driving the Astro commanded two deputies to run to the ends of the bridge.

"See if he's alive," he yelled.

The marshal called headquarters. With disgust he heard himself say, "This is Dougherty. We've got an escape. On the Crown Point Bridge. Send back-up."

The fourth deputy, his gun still drawn, peered over the edge, scared just looking down. He could see the hole in the ice, which appeared like an eye looking up at him. Even if Klocks survived the impact, and somehow managed to swim to the surface, the deputy knew he would never make it back up to that exact hole.

"He's dead," he heard himself saying, shaking his head, flabbergasted at what had just happened.

Then the lady in the car walked over in a nervous state. "Is he dead?" she asked trembling. "Why was he in chains? What did he do?"

"He jumped," said the deputy still in a state of disbelief.

Forty-three

Three ice shanties clung to the ice floe two hundred fifty feet north of the bridge. In the faded red shanty, Striker, Parker and his son were jigging for smelt. For bait, Parker picked out a shiner. Right after he set the hook in the fin, a plunging sound made all of three of them sit up straight. It was like someone dropped a safe through the ice. Bending over, Striker and Parker emerged out of the shanty.

"Bobby, you watch the lines," his dad called back.

"What happened?" Striker asked looking around.

Parker turned his head every which way, standing like a scarecrow in the middle of the ice. He looked up toward the bridge, and saw two heads gazing down and heard some yelling.

Striker was pointing with his beer. "Parker, there's a hole in the ice over there. Right below the bridge."

Parker put the pieces together. "Get the ropes. Somebody jumped."

Up on the bridge, the carpenter from the pickup told the 911 operator that he was crossing the Crown Point Bridge and saw a man escape from a police van and dive off the bridge. At first the operator thought it was a crank call.

"You're where?" she asked.

"Standing on top of the Crown Point Bridge."

Then the lead marshal, his anger building, snatched the cell phone and barked, "This is a federal marshal. There's been an escape. The prisoner is dead. There's no body. We've already called our own people. We need state and local police out here to seal off the crime scene." He looked back at the vehicles angled over the double yellow line. "And the bridge will probably be closed for some time."

Cars and trucks were backing up on both sides of the bridge. Troopers from Westport raced along the same route the federal marshals had taken, sirens blaring, red lights blinking. The Vermont police roared down route 17 from Vergennes. The New York dispatcher radioed the Crown Point sub-station, and a pulsating wail could be heard coming from the south.

The marshals on shore saw no sign of Klocks. All they saw were a cluster of foolhardy fishermen standing on the ice next to their shanties.

Parker and Striker, hauling ropes, rushed over towards the hole beneath the bridge. They hesitated and then stopped. The black ice was getting too thin to support them. The only other holes in the ice were inside their shanties, almost a hundred yards away, where the current dissipated and the ice froze thicker.

Under the bridge the cold water was as deep as the ninety feet Klocks had jumped from. Two strong currents flowed through there. The fishermen set up their shanties a ways off, at The Hole, which was between the east and west channels, where the currents played out. That's where most of the fish ended up, pushed there by the currents.

The same thing happened to Klocks.

The icy water jolted Klocks. He didn't know ice was on the lake. Pure luck that the weight of the chains cartwheeled him around, sending him through feet first. Head first and he would have died on impact.

But now the chains acted like an anchor dragging him to the depths. He fought the weight, while the current pushed him towards the shanties. He struggled upwards, frantic to break the surface and breathe. But his head hit something. His mouth pressed against a clear substance that baffled him. It was ice. His lungs exploding, he opened his mouth inhaling water and a pocket of air too, beautiful bubbles trapped beneath by the quick freeze.

In his waning consciousness, he saw the white lights from two holes streaming down into the depths. Two marbled columns of light dancing through the dark water, two shimmering shafts of light calling to him.

Drawn to those portals from heaven, Klocks writhed along underneath the ice, his breath gone, the chains pulling him down. As he blacked out, he threw an arm, twitching with the last spasms of life, up into a hole, a twelve-inch square, and it clung there, stubbornly, like a tentacle, squirming, refusing to die.

Parker and Striker were outside with the ropes scouring the surface for signs of the man who had jumped.

Inside the shanty, Bobby gaped and stepped back. He thought an eel had jumped through the hole. Or that he was face to face with the snout of a prehistoric sturgeon.

The hand flattened, the arm collapsed, slipping back into the icy water. Bobby leaped and caught the wrist, struggling to hold it. He screamed, "Help! Help! Dad! Help!"

His dad, Parker, was scanning the open water, a rope around his waist. With all the commotion on the bridge - sirens wailing, deputies yelling, onlookers gawking - only Parker heard his son's cry for help.

Parker raced back to the ice shanty. No one paid attention to his running except for Striker, who came trotting after him, holding the other end of the rope. The boy was prone, both hands down in the hole beneath the water holding onto a wrist. Parker thought he had caught a lunker, a huge lake trout.

"Help Dad, I'm losing him."

Parker whipped off his jacket, plopped down next to his son, followed his arm underwater and grabbed what his boy was holding. Parker's eyes took on a look of horror. "Striker, help me," Parker called.

Striker couldn't believe Parker was asking for help. Parker could pull in anything.

"Get the saw!" Parker said through clenched teeth. "It's him," said Parker, jerking his head up in the direction of the bridge.

Bobby had been holding that arm for a minute and a half. Striker feverishly sawed the hole wider. In another thirty seconds Parker and Bobby dragged the frozen Klocks up through the hole.

Parker, who was a town fireman, immediately began CPR turning the body on its back, rhythmically pounding on its chest. He didn't want to do mouth to mouth, but when the body lay there lifeless, he started.

Striker and Parker had worked side by side in the mines and Striker had seen him save a man before. "Come on, Parker, steady, baby, steady."

"Striker, you do the compressions."

Parker was counting on something called mammalian reflex, which takes place in extreme cold water, where oxygen and blood retreat from the extremities going to the heart and brain in a reflexive attempt by the body to save itself.

Klocks sputtered. Striker turned the head aside. Watery vomit gurgled out of the corner of Klocks's mouth. In with the slime, a tiny object tumbled out. Klocks must have swallowed the key.

He was in bad shape, but he was breathing. His eyes opened but didn't focus.

The three of them stared at the gleaming chains around his waist and ankles.

Then Parker got a strange look on his face. "I know who this is," he said. "He was in the papers. This is the fellow that stole the Rodin."

"Yeah, and didn't return it," Striker said.

Parker, who felt he had never caught a break in his life, never won the lottery, narrowed his eyes and stood up, kicking away a bunch of sausage and crackers. "Nobody say anything. Nobody do anything. I've got a plan."

Klocks wasn't functioning. His mind and body were numb.

Parker closed the shanty door. "Shove him over on the blanket next to the heater. Striker, you and Bobby go outside, as if you're just watching the bridge. No one comes in here. No one even gets close."

Parker grinned at Klocks. "You're my winning ticket." Parker picked up his dry coat and lay it across Klocks. "We're going to take good care of you."

#